Neck and Neck

Neck and Neck

LEO BRUCE

ACADEMY

CHICAGO

This edition published in 2019 by Academy Chicago Publishers
An imprint of Chicago Review Press Incorporated
814 North Franklin Street
Chicago, Illinois 60610
ISBN 978-0-89733-040-4

The Library of Congress has cataloged the previous edition as follows:
Croft-Cooke, Rupert, 1903-
    Neck and neck.
    Reprint of the 1976 ed. published by I. Henry
Publications, Hornchurch, Eng.
    I. Title.
PR6005.R673N4   1980   823'.912   80-24002
ISBN 0-89733-041-2
ISBN 0-89733-040-2 (pbk.)

Cover design: Lindsey Cleworth Schauer
Interior design: Nord Compo

Printed in the United States of America

1

My brother Vincent's telegram was on the breakfast table. It had been addressed, I noticed, to the telephone number of my London flat and must have been delivered by the first post. I had been out all the day before and there had been nobody in the flat to answer the telephone. It was marked as being handed in at 4.30 p.m. at Hastings. I read it again.

"Aunt Aurora died suddenly this afternoon. Can get no answer from your phone. Will try in the morning. Vincent."

I had hardly finished breakfast when the telephone bell rang and I heard Vincent's voice at the other end. It was not, I thought, quite his usual tone, which I am afraid I always found a little too self-satisfied and pedagogic.

"This is Vincent." He began assertively enough, but became rather shaky as he went on. "This is a most frightful business, Lionel. No, no, I don't mean her death—she wasn't a young woman. It's that Dr. Rowley won't sign the death certificate and there's a police doctor here now. I do wish you'd come down as soon as you can. Yes, there are policemen here, too."

"Of course I'll come," I answered at once. "When I got your telegram I planned to do so, anyway. But, Vincent,

1

what was wrong with her? Aunt Aurora was never ill in her life."

"I think I'd better tell you everything when you get here. Briefly, she felt terribly ill just after lunch, and by tea-time she was dead. Now when can you get here?"

"I'll be down by lunch-time," I replied, and rang off.

Vincent had sounded more flustered than I had ever known him to be. As I packed my bag I was suddenly struck by an odd thought. I wondered how Vincent had been able to get all the way from Gorridge in Essex in time to be at Aunt Aurora's house if she had not been taken ill till after lunch. Only a week ago Vincent and I had spent a few days with her in Hastings, after which I had left for London knowing that Vincent was to leave later for Penshurst, the Essex public school where he had just been appointed housemaster.

I was soon on my way to Hastings, and as I drove down past Tonbridge and Pembury through the pale September sunlight I kept thinking about Aunt Aurora. She had seemed in such good health and spirits seven days ago on our visit to her comfortable Victorian house, and, after all, she could only be just over sixty. It was almost a traditional saying in our family that Aunt Aurora was never ill.

Aunt Aurora (her full name was Aurora Fielding) should have been a narrow-minded desiccated Victorian spinster, but somehow she was never anything of the kind. She had been brought up by governesses, her own mother having died when Aurora was three. Our grandfather, a well-known local doctor, had left almost everything to her, so that at the age of thirty she had inherited a well-furnished house, a large amount of money and no expensive taste other than good food. The house, Camber Lodge, was one of those large redbrick affairs behind the town, as solid and comfortable as the age in which they were built. It was furnished mostly in massive mahogany and there was a great deal of heavy silver everywhere, but now and then one was surprised at the sight of a delicate Sheraton table or an eighteenth-century mirror, a book or picture that did not quite belong to the rest, relics perhaps of earlier Fieldings.

As boys Vincent and I had loved to spend our holidays at Camber Lodge, for Aunt Aurora had a wonderful way of treating us which perhaps was so successful because it was unconscious. She never talked down to us as children but chatted away to us as equals, asking us our plans for the day and whether we had slept well. She had been brought up in the very strictest Low Church atmosphere, and even when we stayed with her in the early twenties there were still family prayers, which her servants attended—they had all been with her for years. I can still remember the delicious smell of breakfast, a blend of coffee, hot rolls, eggs and bacon, coming into the room, and I know that I hoped against hope, as only a hungry boy could, that the extract from the Bible would be short that morning and that there would not be too many references to look up in the Concordance.

Apart from these prayers and one morning visit with her on Sunday to St. Luke's for the eleven o'clock service, we could do what we liked. Whether we wished to fish all day from the pier or explore the country on our bicycles or walk to Fairlight Glen, Aunt Aurora would always make sure that ample hard-boiled eggs, sandwiches and fruit were packed up for us, and she usually gave Lionel a shilling or two to spend on lemonade or sweets for the two of us. At other times she would arrange to meet us at Addison's and buy us chocolate éclairs or meringues and large cream cakes. There was always, too, the old town to explore with its unfailing smell of fish, the old fishermen with their blue jerseys and the lifeboat. There was even the hope, unhappily never fulfilled, of seeing this being launched.

I am afraid I have allowed myself to run away with these old memories of our childhood, but I wanted you to know what sort of a person Aunt Aurora was and the life she lived, and what reasons Lionel and I had for being grateful to her memory.

As soon as Ellen let me into the house and I saw a uniformed policeman standing by the staircase and my brother coming forward nervously and self-consciously to greet me, I knew there was something terribly familiar about the whole atmosphere. Somehow I had known it all before. I suddenly realised that it was, of course, a scene I had encountered so often in fiction and had myself described in my chronicles of Sergeant Beef. A house a day after someone had died in suspicious circumstances. I had entered it in a hundred detective stories. But to enter it in fact, to be a relation of the deceased (for that was what poor Aunt Aurora had become), seemed a little unreal and certainly most unfair. Why, I said to myself, as I tried to act naturally in greeting my brother and Doctor Rowley, the police may even be suspecting me of having a hand in her death!

"Hullo, Lionel," my brother said. "There's half an hour before lunch. Come into the morning-room. Will you come too, Doctor?" he asked Doctor Rowley.

The latter shook his head.

"I've got to see the Inspector and Dr. Clark, the police doctor, in a few minutes, but I'll see you both before I go."

Doctor Rowley had been Aunt Aurora's doctor for many years and had known us since childhood.

When we were comfortably seated in the morning-room, and Vincent had poured out two glasses of sherry, he began to tell of Aunt Aurora's sudden illness, but I interrupted him.

"Vincent, before you begin, I must know something. However did you manage to be here so quickly yesterday if Aunt Aurora only fell ill suddenly after lunch?"

Vincent coloured. "I've been here all the week," he replied, in a rather unnecessarily defensive tone.

"All the week!" I echoed incredulously. "But when I left you six days ago you were just packing up to go back to your new house at Penshurst!"

"I changed my mind. I had a few things to attend to in Hastings and Aunt Aurora wanted me to stay on. But don't let's waste time discussing my movements. I want to tell you about yesterday."

From his story I learnt that the morning had passed without incident. Aunt Aurora had spent it as she must have spent countless mornings. There had been, of course, family prayers, followed by breakfast. Vincent had gone out for a walk, but he had since learnt that Aunt Aurora followed her usual routine. She had spent two hours or so in the room we were sitting in, settling minor household details and accounts and writing one or two letters. There had been a few callers but none of them were unusual: the vicar, who was an old friend of my aunt, and the two Miss Graves, elderly spinsters who attended the same church and were also friends of many years' standing, a lady collecting for some missionary work, and my aunt's dressmaker. My aunt had then taken Spot, her wire-haired terrier, for a walk. She had gone alone, but she had been seen taking him on to the common at the end of her road, as usual and had come back at a quarter to one—her accustomed time. It was during lunch that Vincent had first noticed that there was something wrong with Aunt Aurora. As always she sat in that upright and dignified manner that belonged to the last century, but when some stewed pears were being served she seemed suddenly to slump and Vincent noticed a strained expression in her face. Eventually she hurriedly excused herself. Miss Payne, her companion, had followed her out and come back shortly after.

"I think we'd better send for Doctor Rowley at once, Vincent," she said. "I don't like the look of her."

Vincent had telephoned Doctor Rowley and luckily found him in. He spent most of the afternoon with my aunt, coming in at intervals with a grave face and asking Vincent about what Aunt Aurora had had for lunch, looking more worried each time.

At four o'clock he had come in, and by the look on his face Vincent knew that Aunt Aurora was dead. The doctor seemed extremely upset, and Vincent said that at the time he put this down to Rowley's being an old friend of my aunt's. It was not until he announced that he had sent for Doctor Clark, the police doctor, that my brother had any suspicion that Aunt Aurora's illness was not perfectly natural. It had seemed very sudden, but he had imagined heart failure, and poison had never entered his mind. Doctor Clark arrived and with him a plain-clothes detective. The police doctor must have confirmed Dr. Rowley's suspicions because soon after that a uniformed policeman arrived and Aunt Aurora's bedroom was locked up. Vincent gave his account of what had happened when he was interviewed by the plain-clothes Inspector, whose name was Arnold, and that was all he knew.

He had just finished telling me his story when the door opened and Ellen the parlourmaid came in. "Inspector Arnold would like a word with you and Mr. Lionel. May I show him in, sir?" she asked.

Inspector Arnold was a brisk business-like man. Neither his clothes, a neat blue suit, nor his face gave much away. Refusing a glass of sherry, he addressed us at once.

"I'm afraid there will have to be an autopsy and probably an inquest. Neither Doctor Rowley nor our police doctor are satisfied about your aunt's death. I must go down to the station now, but I would like to have a word with all the staff after lunch, and perhaps you and your brother could be available this afternoon. I shall leave two of my men here. Your aunt's body has been taken away already."

"Of course," Vincent replied. "We shan't be going out."

"Well, in that case, I'll be going," Inspector Arnold said. "I'll make all the arrangements about the autopsy. The funeral had better be next Wednesday, if that would be convenient to you. By the way, before I go, I should just like a list of everyone in the house."

Vincent gazed at the ceiling and began enumerating them. "First there's Miss Payne, my aunt's companion. A very distant relation of ours. The staff consists of Mary, the cook, Ellen, the parlourmaid, and young Charlie, Mary's son, who drives the old Daimler and helps the gardener and in the house. The gardener comes daily. I think that's all. Oh, well," he went on, "of course there's Mary's husband, Tom Raikes. My aunt allowed him to sleep in the house when he was at home, but he's often away for weeks at a time. He's working as a bookmaker's clerk, and it was only because Mary is such an old servant that Aunt Aurora allowed him near the place."

"All right, thank you. I'll see them this afternoon," said the Inspector as he left us. I looked quickly across at Vincent and caught a very worried expression in his eyes, which I could not understand. I mean, much as he often irritated me, I just could not begin to suspect my brother of having anything to do with Aunt Aurora's death. Yet something was troubling him and I did not quite believe that he had told me the whole truth about his extended stay in Hastings.

Edith Payne joined us for lunch and nobody did much talking. There seemed to be an air of constraint between Edith and my brother, though I always thought they were friendly enough. I must confess that I never liked Edith. She was a distant cousin of ours and about the same age. She was the daughter of a parson who together with his wife had succumbed to Spanish influenza after the first world war, leaving Edith unprovided for. Aunt Aurora had brought her up and she had lived with my aunt ever since, helping her with church bazaars and charities, accompanying her shopping and doing all the odd things that fall to the lot of poor relations. But she was not the faded quiet mousy type at all. She always had plenty to say, prefacing most of her remarks with "Your dear aunt thinks . . ." or "Your dear aunt wishes . . ." Though she appeared to share my aunt's interest in church affairs and charities, I could not help feeling that some at least of her Christian humility was put on for my aunt's benefit. There was something unnatural in her invariable good humour, and I thought I had caught quite a different expression now and again behind her thick-lensed glasses. Perhaps I was prejudiced, for Vincent did not share my dislike. They were exactly of the same age, and that made a difference when we were kids. I had been two years younger, and often jealous at being left out as too young for a visit to a theatre or a party, while Edith and Vincent, in those days, had sometimes shared secrets denied to me. I could not help noticing on our last visit that Edith did not seem to annoy Vincent as she did me. In fact they spent a lot of time together. It was because of this that I noticed how little they spoke to one another now.

Soon after lunch Inspector Arnold returned and was given the morning-room for his interviews. To my surprise he called me in first.

"I've asked you to come here first, because I don't think I need keep you long. Let me see, you're Mr. Lionel Townsend. Now, sir, I would just like you to tell me what you did all yesterday. Your brother tells me he tried to get you by phone at your flat in London but was unsuccessful."

He looked across at me, balancing a fountain-pen between his fingers.

"Just a few details of your day that we can verify, and then we needn't trouble you further."

"Well, Inspector," I answered, "I'll certainly tell you what I did. It was such a lovely day that I thought I'd have a day in the country. The woman who comes to my flat for two hours every morning cut me some sandwiches. I took a couple of bottles of beer and drove off. I took the Henley road and just toured round."

"Didn't you speak to anyone? Buy cigarettes or petrol?"

"I'm afraid not. Mine is a very small car and the tank holds enough for two hundred miles. I don't even know the villages I passed through. I had my lunch in a wood and got home about seven o'clock, had some food and went to the cinema."

"H'm," said the Inspector. "Your statement doesn't help us much. Well, if that's all you can tell me . . . ."

"I'm afraid it is," I interrupted. "You see, I didn't know I should have to account for my day or I could have so easily done better."

I was glad to get out of the room. The Inspector's cold questioning upset me. As everyone else was going to be busy being questioned I took the terrier Spot out on the common, and there in the open, throwing sticks for the dog, I felt better. Spot did not seem as upset as I expected by the absence of his mistress, but I noticed that when I turned homewards he scurried back to the house, and I found him scratching at the drawing-room door where normally Aunt Aurora would be at that time of the afternoon.

It was just before dinner that Doctor Rowley called. The Inspector had been gone some time. Vincent and I took him into the morning-room, but from his face I think we had already guessed what he had to tell us.

"I fear my suspicions were correct. We found a large quantity of morphia in your aunt's body. That's not a poison that could be taken by accident, at least not in that quantity. I'm sure you'll agree that the very idea of your aunt attempting suicide is unthinkable. I'm afraid it looks very, very serious to me."

When he had gone Vincent sank into an armchair. "Well," he said, "we know the worst now." He seemed almost relieved that any doubt about my aunt's death had vanished. "Whoever could have wanted to murder poor old Aunt Aurora?"

Just then the bell rang for dinner. "We'd better have a chat after dinner," he said, leading the way to the dining-room.

"Where's Edith?" I asked Ellen, noticing that only two places were laid.

"Oh, Miss Edith is not feeling well and has gone to bed," Ellen replied.

"Nothing serious?" Vincent queried anxiously.

"Oh no, sir. It has been too much for her, that's all. Detectives, doctors and policemen—ambulances and questions."

Ellen sailed out of the room, managing to convey with a slight sniff and head held high that she found the way in which my aunt's death was being treated rather vulgar and disrespectful in this ordered household.

"Look here, Vincent, I'm going to call in Beef," I began, as soon as we were settled comfortably in front of a fire.

By this curious sentence I meant that I felt it high time to consult my old friend ex-Sergeant Beef. Whatever mystery might attach itself to the death of Aunt Aurora would be dissolved as soon as he had investigated it. I could no longer blind myself to the fact that Beef was a genius. I had known him first as a heavy-footed country policeman whose ginger moustache seemed nourished by the beer into which it was all too frequently dipped. Like others I had refused to take him seriously as a detective, for his methods seemed outwardly slap-dash and he himself openly scorned the modern scientific methods—"mucking about with microscopes" as he called them. But his hardy common sense, so blunt and English, so boorish as I sometimes thought, had prevailed too often to leave any doubt about his really profound cleverness. I had seen him shoulder his way into some delicate investigation, lay his great hand on a clue and triumphantly point out the murderer, while brains which appeared more subtle and polished remained bewildered.

I had chronicled a number of his successful cases, but it was not with the hope of finding material for a book that I wanted to summon him. It was because I was deeply troubled, even a little scared, and I wanted the comfort of his gross but reassuring personality.

Vincent, however, took the most cynical view of my motives.

"I am surprised at you, Lionel," he said, with a rekindling of some of his old sarcastic fire. "I shouldn't have thought you would wish to make a detective-story-fan's holiday out of Aunt Aurora's death. Is nothing secure from being used as grist to your mill?"

I began to protest, but he ignored this.

"Oh, I've no doubt it will make an excellent novel," he said loftily. "And I admit that Beef will as usual get to the bottom of it. But in such a personal case I should have preferred to leave it to the police."

"Well, you know what the police will look for. Motive. And the only motive that anyone could have for doing away with Aunt Aurora is money."

Vincent winced. "Yes, yes, I know, but we don't *know* it's murder," he said; but I knew from his voice that he was only trying to persuade himself of a possibility of which there was little hope.

"Well, assuming Aunt Aurora has been poisoned, who are the chief suspects? You and I. You're her executor, and you've always told me that she'd left the bulk of her money to us."

"And cousin Hilton Gupp," Vincent added. "You're forgetting Hilton. He is the only other close relative of Aunt Aurora's, and the money was divided more or less equally between us."

"The only trouble about Hilton as a suspect," I replied nastily, "is that you were on the spot and he wasn't."

"I don't know," Vincent countered in his most superior tone, "where either Hilton or you were yesterday. For all I know—"

"This won't do, Vincent. We shall start suspecting each other soon. I can't think why you don't want to have Beef. You welcomed him at Penshurst School, and he solved the case. Now when there's a case which is vital to us you discourage the idea. I don't understand you."

Vincent stared for some time into the fire.

"All right, Lionel. Perhaps you are right." His voice sounded weary. "Send for him if you like. I'm going to bed."

Before I retired I wrote a letter to Beef, giving him an outline of the matter and begging him to come down to Hastings as soon as he could. I pleaded the fact that I myself was so closely involved to persuade him to come.

As I fell asleep, I could not help wondering exactly how much money we should inherit from Aunt Aurora.

2

Next day I received a most extraordinary communication from Beef—a telegram dispatched from Gloucestershire to me:

"Regret investigating other case very very interesting can only suggest you confess everything to police hiding nothing always the best way Beef."

The infamous suggestion here was not lost upon me, but all my knowledge of Beef could not tell me whether this was the result of his coarse sense of humour or of genuine if perverted concern for me. I wired back:

"No laughing matter please drop everything and come stop this also promises interesting case Townsend."

I received no reply to this, but while we all stood around the grave, watching the coffin bearing Aunt Aurora's body being lowered, I became aware of his arrival. He stood a little aside, bowler hat in hand, and he was mopping his brow with a large handkerchief. It certainly was a warm afternoon for September, but knowing Beef I suspected that he had spent what he still called his dinner hour in the pub nearest to the cemetery. However, I was glad to see him and grateful that he had come so quickly. In addition to all the staff, Mary, Ellen, the gardener and young Charlie, there was present at the funeral a crowd of friends and fellow parishioners from St. Luke's. I noticed particularly the two Misses Graves, Aunt Aurora's great friends. They were almost always sombre in dress, but today they seemed to have surpassed themselves. Everything was black down to the knobs on their hat pins and the ugly great ornaments they pinned in their dresses.

In our party there was Vincent, of course, and Hilton Gupp, who had only arrived the night before and had had a long interview with Inspector Arnold before the funeral. He had not changed as much as I had expected since he had been out East. True, his features had coarsened and his large brawny body had grown gross and fleshy, yet he would still, I imagined, be accounted good-looking in a heavy, rather animal way. Edith Payne was there. Ever since Aunt Aurora's death she seemed to have lost her colour and her flow of cheering commonplaces. She and Vincent were still, I felt, avoiding one another. Vincent had introduced me to Mr. Money-penny, Aunt Aurora's solicitor and fellow executor with Vincent.

As we wandered away from the grave to where the cars were waiting, I approached Sergeant Beef and thanked him for coming so promptly.

"Couldn't very well help it, could I?" he said. "I couldn't have you arrested just when I may need you to write a nice little case up for me. I've been taking an interest in a little affair in the Cotswolds, you see, which looks like making a first-class story for you."

He suddenly caught sight of the two Misses Graves about to enter their car.

"Here," he said to me, in what he imagined to be a whisper, "whoever are those old girls? Funerals look as if they was just about their meat. Black handkerchiefs, too, see?" he added triumphantly.

I hurried him into the car that had brought Vincent and myself to the funeral.

"Afternoon, Townsend," Beef greeted my brother. "Bit different sort of turn-out from that affair at your school, but I dare say we'll sort it all out."

"Beef," my brother replied rather irritably, "please remember that we have just buried my aunt. Miss Fielding was a member of our family. We were very fond of her. We shall be very grateful," he went on in a more conciliatory tone, "for any help you can give us in clearing up this horrible situation. Personally, I think the police will find it is due to some tragic mistake. When we get back to her house, Mr. Moneypenny, the solicitor, will read the Will, and after that I'll tell you all I know of the matter."

We came to the house and Vincent went to have a few words with Moneypenny. Beef drew me aside.

"What's up with your brother?" he asked. "He didn't seem as pleased to see me as he did over that affair at his school. Cut up, is he, over the old girl's death? Should be a bit of cash somewhere," he added, looking round the hall.

Everyone, including the staff and the two Misses Graves, were seated in my aunt's drawing-room as Beef and I entered. Moneypenny wasted no time, but began to read the Will at once. It began exactly as I expected with bequests to the servants (rather more generous than necessary, I felt); a thousand pounds to the Misses Graves "in memory of their life-long Christian devotion"; an annuity of two hundred a year to Miss Edith Payne (yes, I thought, that was wise of my aunt); and five hundred pounds for the St. Luke's Restoration Fund. Then came the surprise. "The residue of my estate I leave equally between my nephews Vincent Harvey Townsend and Lionel Johnson Townsend," I heard Moneypenny's voice saying. But there was no mention of Hilton Gupp. I looked across at Vincent and could see that he appeared equally taken aback, though he, after all, was an executor. I hardly dared look across to where Gupp was sitting. At first I thought he had fainted. His face was white. He suddenly seemed to pull himself together.

"But I know my aunt left her money in three equal shares," he shouted at Moneypenny. "I *saw* it."

Mr. Moneypenny shook his head sadly. "No, Mr. Gupp," he said, "your aunt's instructions were quite implicit. She added a codicil to her Will on the twentieth of August. That was the day after you visited her on your return from the East Indies, I believe."

Edith seemed to think that she should relieve the tension and began to lead everyone to the drawing-room where tea was to be served. The staff hurried to their quarters, and only Vincent, Gupp, myself, Sergeant Beef and Inspector Arnold were left. Moneypenny was gathering up his papers.

Gupp went up to the solicitor. "I would like to have a look at the Will," he said in a flat voice. Moneypenny opened the pages again. There was silence as he looked at it, and then he turned to go. "I'll get my own solicitor to look into this," he said rudely to old Moneypenny. "I still think there's a trick in it somewhere."

As he was leaving the room, Inspector Arnold stepped across to him. "Where are you staying for the next few days, Mr. Gupp?" he asked politely.

"Not here, anyhow," he said, looking angrily at Vincent and myself.

"I'd like to know," persisted the Inspector.

"The East Indian Club will find me. Any objections?"

"None," replied the Inspector, but I noticed that he followed Gupp from the room.

When they had gone, Vincent introduced Beef to Moneypenny. He had obviously prepared the solicitor for Beef beforehand, for Moneypenny did not turn a hair when Beef asked eagerly, "Roughly, after paying out, how much would you say there was in the kitty?"

I must say, that although I thought this was hardly the time to go into details of money with my aunt only just buried, I could not help being interested in what Moneypenny's answer would be.

"When death duties and all the bequests are paid, there should be between fifty and sixty thousand to divide between the Messrs. Vincent and Lionel Townsend, in addition to the house and personal effects."

"Yes, I thought there'd be quite a lot," Beef said, nodding his head sagely. "You can always tell. Look at this room. Look at the servants. Good solid comfort and no extravagance. I shouldn't think your aunt spent half her income all these years. Nice tidy sum."

As we entered the drawing-room to join the others for tea, I heard Edith Payne saying to the Misses Graves how kind it was of dear Aunt Aurora to remember her. The Misses Graves nodded their heads sadly. "She was so good to everybody," one of them said.

I had arranged for Beef to have a talk with Inspector Arnold, and after swallowing a quick cup of tea I led Beef to the morning-room, which the Inspector had come to use for all his official work. The Inspector greeted Beef in the impersonal manner that he used with everyone. But he seemed ready enough to discuss the facts of the case. I was interested, too, to know what the police had been doing and, as the Inspector seemed to raise no objection, I stayed in the room.

The Inspector ran over very clearly the events up to the time when my aunt was taken suddenly ill, the morning spent with letters and accounts, the list of visitors, and the walk with Spot the terrier.

"Did she have anything in the middle of the morning?" Beef asked. "Most of these old ladies like their elevenses."

"Yes, she had a glass of sherry and some biscuits," the Inspector answered. "She always had a decanter and half a dozen glasses left out every morning. Someone usually came to see her. Don't wonder. It was good sherry."

This was the first human remark that the Inspector had made, and I wondered how far his cold manner was assumed.

"Fingerprints?" Beef queried.

"Yes, we were lucky. The glasses hadn't been washed up. I've got them all, but I don't think they'll be much help. We had all the glasses and the decanter tested, but there was no trace of morphia in any of them. They had used six glasses in all. You remember there were all those visitors."

"What about her dinner?" Beef went on to ask.

"Lunch was soup, fried plaice and some fruit," the Inspector replied. "Miss Payne and Mr. Vincent Townsend had the same as your aunt. So did the servants. They were all right."

The Inspector went on to describe how Doctor Rowley had summoned the police, and how the police doctor agreed with Rowley's suspicions and how this was confirmed by the autopsy.

"What about her?" Beef asked. "Didn't she say anything before she died?"

"She was half unconscious most of the afternoon. She had no suspicion that it wasn't just a natural attack."

"Now, what about this chap Gupp?" Beef asked. "He seems a likely customer. There'd been some funny business with his aunt on that last visit. You could tell that by old Moneypenny's manner."

"He's got an apparently cast-iron alibi for the whole day from ten o'clock in the morning till after Miss Fielding's death. I shall, of course, investigate his movements, but I somehow felt he was telling the truth. He seemed almost too eager to tell me about where he was."

"He obviously didn't know he'd been cut out of the Will," I said.

"In which case, if you think the motive was money, he thought he had exactly the same amount to gain as you and your brother."

I looked up quickly at the Inspector as he said this, but his expression was unchanged.

It was at this point that Vincent came in and asked me to spare him a few minutes with the solicitor before he departed for London.

I left Beef with Inspector Arnold, and when I had settled a few points with Moneypenny, I found Beef alone.

"Did you get all the facts you wanted, Beef?" I asked.

"Oh yes. Good chap, that Inspector. There's a lot of things I want to find out that I can't ask him. I shall just have to nose round by myself. I say, look at the time. It's six o'clock. Coming to have a look at the pub I'm staying at?"

"How do you think I could be seen in this town drinking on the day of my aunt's funeral? It wouldn't be decent."

"All right," Beef replied affably, "I only thought you might like to get away from this house for a bit. Your aunt's body only just removed and all this mourning and drawn curtains.

Couldn't stand it myself. Besides, there's that money that's coming to you. Ought to have a drink on that."

I must say I was greatly tempted to follow Beef's lead and go out with him. My brother and Edith Payne in their present mood were poor company.

"All right, Beef," I said, feeling I was being weak. "Just wait till I change this black tie. But, mind you, we'll have to take my car and go out of the town, and no low pub-crawling."

"Suppose you're worried what those old girls in black would think if they heard you'd been seen in a boozer."

"Of course not," I replied indignantly.

We drove over to Battle, and on the way Beef questioned me about Aunt Aurora. He wanted to know all about the family and the relationship of Hilton Gupp, Edith Payne and ourselves. He seemed more interested in the past than what had just happened. I told him stories of our visits to our aunt, of my dislike of Edith, and confessed the reasons. About Gupp I had no strong feelings. He had occasionally stayed with my aunt while Vincent and I were there. He was a strong, well-developed, but a rather gross boy at that time and used to beat us both at the games we played. He was a strong swimmer and had a passion for the silent films of those days. He would tell wild tales of his escapades at school—he was a day-boy at a London school—in which he figured as hero, and often I felt he must have been a bully. When he left to go into a bank, and later to go to a foreign branch in Sumatra, we lost sight of each other and during these years had hardly given him a thought. Vincent had once told me that Hilton Gupp and ourselves would eventually divide Aunt Aurora's money between us, but that her death had always seemed to be something so distant and unlikely that I had not given the matter much thought.

Beef seemed so interested in all this, in Gupp and how Edith first came to Aunt Aurora, that I lost sense of time and was surprised to find that we were in Battle already. I managed to persuade Beef to patronise the saloon bar, but I noticed him casting an eye every now and then at the public bar, where we could just see a four playing darts. I took a roundabout route back, and it was after eleven when I got back to the house, dropping Beef on the way. I tried to persuade him to move to the house, but he would not hear of it. I noticed that all the lights were out in Camber Lodge as I drove to the garage, which was away from the house. I had borrowed from Ellen a key of the garden door and entered as silently as I could. The house looked so quiet and respectable that I felt I did not want to meet anyone after my outing.

I got to my bedroom and undressed. Aunt Aurora had never had the bedrooms modernised with wash-basins and running water, so I had to go along to the bathroom to clean my teeth. As I crept along the heavy carpeted passage, I noticed a light flickering ahead, and as I approached I realised that someone was in the bathroom. The door was half open and I could tell from the way the shadows moved that the light was a candle held in someone's hand. I felt suddenly a bit nervous as I advanced cautiously to the door. A mirror hung on the wall, and reflected in it I saw my cousin Edith, the candlestick in one hand and a small wicker basket in the other. She could not, even if she looked in the mirror, see me because I was in the darkness. The light of the candle rose for a moment and I realised what she was doing. She had my aunt's key basket in her hand and she was trying key after key in the hope of unlocking the medicine cupboard. I did not like to be caught spying but I was not content to leave her there, so I went along the passage, then came back whistling. I burst straight into the bathroom, turning on the electric light as I did so.

"Hullo, Edith," I said. "Whatever are you doing at this time of night?"

She turned very pale and for a moment I thought she was going to faint.

"Oh, Lionel, what a fright you gave me," she answered. "I've got such a headache and I was trying to find some aspirin."

"I've got some I can give you, Edith. But why all the keys? Where's the key of the medicine cupboard? My aunt always kept it on her special ring, didn't she?"

Edith looked terribly ill, and I thought it was unkind to question her further and I went to fetch some tablets from my room. When I returned I found her looking a little better.

"Lionel dear, I'm afraid it was my fault. I lost Auntie's key some days ago and I'm frightened to tell the police. Please don't say anything to them about tonight."

She took the bottle of aspirin I had brought and went out. I lay in bed for a long time thinking about Edith and the medicine cupboard. I was quite sure my aunt did not keep poison there, but there were numerous bottles. Patent medicine had been a weakness of Aunt Aurora's, and I supposed that some of them might contain poison in some form. But perhaps Edith really just had a headache and no aspirin. In that case it was curious about the loss of the key. I would have to tell Beef in the morning, but somehow I did not think I would tell Vincent.

3

At breakfast Vincent announced that he was going back to his school, Penshurst, for a few days to arrange matters about his new House. The school was due to open in ten days and there was a great deal to do.

"I've told the Inspector," Vincent said. "Let's see, it's Thursday today," he went on glancing at the paper. "I'll be back Saturday evening."

Edith was not down and Ellen told us that she was having breakfast in her room. I did not say anything to Vincent about the events of the night before. He looked as if he had enough on his mind already. It was awkward for him, I realised. There would be the unpleasant publicity for one thing, just as he was taking over a House at Penshurst and he must have a hundred details to arrange.

Beef arrived soon after Vincent had been driven off to the station and I told him at once what I had seen the evening before.

"I'll ask the Inspector about that cupboard. Bet you he's had it open with a skeleton key. I think I'll just stay around the house today and have a word with your aunt's servants. I don't want a proper interview with them. Just chat to them at their jobs. You can fix it for me."

"I think we'd better start with Ellen, the parlourmaid," I replied, and rang the bell.

"Ellen," I said, when she came into the room, "this is Sergeant Beef. He's a private detective and friend of mine. He's investigating your mistress's death on our behalf so I want you to give him all the help you can."

"Yes, sir," she answered unsmilingly. I had always respected rather than liked Ellen. She had not altered in the last twenty years. She was an ardent chapelgoer and carried a general air of disapproval around with her, so unlike the cook, Mary, for while Ellen was tall, spare and erect, with thin pointed features, Mary was short and fat with a round red good-natured face. She had loved to spoil us as kids. "Mary," Ellen used to say, "you know those boys shouldn't be in the kitchen. What would the Missus say? And they'll spoil their lunch with all those new cakes . . ."

"Never mind, Ellen, they're only young once. Why, I remember . . ." and Mary would launch into a long racy tale of her girlhood at Portsmouth, of her father and brothers in the Navy, while Ellen would stalk off, muttering that she had work to do.

"Good morning, Miss," Beef began. "Have a seat. There are a few things I'd like to know about. First I'd like to hear all about the visit Miss Fielding's other nephew paid her back in August. Was she expecting him?"

"Oh yes, Mr. Beef," Ellen replied. "Miss Fielding told Mary and me that Mr. Gupp was coming to stay for a few days and to get a room ready. That was why we was so surprised he went off the day after he arrived. He didn't even stop for lunch, and Miss Fielding never came into the hall to see him off. We thought it funny at the time."

"Anything else you noticed?" Beef went on.

"Well, there was. Miss Fielding seemed ever so upset all that day, and about tea-time Mr. Moneypenny called. He used to call to see Miss Fielding every few months, you know. We thought perhaps she wouldn't want to talk business then, but she saw him. Mary and me was called in later to witness her signature and we said at the time that Mr. Hilton hadn't done himself any good. But we never thought he'd be cut right out like that. She'd always been the same to her three nephews. What she gave one she gave the others. You know that, Mr. Lionel."

I nodded.

"You never heard any row between them, did you?" Beef asked.

"Nothing like that," Ellen replied, shaking her head. "When I took her up her cup of Ovaltine in bed, she looked a bit pale and worried like. 'Ellen, I'll have one of my sleeping tablets tonight,' she said, and gave me the key to her medicine cupboard. I went and fetched her the bottle. 'Oh dear,' she said to me, 'what a few there are left. I didn't realise I was taking so many. Remind me to get some more tomorrow,' and I did."

Beef paused, fingering his ginger moustache.

"Now let's get on to the day of her death. I know you've given the Inspector all the facts, but perhaps there are one or two little things you may have noticed, Miss, since you knew Miss Fielding such a long time."

Beef certainly seemed to be getting along much better with Ellen than I had foreseen. I had rather felt that I should have to help him overcome Ellen's reticence, but as it was they both seemed to have forgotten me.

"Notice anything queer about her the day before or when she got up?"

"No, Mr. Beef. She was just the same. She seemed to have forgotten her upset over Mr. Hilton, especially after Mr. Vincent and you, sir," Ellen replied, turning to me, "had been staying for a few days. She got up as usual, read prayers, and had her breakfast. Miss Edith and Mr. Vincent were there, and they all seemed happy together. After breakfast the Missus went as usual to the morning-room, which I always did before breakfast, ready for her. It was just like any other day. That's why it came as such a shock . . ."

"About them visitors. You let 'em in, I suppose? Mind if I smoke here?" Beef started filling his pipe.

"Yes, I opened the front door to them and showed them in. Let me see now. The vicar was the first. About eleven o'clock . . . I remember the time as I'd just brought in the tray with the sherry decanter and the glasses. He didn't stay long, and then the lady came to collect for some missionary society. I didn't know her face, but she seemed to know all about Miss Fielding. 'I was told I should find her in at this time,' she said and followed me in as I went to announce her. She stayed quite a time. In fact the Misses Graves had already arrived when she left, and no sooner had she gone when Miss Pinhole, who did a lot of dressmaking for Miss Fielding, rang the bell. It was nearly twelve o'clock by the time she was free from all her visitors, because I remember her saying, 'I've just got time to take Spot for a nice run before lunch.'"

"Sure there was no one else?" Beef asked. Ellen thought for a moment. "Well, of course, Miss Edith was in and out all the morning, and Raikes, that's Cook's husband—was cleaning the windows. But not what you'd call visitors."

"How many of them had a drink?"

"All six glasses had been used, I noticed, when I fetched the tray for the Inspector," Ellen replied, "but I'm afraid I don't know who used them. The Missus, Miss Edith and the two Misses Graves always liked a glass in the morning, and I can't see Miss Pinhole refusing if she had a chance. Sometimes the vicar did, sometimes he didn't. The charity lady did because I heard her thanking Miss Fielding for her generous contribution and for the delicious sherry. 'Such an unexpected treat,' she said, but I wondered whether she'd heard about Miss Fielding's sherry before ever she came."

I saw Beef make a few notes at this point, and then he went on to ask about lunch (or dinner as he called it). Ellen could offer no further details than she had given to the Inspector. All three, Miss Fielding, Vincent and Edith, had the same food, and the kitchen staff also—vegetable soup, fried fillets of plaice, and some fruit to follow. No fresh facts came from her recital of the events leading up to my aunt's death, and Beef, after thanking her, let Ellen go.

"Who's this fellow Raikes?" Beef asked, as soon as Ellen had shut the door. I told him all I knew of Mary's husband. Tom Raikes had been quite a hero of ours when we were young. He was always full of life and had many accomplishments that appealed to us boys. He was a bit of a ventriloquist, and could do conjuring tricks and card tricks that would hold us spellbound. He was a good-looking fellow then, but, as we learnt later, he never kept his jobs. When he was short of money, which was frequently, he used to come back to Mary, and my aunt, who had a weak spot for him, allowed him to stay with Mary until he found another. For some time now he had been acting as bookmaker's clerk, Mary had told us, and as he was away most of the time he appeared to be earning a living.

Beef nodded thoughtfully. "We'll have a word or two with him some time. Better find out what pub he uses," was his only comment.

We were just wandering through the hall on the way to the garden when I saw Edith Payne coming downstairs. She looked pale and ill and I asked at once after her headache.

"Oh, it's better, thank you, Lionel," she replied nervously. "I must really try and pull myself together today. So much to do." She began to edge away towards the kitchen. Beef nudged me. "Want to talk to her now, while she's scared," he whispered.

"Edith," I called after her. "I don't think you've met Sergeant Beef, who is looking into aunt's death for us."

"Morning, Miss," Beef said. "Could you spare me a few moments?" Without waiting for her reply he got home his first question. "Now what's all this about a missing key?" he began, rather brusquely I thought.

Edith looked across at me accusingly, her eyes behind the thick lenses like pin-points.

"It's all right, Edith," I reassured her, "I haven't told the police. Sergeant Beef is acting for us. I'm sure we all want to know the truth about Aunt Aurora's death. It would be awful for any of us to go on being suspected. You must tell Sergeant Beef everything."

Edith did not answer for a moment, and then, seeming to pull herself together, she began to speak. "I suppose, Sergeant, that Mr. Townsend told you that he saw me last night trying to open the medicine cupboard. I had a terrible headache and I wanted some aspirin. I was foolish not to speak out at the beginning and tell the Inspector I had lost the key of the cupboard when he asked about it. You see I had taken that particular key off Aunt Aurora's ring—they all had little ivory labels, you know—and I was going to get another made by a locksmith. The first-aid equipment was kept there and I thought I ought to have a duplicate key in case of an accident."

"Did you speak to Miss Fielding about this?" Beef asked.

"I didn't want to worry her with unnecessary details. I thought I could put it back before it was . . . needed."

"When was this?" Beef questioned.

"The day before Aunt Aurora died. I took the key off the ring and meant to take it that afternoon. When I tried to find it, I couldn't. I must have dropped it in the garden somewhere. Then that awful afternoon when Aunt died, Doctor Rowley wanted something out of the medicine cupboard, and of course the key couldn't be found. Doctor Rowley must have told the Inspector, because he asked me about the key. I was frightened then and told him I didn't know anything about it. I've been worried ever since. Lionel, do get Sergeant Beef to explain it all to the Inspector."

Beef said that he would be speaking to Inspector Arnold about a lot of things and would bear her story in mind.

"Did you have a glass of sherry with her the morning Miss Fielding died?" Beef asked.

"Oh yes, Sergeant. I remember distinctly. I came in when the Misses Graves were there to ask Miss Fielding something and had a glass. I remember wondering, with all those visitors, whether there would be enough clean glasses."

"I think I'd like to see that decanter," Beef went on. "Supposing you have it sent in just as Miss Fielding did."

"Certainly, Sergeant," Edith said. She seemed more at ease now and turned to leave the room.

"Full, of course," Beef added, and winked at me. "Dry work all this questioning," he added. "It's just about eleven now. I feel I need something."

When Ellen had brought in the tray, Beef filled two glasses and sipped his noisily. "Too sweet, this stuff, for me, but it's better than nothing," he said, but I noticed that he was refilling his glass. "Let's see now," Beef said, getting out his notebook. "We've seen Ellen and Edith Payne. That leaves Mary and Tom Raikes and young Charlie Raikes, their son, and the gardener."

"I don't think you need worry about the gardener because he only comes daily and never enters the house. I don't think young Charlie could help you much. He's always out in the garage tinkering with the car or the motor-cycle my aunt bought him. However," I said, "Mary will be busy now so we'll just wander round the garden and the outbuildings. I should like some fresh air before lunch."

Sergeant Beef got up, gave one reluctant glance at the decanter of sherry still three-quarters full, and followed me through the french windows into the garden. It was pleasant to be out on this warm September morning. Only dahlias and giant sunflowers seemed still to be in bloom, with here and there an occasional late rose. The garden sloped away from the back of the house and one could see the town of Hastings a mass of roofs, below. Beyond, merging impercepti- bly into one another, stretched sea and sky. As we came into the courtyard, around which were built the old stables now used as a garage, potting shed, coal-shed and other domestic offices, I saw young Charlie talking to his mother through the kitchen-window. Mary Raikes came out through the kitchen door as we approached and I introduced Sergeant Beef.

"How do you do, Mrs. Raikes," Beef began. "This your lad? I don't think I need trouble you two. It's your husband I'd like a few words with. Know where I can find him?"

"My husband, Sergeant?" Mary's usually beaming round face looked troubled. "He went away after the funeral. I don't know where, but he said he'd be home tonight."

"What pub's he use, Charlie?" Beef asked Mary's good-looking young son. Charlie blushed slightly.

"King and Queen in Old Town Road," Charlie replied.

"Tell him I'll look for him there about eight-thirty," Beef told the young chauffeur. "Public bar," he added.

Beef smiled as he walked away. "Guessed he was a booser when I heard about him. Well, I think that about covers all those in the house. I haven't heard what you were doing all that day."

I repeated the story I had told Inspector Arnold, but Beef did not seem to be listening.

"There's the Inspector," he interrupted. "I must have a few words with him." He left me and joined the Inspector, who was going towards his car.

I went back into the house, thinking over what we had heard that morning. It had often struck me in detective stories how, the moment a crime was committed and the police appeared, everybody seemed to have something to hide. I used to think this was unnatural, but now I realised the truth of it. Everyone, even my brother, seemed to have changed since my aunt's death. Nobody was behaving naturally, even such open-hearted people as Mary and her son. It was, I supposed, the searchlight that was suddenly thrown on all our lives. Why, even I had my little secret.

Some twenty minutes later Beef came back to the house. "Know that missing key?" he said. "Know where the police found it? Well, I'll tell you, but I shouldn't really. Hidden on the top of a big wardrobe in your brother's room. Now don't say nothing to anyone. He's a smart fellow, that Inspector."

I was trying to think what this piece of information meant when Beef spoke again.

"That alibi of your cousin Hilton's is cast-iron. Can't be broken, says the Inspector. Still, I must have a word with him sometime. I still think he knows a bit more than he says. Well, I must go and get my dinner."

After lunch I was just sitting down to do *The Times* crossword when Edith Payne came into the room.

"Lionel, could you let me have some money for housekeeping? I've been using some of my own, but I've run short. Auntie always gave me money weekly on Wednesdays or Thursdays, but of course . . . ."

I took out my wallet and gave her a few pounds. When she had gone, I began to wonder whether a check had been made by the police as to whether anything was missing. The police had not been to the house all day, so I telephoned to the station and asked for Inspector Arnold. When I explained what had occurred to me he answered at once.

"Yes, Mr. Townsend, that's all being looked after. Miss Payne went through your aunt's jewellery with us and nothing was missing. We haven't yet been able to trace what your aunt did with the twenty pounds she drew from the bank the day before her death. No doubt that was partly for housekeeping."

"Does Sergeant Beef know about this?" I asked him.

"One of the first things he asked me," the Inspector replied. "We don't miss much, Mr. Townsend. Everything is checked up."

I did not altogether like his tone of voice, but he had rung off before I could think of anything to say. I returned to my crossword, but kept wondering what my aunt had done with the twenty pounds. Blackmail? I remembered so often reading in detective stories of a cheque for several hundred having been drawn for cash shortly before a murder by the victim and to discovering that blackmail had been going on for months, but here in real life I could not think of anyone less likely to be a victim of blackmail (unless some of the demands on my aunt for charity came vaguely under that heading) than Aunt Aurora.

I had just solved a clue to finish the top right corner of the crossword (Not a wild party in a gondola. 8 and 5, turned out to be Venetian Blind) when Beef returned. I at once asked him about the missing money. "Oh, that," he said. "It may not be anything to do with the murder. I've lots of things to clear up yet besides that. I'd like to know what's happening between that Miss Payne and your brother . . . ."

"But," I protested strongly, "there's nothing going on between them. They hardly speak to one another."

"That's what I mean," Beef replied. "It's like the old Sherlock Holmes gag of the behaviour of the dog in the night. A week ago, when you were staying here, you said they was as thick as thieves. Now they hardly seem to look at one another. There's something funny there, but I'll find out. The cook—what's her name?—Mary Raikes, and young Charlie didn't look too happy this morning when we came on them suddenly in the yard. Then there's the key of the medicine chest. Oh yes," Beef went on, puffing at his pipe, "there are lots of puzzles in this case, but I think I begin to see the wood from the trees."

"I'm very glad you do, Beef," I said. "It's very worrying for us, you know. This is not just one of our ordinary cases where it's only question of your reputation to keep up. My brother and I are in a very awkward position . . . ."

"You're telling me," Beef said, using an unaccustomed Americanism. He seemed to be pleased with it and repeated it thoughtfully. "You're telling me."

4

After breakfast I strolled out to the garage and found young Charlie cleaning the Daimler. He seemed much more cheerful and greeted me with a smile. "Morning, Mr. Lionel. Thought I'd get the car clean in case it was wanted. I hardly like to ask so soon after Miss Fielding's death, but I wondered what was going to happen like. Mum and I was talking last night. I'd like to take her to Canada. We could manage that on what Miss Fielding left her. It *was* left to her, sir, not to Dad, wasn't it? I mean, there'd be no trouble about her collecting it?"

He looked very young and earnest as he waited for my reply.

"Oh no, Charlie, there's no trouble about that, as soon as this is all cleared up. It's your mother's money absolutely, and, besides, Miss Fielding left you a hundred pounds too. But it's your father I want to ask you about. He never turned up for his appointment with Beef. Did he come home last night?"

The same expression that I had seen in his face when Beef and I were questioning his mother returned. "No, he didn't sleep here, Mr. Lionel. He came back for his tea about five. I gave

34

him your message and I'm afraid we had a bit of an up-and-a-downer and he cleared off. I haven't seen him since. Can't say I want to much. Sooner Mum and I get away, the better."

As he was speaking I had been looking round, conscious that there was something unusual about the garage. I suddenly realised what it was. Charlie's motor-cycle was missing. It always stood looking so clean and bright, the aluminium exhaust pipes shining as brightly as the silver when Ellen had polished it.

"Where's your bike, Charlie?" I asked.

Charlie busied himself cleaning the headlights and did not look up.

"Oh, I sold it," he replied.

"When?" I asked incredulously. "I saw it here yesterday."

"Yesterday," he answered almost irritably. "Got a good offer and let it go. I can always get another," he added, but I knew he was lying. Vincent and I had known the boy since childhood, and now for the first time that I could remember he was not being open. As I turned to go I caught his eye for a moment and was worried at the hurt look. "Anything my brother and I can do, we always will, you know. We must get the question of my aunt's death cleared up first."

"Thanks," he replied, and went on cleaning the car.

Beef had arrived when I returned to the house and I told him of my talk with Charlie. He made no comment, however, but got out his notebook. "I want to have a little stroll round this morning," he announced. "I'm going to have a word with the people who visited your aunt the day she died. I've got all the addresses from the Inspector—that is, all except the lady who came collecting for charity. He can't trace her yet. Anyway, we've got a few for a start. There's the vicar, the two Misses Graves and Miss Pinhole her dressmaker. Like to come along?"

As he walked towards the vicarage, I began to question Beef. "Do you really think one of my aunt's friends could possibly have poisoned her?" I asked. "I know it has been proved that she died of poisoning, but I can't help feeling that it will turn out that it was all due to some mistake," echoing Vincent's words.

"According to the doctors," Beef replied, "the poison was probably taken in the morning, and I'm just following the ordinary routine. After all, the only thing we do know that your aunt had to eat or drink between breakfast and lunch was her glass of sherry. They all seem to have known about that. Easy as wink just to put a little morphia into her glass. I know some very funny things happen among these church people. But it's the motive you want to keep your eye on. What about these Misses Graves? They got a thousand, didn't they? Were they hard-up?"

"I really don't know, Beef," I replied. "They always seemed to live fairly comfortably. Here's the St. Luke's vicarage, anyway," and I opened the gate.

The vicar of St. Luke's was tall, thin, and grey-haired. His clothes, which needed brushing, hung loosely and untidily about his spare figure. He looked as if he needed a month on the sort of meals that Mary had always prepared for my aunt. I had met him at my aunt's funeral and introduced Beef.

"Dear, dear. Private detectives now," he said, and could not conceal the distaste he seemed to feel at the thought. "I felt it was bad enough when the police came to question me. Poor Miss Fielding! How she would have hated all this . . . er . . . vulgar publicity."

Beef did not seem to notice the vicar's cold reception.

"You went to see Miss Fielding, didn't you, sir, the day she died?" he began in his usual blunt way. "May I ask what you went to see her about?"

Vicar gave Beef a look of obvious dislike. "Parish matters, my dear sir, parish matters. Miss Fielding was always so good at understanding difficulties."

"Contributed a lot, didn't she, to your church?" Beef went on.

"Most generous, always, dear Miss Fielding. We shall miss her deeply. Thanks to her legacy I can now finish my life's work and the restoration of those fine old murals that have been covered for over a century. Some of the finest in the country. Just allowed to go to rot and ruin. Absolutely wicked."

As he spoke of the murals the vicar seemed to forget all about us. His eyes lit with a kind of fanatical light. The quiet, untidy, underfed figure appeared transformed for a moment and I thought that even he, whom I had always considered a rather dull disappointed parson, had his splendid vision. It soon passed, however, as Beef began to question him about his last visit to my aunt.

"Did you have a glass of sherry with Miss Fielding that morning?"

The vicar paused, and I saw him look swiftly at Beef. "Let me see now," he replied slowly, and he appeared to be thinking deeply. "Yes, I remember now. Your dear aunt pressed me. She said she thought I looked as if I needed a tonic. It was a special medicinal sherry, she told me."

"What about her?" Beef continued. "Did she have one?"

"I seem to remember that she poured herself out a glass, but only had a sip out of it. I didn't take much notice. I was in a hurry to be off, as I had much to do."

Beef did not seem to have any further questions to ask, so as I rose to go I asked him whether he had begun further work on the restoration.

"Yes, yes indeed. I gave orders at once," he answered eagerly. "We must lose no time. I don't know how long I shall be spared, but I have vowed that I will see it completed."

He ushered us out. I felt sorry for the vicar. A poisoned parishioner was so out of his experience.

"Very keen on this restoration work, isn't he?" Beef asked as I led the way to where the Misses Graves lived. "Never think he had it in him, would you, to look at him? Do with a good square meal and a pint of Guinness. Bachelor, I suppose?"

"Yes," I replied.

"Thought so," Beef said, and relapsed into silence. I still felt the air of cheerlessness in that room, of the dusty theological books that lined the walls and the stuffy atmosphere that still lingered in my nostrils.

The two Misses Graves had been life-long friends of my aunt. I had been told that they had all three been educated together and, as none of them had ever married and as they all had St. Luke's as their chief interest, they had remained close friends ever since. If ever my aunt took a holiday, the two Misses Graves would go too. I often suspected that most of the expenses of such trips—once I remember they had ventured as far as the Holy Land—were paid by my aunt. I had heard my aunt say when we were out shopping, "That's the very material the poor Misses Graves want for their new curtains. I must see what I can do", and whenever she bought bulbs for the garden or some special delicacy for the table, she would give an extra order for some to be sent to these two sisters.

We as boys candidly disliked them, with their funereal black clothes and prim air of disapproval, and as we grew up we saw no reason to change our opinion. Their house always seemed dark and dingy, and in the last years, though my visits had been few and then only for the sake of my aunt, I could detect an air of unkemptness about the place due either to poverty or lack of care. The paint on the woodwork was peeling, though what was left retained its ugly dark chocolate colour, and in the small garden the grass was unmown and the flowerbeds untended.

I was surprised, therefore, as I led Beef up the gravel path, to see a man on a ladder painting and a gardener busily pruning the overgrown trees. I remembered then, of course, my aunt's legacy of a thousand pounds.

"They've not wasted much time in anticipating getting my aunt's money," I said to Beef, and pointed out how far the place had been let go.

Beef seemed more than ever out of place in the poky little rooms over-crowded with Victorian knick-knackery. The two Misses Graves sat upright in uncomfortable-looking chairs and eyed Beef as if he were some monster.

"Got the painters in, I see," Beef began cheerfully.

"Yes," the elder Miss Graves replied. "I'm afraid the place was getting in a sad state. I'm sure your dear aunt"—she turned to me—"will look down with approval and know her kindness to us is already bearing fruit."

Beef looked around, literally like a bull in a china shop, and I could tell he was anxious to escape. He questioned them about their visit the last morning of my aunt's life, but they said that they had noticed nothing unusual. My aunt had seemed exactly as she always was.

"Did you both have a glass of sherry that morning?" Beef asked.

"Oh yes," Miss Graves replied. "Miss Fielding insisted. "Only a very small glass, of course, just to please her. Miss Payne came in while we were there, so we left."

I could tell from the nasty smug expression that there was no love lost between my aunt's friends and her companion. As we walked out of the gate I said to Beef, "Much as I dislike the Misses Graves I can't see them poisoning my aunt, even for a thousand pounds. She was their only friend and, more or less, the goose that laid the golden eggs for them." I explained about the numerous gifts my aunt was in the habit of making them.

"No more can I," Beef replied. "But you never can tell with old girls like that. They're a bit cranky to start with. Look at that room we were in. More like a third-rate museum. They didn't waste much time spending money, either, before they could have even got their hands on a penny."

"The place certainly needed cleaning up," I said, remembering how bedraggled it had looked. "People must have started talking about them soon."

Beef nodded. "And tradesmen had begun to wonder, I daresay, how long they could go on giving the two old girls tick," he said.

As Miss Pinhole, the last on Beef's list, lived on the other side of the town, we walked back to my aunt's house and picked up my car. We eventually found the address and saw a small wooden plate on the wall beside the door: "Miss Amelia Pinhole. Ladies' Dressmaker." The street was in the old town and, though in a poor district, was cheerful enough—a district of shrimps for tea and jugs of beer from the local pub. I had never met my aunt's dressmaker, and somehow I imagined another thin faded spinster.

Miss Amelia Pinhole opened the door herself, and her bulk filled the whole passage behind her. Over her broad bosom hung a heavy necklace of pink coral that seemed faded as one looked up at her large made-up face.

"Well," she said, in a deep, slightly husky voice, "what's it this time? I've paid my rent *and* the water-rate . . ."

I hastened to assure her that our visit had no such object. "I came to see if you would be kind enough to help us. I am the late Miss Fielding's nephew, and this is Sergeant Beef, a private investigator. He is looking into the unfortunate circumstances on behalf of the family."

She beamed, and Beef coughed slightly.

"I daresay it's been a bit of a shock to you, what with one worry and another. Supposing you just put on your hat and coat and we go where we get you something warming?"

I could see them almost winking at one another as she hurried into the house, and I felt angry with Beef.

"Beef," I said sternly, "this is a serious enquiry. There was no need for that."

"Get twice the amount out of that old girl with a large gin in her hand," he replied unrepentantly. "Tell that as soon as I saw her, let alone heard her voice."

"Well, I will have a drop of gin, as you suggest, Sergeant," she said, as we settled into three chairs in the saloon of the nearest public house. "I feel I need it, after all I've been through. First the police—though I must say that that Inspector Arnold was as nice as pie. But it makes the neighbours talk. Then, just because I was a week or two overdue, they had to come and turn the water off. 'Course, I settled it all up. But there, I mustn't talk about myself, though I will say some people are never satisfied. I've lived here for close on twenty years, ever since I came from Cheltenham. You'd think they could trust me now. I hardly look as if I'd fly away, do I?"

She laughed heartily and swallowed the gin. I ordered another round while Sergeant Beef condoled with the garrulous but likeable old thing, and then switched the conversation to the morning of my aunt's death.

"Yes," she said, "remember it well. I was fitting her a new wine-colour dress. Your aunt always had beautiful materials, Mr. Townsend," she said to me. "But I could never persuade her to alter her style. Dignified, she always looked, I will say. Now where was I? Oh yes, that morning I remember because I thought I caught sight of an old friend of mine as I was going in, but it must have been someone else. No, your aunt was quite alone when I went in. We worked away some time. Sherry? Yes, she always gave me a glass. Very generous woman, Miss Fielding."

"Did she leave you alone at all while you were there?" Beef asked, and I saw her look up warily. Then she burst into laughter. "How did you know? Yes, I did help myself to another glass or two while she went to the kitchen to give some order."

As we drove back from the old town, after dropping Miss Pinhole at her small house, I asked Beef how he knew that the dressmaker had helped herself to the sherry.

"Measured out the decanter with the number of people," he replied. "Ellen told me it was filled up every morning, and I found quite a lot extra had gone, and none of the others looked likely customers."

When we got back to my aunt's house we met Inspector Arnold in the hall.

"The inquest is fixed for Monday, ten o'clock," he said to me. "You'll be there, of course. I've arranged for all the witnesses, and naturally your brother and Mr. Gupp will attend. What about you, Beef?" the Inspector went on. "You coming along?"

"I shall probably look in," Beef replied, "but I don't expect much from it."

The Inspector smiled. "We'll see," he said, and then more pleasantly asked how Beef's enquiries were going.

"Covering much the same ground as you, Inspector, as far as I can see. I want a word with that fellow Gupp. When's he coming down for the inquest?" Beef asked.

"He'll be here, but I'm afraid you won't get far there. Cast-iron alibi. Had the Yard on it. Can't be shaken."

"Still, I'd like a word with him," Beef persisted. "Get any further in tracing that woman who came collecting for charity, Inspector? She's another I'd like to find."

The Inspector shook his head. "Afraid not," he said. "Lots of them came here, and the parlourmaid said this lady knew the lay-out here, so she'd probably been before. I'm concentrating on motive, Beef. I advise you to do the same. Once you've got that the rest usually falls into place with a few enquiries."

Beef laughed as the Inspector shut the front door. "What's he think I'm doing?" he said. "But he's no fool, you know. Not much misses him."

"Well, Beef," I could not help saying, "he is an inspector and you were only a sergeant when you left the Force."

"Yes," said Beef triumphantly, "but who's ever heard of Inspector Arnold, whereas Sergeant Beef is what you might call a household word."

"I wish it were," I replied, rather nettled.

"Well, it should be," he replied. "I don't know whose fault it is. I go round finding the murderers for you. Either you can't write 'em up the way they like or it's your publisher's fault. I shall have to look into it all."

He paused. Then he added, in what I thought rather a nasty tone, "Anyway, perhaps I shall need a new biographer in any case, after this. You've never told me what you was up to all that day your aunt was murdered."

5

Ellen brought me Hilton Gupp's telegram as I was walking in the garden. "Townsend, Camber Lodge, Highview Road, Hastings," it ran. "Coming down for inquest. Should like to spend weekend Camber Lodge. Shall arrive Saturday evening. Please wire that this is convenient and that Vincent will be there. Hilton. East Indian Club." As the boy was waiting, I sent the necessary reply. After all, I could not refuse my cousin a room here, however much he had offended Aunt Aurora. As I read it through again I began to wonder why Hilton wanted to see my brother, especially after his last words when the Will had been read. Since that scene I had never really had time to think about Hilton and why Aunt Aurora had cut him out of her Will. Had Vincent known about this, I wondered, before my aunt's death? He had appeared as surprised as I was.

The sight of Beef's bowler hat over the hedge of the drive put a stop to these unpleasant thoughts. "Beef," I shouted, "I have something I think you'd like to see," for although I was still annoyed with him after our last conversation, I felt he ought to know of Gupp's intended arrival.

"I wonder what he's after," he said, when he had read the telegram. "Anyhow, it suits my book. I've got to go to London tonight on my other case, but I'll be back Sunday before dinner. Keep him around till I have a word with him."

Assuming that Beef meant that he would be back Sunday morning, I began to think it would be a good idea if I went up to town for a night. Among other reasons I had only brought a small case and needed some clean clothes, and I was glad of an excuse to be free for a night in town. Beef wanted a lift, and after lunch we set off. I dropped him near Trafalgar Square, where he said he had a call to make, and drove straight to my flat.

I lived in a small service flat near Marble Arch. I had found, since I had become the chronicler of Beef's cases, that my life was a pleasantly busy one. I was either following him around while he did his investigations—and this I admit was the part I preferred—or sitting down in the flat recording what I had seen. However, these periods of writing were often interrupted by a surprise ring on the telephone, and I would hear Beef's voice booming down the earpiece: "Got something that might interest you. Nice little bit of black," he would say. "Meet me in the—(and he would name some pub or other) at six o'clock," and I would happily put together what I had written that day, jump in my car, and set out to see what this new story, on this occasion blackmail, would turn out to be.

Much as I missed Aunt Aurora and felt how sad it was that never again would Vincent and I be able to invite ourselves down to Camber Lodge and enjoy her kindly hospitality in that comfortable house, I could not help thinking as I entered through the swing-doors of the large block in which my flat was, how different my life could be when her estate was settled up.

I had not been in the flat many minutes, when there was a ring at the bell. When I opened the door I found George, one of the porters who kept an eye on the flat when I was not there. "Come in, George," I said. "I'm only here till tomorrow." He shuffled awkwardly and I was afraid he was going to offer condolences on my aunt's death, until I remembered that there was nothing yet as far as the public were concerned to connect the name Fielding with that of Townsend.

"It's not that, sir," he began. "I don't hardly know what to say, but you've always treated me well, so I thought I ought to tip you off. It's the police. Plain-clothes C.I.D. They were here quite a time yesterday, asking all sorts of questions about you."

"Really," I replied, trying to reply with an ease which I did not feel. "I expect they are checking up on my car or something."

"Oh no, sir," George went on, and I could see that now he had broached the subject he was beginning to enjoy the situation. "They questioned all the porters. Asking them when you came in and went out. They seemed especially interested in last Saturday. You were out all day, I remember. Wanted to know if you owed money round here. Asked all sorts of questions, they did. 'Course we haven't said a word, but I thought you ought to know."

"Thanks, George. I'll have to look into this," I said, handing over the expected note and dismissing him. After I had washed I walked round to the garage where I kept my car, and by a few enquiries discovered that similar questions had been asked there. It was easy enough to see what line Inspector Arnold's investigation was taking, and I wondered if the same check-up was being made on Vincent. He was calling in the morning and I was driving him down to Hastings, so

I thought I would forget for one night Aunt Aurora's death. I put a toll call through and then booked a table for two at Marinetti's.

Vincent did not seem at all worried when I told him about the police making enquiries about me at the flat, and I began to feel ashamed at even having the smallest suspicion about him. We were just entering Tunbridge Wells when I told him this, for the first part of the journey had been occupied with a detailed account of his new House at Penshurst School and all that he planned to do when he received his share of Aunt Aurora's money. On the contrary, he seemed pleased at my discomfiture, so I changed the subject and showed him Hilton Gupp's telegram.

"Slight change of front since he went off in a huff after the funeral," was his only comment.

"Beef still wants to question him," I went on, "but I don't see how he can have anything to do with Aunt Aurora's death. His alibi, the Inspector says, is cast-iron, and the doctors agree that the poison must have been taken that morning. It's not like one of those cases where the pill is put in the middle of the bottle and the murderer is miles away when the poison is actually taken."

"You know my view, Lionel," Vincent answered, as he lighted his pipe. "I still think the whole thing was some ghastly mistake. Some drugs or something got mixed up. I hope the police will drop the affair."

"What about Beef?" I asked. "He won't be satisfied till he gets at the truth. Don't you want it all cleared up? I mean, it puts us in a most invidious position. There'll be detectives ferreting round your House at Penshurst next."

"Yes, there's that," Vincent replied thoughtfully, and lapsed into silence until we reached Camber Lodge.

Edith Payne joined us for lunch, and I was astonished at the change which had come over her. Gone was all that bright and chirpy manner that had always irritated me, so far vanished that, I must confess, I could not help feeling sorry for her. Her complexion, which normally was positively ruddy and shining as if she had just washed with carbolic soap, looked splotchy, and her eyes behind the thick lenses seemed suspicious and furtive. She used in the old days to welcome us heartily when we came into the house, as if we were her brothers, and, although I knew she disliked me intensely, she tried to behave in the same way to both of us. She hardly said a word during lunch, but as soon as Vincent had gone out of the room, saying he had some papers of Aunt Aurora's to look through, she began to talk to me.

"Lionel," she said, "that Inspector was up here again this morning looking round, asking me questions. I'm so glad you and Vincent are back. What do you think the police are looking for? I feel frightened every time they come."

"Oh," I replied, trying to reassure her, "it's only routine. After all, Aunt Aurora *was* poisoned. They've got to do their duty. We've got nothing to hide, have we?"

"No, of course not," she answered quickly. She was just leaving the room when she turned back. "Lionel, you remember I asked you for some money for housekeeping and you gave me four pounds? Here it is back. A most extraordinary thing has happened. I still can't understand it. I'm sure there was no money in Aunt Aurora's bag when I looked the day after her death, but yesterday when I was collecting all her personal things I opened the bag again and there were twenty one-pound notes."

"Thank you," I replied. "How odd. You must have over-looked them, but I'll tell the Inspector. Vincent will let you have any money you want until things are settled."

I went out into the garden wondering at yet another strange occurrence in this house. It had been for me one of the charms of the place that nothing ever used to occur to spoil the peaceful orderly routine of life at Camber Lodge, and I still believed that Inspector Arnold would ultimately come to the conclusion that my aunt's death, even if due to poison, was not contrived purposely by anybody.

I found young Charlie in the garden, clearing a bed of dead flowers. He looked up cheerfully as I approached. Whatever trouble had been worrying him seemed to have disappeared. Knowing how much he disliked gardening I suggested he might like to clean my car. "You might check the tyres, too," I added. "I don't suppose my garage people have looked at the oil in the gearbox and back axle for some time."

"Rather, Mr. Lionel," he cried, throwing down the spade and preparing to leave his work.

"You must finish that bed first," I said, "or I'll get into trouble with the gardener."

"Oh, very well," he answered resignedly. "I'd better do a proper job on your car, when I start. What about a decoke?" he asked.

"You'd better leave that for a day or two, Charlie," I answered. "I may need the car in a hurry. But you've got enough to keep you from gardening for a little while. Oh yes, and by the way, I want you to meet Mr. Gupp, who's arriving on the six ten."

By the expressive noise he made as he started to dig again I gathered that Hilton Gupp was not one of his favourites.

Hilton Gupp arrived in time for dinner. Mary, the cook, surpassed herself that evening and, accustomed as I was to good food at Camber Lodge, I could not help feeling that for Mary, too, like her son Charlie, her cares had vanished. Our cousin Hilton ate as usual with gusto, and I found myself contrasting him with Edith, who hardly ate anything and did not appear to notice what was on her plate. She left us three together as soon as she could, and I produced some brandy which I had found that afternoon in Aunt Aurora's cellar. Someone, our grandfather probably, had laid down a nice little collection sometime, and, though much of the wine would have gone off, there were bins of port, brandy, and rum, that promised well.

Hilton did not keep us waiting long before revealing the object of his visit.

"Look here, Vincent," he said, putting down his glass. "I know I was rather hasty last time you saw me, but you must realise my feelings. I've been living for years, slaving away at the bank, on the assumption that one day I'd have enough money to be free. I wonder how you'd have felt if Aunt Aurora had cut you out completely?"

Vincent paused for a second and poured himself out another glass of brandy.

"I don't know, Hilton," he said, looking steadily at our cousin. "I think it would rather depend on *why* I was cut out."

I felt that Hilton knew this question must come and had prepared for it for his next speech came so pat. "I tried to touch the old girl for a loan," he said. "Nothing very much. A few hundred. Told her it would save death duties. I never thought she would take it like that, though she did seem a bit cold. I cleared off next morning and she never even came down to say goodbye. But I needed the money badly, and I need it now. That's what I came down tonight for. I don't want to make any trouble or contest the Will—though I know you, Vincent, were down here the whole week before she died. It wouldn't sound very well in court. You two must know the whole thing's unfair." He looked round at both of us and puffed for a moment at his cigar.

"Tell you what," he began again. "This is what I propose and what I think would be best for all concerned. You give me five thousand out of your two shares and I'll not cause any trouble."

I had never seen Vincent look so angry. "What the hell do you mean 'cause any trouble'? Are you trying to threaten us?"

Hilton smiled. "Oh no. I just thought there were things best left unsaid. If I fought the Will, it wouldn't look good for you, would it, with the problem of Aunt Aurora's death still unsolved? However, we cousins mustn't quarrel. I'll give you a few days to think about the five thousand, but, Vincent, I must have two hundred pounds right away. You can easily manage that."

"What for?" Vincent asked.

"That's my business, but I think you'd find it advisable to give me a cheque before I go back to town or you may have another family scandal in the papers."

"Hilton," Vincent said in a cold even tone, "you'd better get this quite clear. I don't care what trouble you try to create. You won't get a penny from me until Aunt Aurora's death is cleared up and everything else is explained. Perhaps then, if I feel—and I'm sure Lionel agrees with me—that Aunt Aurora was a bit hard on you, we might be prepared to help you."

"All right, Vincent, I've given you a warning. I've still got one or two arrows to my bow. You'll regret this. Just for the sake of two hundred quid! You *are* a fool. Well, I'm off to bed now. By the way, Raikes told me about the key of the medicine chest being found in your room. Funny, wasn't it?" He got up from his chair. "You always were a sanctimonious couple even when you were kids," was his parting shot as he shut the door.

"Don't worry about him, Vincent," I said. "Have another drink. He was always the same. I think you were quite right. About the money, I mean. Why, it was almost blackmail."

Vincent swallowed the brandy which I had poured out for him in one gulp. "I think I'll go to bed too," he said, and I was left alone.

I listened to the wireless for a time, but, tiring of this, I began reading the novel I had started. I felt in my pockets for a cigarette but I remembered I had left them in my room. As I passed the room on the half-landing, on my way to retrieve my cigarette-case, I heard voices. The sound came from Edith Payne's work room. I paused to listen. At first I thought it must be Vincent with her, but I soon recognised Hilton Gupp's voice, though I could not distinguish what he was saying. I thought no more of it, and, having collected my cigarette-case, I was just settling down to read when Ellen came in and asked if she should lock up. I glanced at my watch and saw it was ten o'clock.

"Certainly, Ellen," I said, and wished her good night.

It was just on midnight when I heard quiet footsteps coming down the stairs. I looked at my watch and was surprised to find it was so late, and I wondered who in this house could be wandering about at this time. As I listened I became aware of something furtive in those footsteps on the stairs, for they advanced very, very slowly and every time a step creaked they would stop for a second before they began once again their slow descent. My first thought was to go out boldly and confront whoever it was, but then the idea struck me that if I waited and watched I might get to know something of the mystery surrounding Camber Lodge. Fortunately the door of the room in which I sat was not quite closed, so that I could follow the sounds fairly distinctly. The footsteps now seemed to have reached the hall. I could hear the different tread as they left the heavy-piled stair-carpet and crossed over the oak floor and the thin Persian rugs. The footsteps began to approach the room in which I sat, and it was then that I began to be uneasy. I had only a shaded reading-lamp alight in the room and I could not be sure whether this could be seen from the hall or not. I sat hardly daring to breathe and with my eyes on the door, expecting to see it gradually opening. I heard the footsteps pause outside the door. Then, slowly, they began to move away. I must admit I was relieved. A metallic grating was the next sound that came to my ears. At first I could not decide what it was; then I heard a bolt being drawn back stealthily and realised that someone had taken off the old-fashioned chain and was opening the front door. I realised that here was a matter which I must investigate myself, though I could not help wishing that I had Beef with me. As I rose from my chair, I heard the front door being softly closed. The hall was dark as I entered, and I hurried to the front door before I should lose sight of whoever had gone out. I could easily distinguish a dark figure walking down the drive and from the gait I could tell it was a woman. I decided to follow.

It was a warm September night with enough moonlight to make my task of trailing easy. It was not until the figure in front came opposite a brightly-lit tram station that I was able to tell for certain that I was following Edith Payne, dressed in an old mackintosh with a hood. I felt a certain relief now that I knew who it was. It was late and I was tired. I was strongly tempted to go back home to bed but I wondered what Beef would say to me if I let this opportunity pass. Besides, I had begun myself to have some curiosity about this midnight jaunt. It was so out of keeping with the sedate hours of Camber Lodge. I remembered again how stealthily Edith had crept out of the house and I kept on the trail. She was setting a good pace now, but I had no difficulty in following at a safe distance. She seemed to be making for the old town, and I wondered what the prim Edith could want there. Was there some secret link between her and the dressmaker, Amelia Pinhole? She never paused, however, and presently she came out on the seafront near the old harbour. My interest was really aroused now and I watched her pressing forward with increased pace as if driven by some urgent purpose. She never gave a glance behind, and I felt it was safe to decrease the distance between us. I hurried forward, and as she came opposite the end of the old harbour I was not more than twenty yards behind. To my amazement she began to clamber over the old stone rampart. It was then I think that I guessed her purpose and began to run towards her.

"Edith!" I shouted. "Stop!" I saw her white face turn towards me for a moment and then she in turn started to run over the rough surface. Suddenly she darted to one side of the stone harbour wall. I saw her figure silhouetted against the moonlit water as she jumped. Then I heard the splash. I was now only a few yards behind and, marking the spot where I had last seen her, I jumped in after her. The tide, fortunately, was only half in and I could feel the bottom with my feet. At that moment the moon came out from a cloud and I could distinguish the figure of Edith rising to the surface only two yards away. In a few seconds I had her in my arms.

She did not struggle and I managed to wade back with her to the beach. I laid her down on the shingle while I got my breath. I saw her eyes slowly open and gaze around.

"Oh God," she cried, weeping, "what will happen to us now? Why didn't you leave me there?"

I was cold, wet and tired. "Come on, Edith," I said impatiently. "Pull yourself together." I seized her arm and dragged her towards the lights of the town. I found a telephone kiosk and managed to telephone for a taxi. I told the driver some story of an accident on the rocks and tipped him heavily.

When we reached Camber Lodge I roused Vincent and gave him a brief account of what had happened. He looked ghastly as he listened but I was too tired to worry.

"All right, Lionel," he said, "I'll get Ellen to look after Edith. You get to bed and we'll talk in the morning."

He seemed in a hurry to get rid of me, and I was in no mood to linger. I wanted a hot bath and bed, but as I came back once again to fetch my book Edith was in Vincent's arms.

"Why did you do it?" I heard Vincent asking.

6

In Aunt Aurora's house when she was alive, unless anyone was ill, breakfast was never served in bed. I was surprised, therefore, to wake and see the prim Ellen entering my bedroom with a tray.

"Good gracious, Ellen," I greeted her, "whatever's the time?"

"Half-past nine, sir," she replied, putting the tray on my bedside table. "Mr. Vincent said you were not to be disturbed and told me to bring up your breakfast. I hope it's all right."

One glance at the tray was enough. Grapefruit, cereal, scrambled eggs, a roll, toast, marmalade, and a large steaming pot of coffee. I could almost hear Mary the cook saying in the kitchen, "Do him good to have a nice lie-in, Ellen, and I'll get him a good breakfast."

I had just finished eating what I could of this enormous tray-load and was lighting a cigarette when Vincent came in.

"How do you feel this morning, after your adventures last night?" he asked.

"Oh, I'm all right," I replied. "How's Edith?"

"Still a bit distraught. Hilton Gupp was the cause of it all, apparently. After he left us he went up to Edith and tried to get some money out of her. Frightened the life out of the girl with his threats. She thought Inspector Arnold was coming any moment to arrest us all for murdering Aunt Aurora. You know how upset she's been since Aunt Aurora's death. She must have felt it more than any of us, living here with her all that time."

"Yes," I said, but I thought somehow Edith's behaviour during these last few days could not be accounted for solely by grief for my aunt, but I did not say so to Vincent.

"I don't think we need say anything to anyone about last night. It's obviously got nothing to do with Aunt Aurora's death. Just a family secret. I don't want Hilton to suspect anything. When he asked what all the noise was last night, I told him Edith had been taken ill in the night and roused Ellen, but that she was better this morning."

"I'll have to tell Beef," I replied. "That reminds me. I must get up. Beef is due here this morning. He wants to see Hilton Gupp. I'd like a few words with Beef first."

Vincent left me, and as I dressed I went over again in my mind the event of the evening before and Vincent's explanation this morning. Somehow I was not quite satisfied about it all. When I came down I found Edith and Vincent together for the first time since Aunt Aurora's death. They seemed on excellent terms. I thought of the sight of Edith in Vincent's arms the night before. "Well, well," I said to myself, "if that's it, sooner he than I, but why have they been avoiding one another since the death of my aunt?"

I was glad when, soon after eleven, Beef arrived. I told him all that had happened. First how I had found that the police had been enquiring about me in town, then about Gupp trying to get money from Vincent, how I had heard the voices of Edith and Gupp in her room, and later of Edith's attempt to throw herself in the sea. He listened to my long recital, nodding his head and every now and then asking a question, until I came to my brother Vincent's explanation this morning.

"Think she's sweet on him, do you? I thought so myself. What about your brother? He keen, do you think?"

"It's very difficult to tell with Vincent," I replied. "He's always very much the schoolmaster."

"Well, what about Gupp? He's the one I want to talk to. Have you fixed it?"

Gupp, curiously enough, had seemed anxious to be on good terms with me when I met him after breakfast, though he avoided Vincent and Edith. I wondered whether he thought that I was the last chance of raising any money left to him and that he had better keep on good terms with at least one member of the family. When I had told him about Beef, who he was and how he was acting for the family, he seemed to be eager to help all he could. "Yes, I'd like a word with your old ex-copper," he said. "That is, as long as your brother and Edith are not there."

When I told Beef about this, I saw him take out his large watch from his waistcoat pocket. "Just nice time," he said, and I knew at once he meant: "Get your car out. We'll run down to the Pier Hotel and have a couple before dinner. No, don't worry. Ellen will get hold of Gupp for me."

I knew it was no use arguing. Twelve o'clock Sunday morning was to Beef what eleven o'clock matins had been to my Aunt Aurora. Neither of them ever missed.

Beef, having got his pint, did not waste much time. "Mr. Gupp, you know who I am and what I'm doing here. Trying to clear the family of anything to do with your auntie's death. The police, of course, were bound to suspect you three. Why? Because of motive. It stands out a mile it wasn't love in this case, so they reckon it was money. I know you'll say you don't get any dough under Miss Fielding's Will, but you

didn't know that then, did you? So you're just as much a
suspect in their eyes as these two brothers. See?"

"Yes, Sergeant," Gupp replied. He seemed quite at ease.
"But I happen to have been a hundred miles away when my
aunt was poisoned. I say, Lionel, get me another large whisky,
will you? I can see your friend Sergeant Beef is going to grill
me, and it's thirsty work."

Beef lowered his pint with remarkable speed and I ordered
their drinks and another Worthington for myself.

"Let's go back a bit," I heard Beef saying as I rejoined them.
"You've just come back from the East Indies, haven't you?"

"Yes," Hilton replied. "I arrived a few weeks ago."

"Did you want to come back?" Beef went on.

"Not particularly. We do three years out there and then
come back on leave. After that it's up to the bank. But what's
all this got to do with Aunt Aurora's death?" he asked.

"Just routine," Beef answered. "Had you finished your three
years out there?"

"Not quite," Gupp admitted, finishing his second double
and signalling to the overworked waiter.

"Did you get into trouble, then?" Beef asked. "Didn't start
embezzling the bank's money?"

"Oh no," Gupp answered. He paused to give his order and
then began confidentially. "You see, it was like this. I lived rather
well out there. Bit above my income. You know how it is in these
hot climates. Drink, cards, women. Began to get into debt. The
clubs started coming down on me and somehow the bank heard
about it. That's why I asked Vincent for that cash last night. If I
don't get it, I'll lose my job. I warn you, if I lose that, I'll make a
hell of a stink for him and his precious new House at Penshurst."

Beef listened to this quietly and then asked him what date
he arrived.

"Early August," he replied. "I can't remember the exact date."

"You didn't waste much time in getting down to see your aunt, then," Beef commented.

"Well, Sergeant, as I explained, I needed the cash. I knew what the bank would say. If you can't clear your debts, you'll have to go."

"Um," Beef said. "Now let's get on to the time of Miss Fielding's death. I've heard about your movements at that time from the Inspector, but I'd like to go through it again with you. See, if I'm acting for the family I must have all the facts."

"I was staying at the Randolph in Oxford for a couple of nights when Aunt Aurora was poisoned," Gupp replied, and I could not help feeling, just as the Inspector had when he first heard Gupp's story, that he was not only speaking the truth, but that there was no tension or fear behind his words.

Beef went into details of how Gupp had spent the day of my aunt's death, and as Beef had been shown the police notes and verifications of his story I could not see what purpose Beef hoped to achieve.

"What did you do in the evening? You've got witnesses of everything up to six o'clock, but what about after that?"

Gupp looked taken aback for a moment. "But Aunt Aurora was dead by then," he cried impatiently. "The police and everyone knew that. However," he went on, in a more even tone as if to conciliate Beef, "there's no mystery about it. I went for a pub crawl."

"Meet anyone you knew?" Beef asked.

Gupp hesitated. "No," he replied. "Remember I've been out of this country for three years, and then there was the war."

Beef seemed satisfied, and I suggested returning to Canber Lodge for lunch. "You certainly seemed to be nicely covered against any suspicion that you had anything to do with poisoning your aunt," Beef said, as he finished his last pint and rose to go.

Gupp looked up rather quickly at the Sergeant, but there was nothing in Beef's expression, as far as I could see, that showed that his words meant more than they said.

On the morning of the inquest everyone at Camber Lodge seemed nervous and irritable, and I felt glad I was unlikely to be called. The inquest itself was the usual long-drawn-out affair, and all the witnesses except the servants—my brother Vincent, Edith Payne, the Misses Graves and the vicar—all seemed to be feeling the strain, and it seemed that, if I were an outsider judging them all, they would all have appeared to be guilty in some way or other.

Nothing new came up. They went thoroughly over the old ground. Everyone agreed that my Aunt Aurora, apart from having no reason, was the last person to take her life. The only point that seemed to be really established on medical evidence was that my aunt had died from morphia poisoning, but how or by whom it had been administered, was not known.

And that was the verdict.

As I left the inquest with Beef we ran into Inspector Arnold, who was just walking towards his car.

"Just as you wanted it, I suppose, Inspector," Beef said as we came up. "Leaves you a nice free hand."

"What are your plans, Beef?" Inspector Arnold asked pleasantly enough. "Staying on?"

Beef took out his pipe and began slowly to fill the huge bowl.

"For a day or two, I think. I'm on another case in the Cotswolds that I ought to get back to, but I think I'll just clear up one or two things here."

"Such as?" the Inspector asked.

"One thing, how Miss Fielding was poisoned, if it wasn't in the sherry. Seven people drank sherry that morning. Miss Fielding herself, the companion, the collector for missionary work, the two Misses Graves, the vicar and the dressmaker. Yet there were only six dirty glasses, no glass missing and none of the glasses nor the decanter had a trace of morphia. The person who did it obviously hoped to get away with accidental death."

"Person or persons," the Inspector said with some emphasis.

"Yes, as you say, Inspector, person or persons," Beef repeated slowly, pausing in the middle of relighting his pipe. Then his manner abruptly changed. "Here, Inspector," he asked, "you never traced any unusual purchase of morphia about that time?"

"We've tried. Had the Yard on it, too," Inspector Arnold replied, "but we've had no luck yet. If I were you, I'd concentrate on motive. Money, in this case. As I said before, if you follow the motive you always get the right people in the end."

"Meaning, Inspector, you think you know who did it," Beef said with a sly chuckle. "You're just hoping to dig up enough evidence to bring a case. Don't blame you. By the way, did you ever trace anything about the woman who came to collect for some missionary work?"

"No local society seems to know anything about her," the Inspector answered. "But, generous though Miss Fielding was, she wasn't the sort to hand over contributions to anyone and, goodness knows, she had a pretty wide knowledge of charities and such like. I shouldn't worry about her, Beef. Remember my words. Stick to the real motive. Goodbye."

Beef lit his pipe and watched Inspector Arnold drive away in the police car. "Nice fellow, that Inspector," he said. "Very helpful, too. He's on to something and he doesn't mean to let go. No fool, either, but I *think* he's barking up the wrong tree."

"You think you know better, I suppose."

"Yes, now I think I know better," Beef said slowly.

Something in the tone of his voice stopped me asking any questions and we drove silently back to Camber Lodge.

"I want to have another look at that room—where your aunt used to spend her mornings."

I showed Beef into the morning-room, which looked so exactly as it always had looked that I had an awful feeling that my aunt might come bustling in and ask us in her usual good-natured way whether we had had a nice morning at the inquest. Beef's voice broke into this grotesque reverie.

"I'd like to be quite satisfied about that sherry drinking," he said. "I feel it must have been in the sherry that the morphia was put, but the Inspector was sure there was no trace of poison either in the glasses or the decanter. You see, that's the only chance I can figure an outsider had of doing it. There's no tap here anywhere, but if my theory is right, one of the glasses, the one with the morphia that was drunk by your aunt, must have been washed out."

"I think we should have Ellen in again," I said to Beef, who was poking into every corner. He agreed, and when Ellen entered he began to question her.

"Is there anywhere around here that someone could have washed a sherry glass," she repeated, shocked at Beef's question. "Why, Mr. Beef, whoever would want to do such a thing?"

For a moment I thought Beef had spoilt the good relations that his first interview had produced, but when he took her more into his confidence and explained what he was looking for, Ellen thawed.

"I see, Mr. Beef," she almost simpered, so unlike the unbending figure I had always known. "You think someone washed the poison out of one of the glasses. Yes, I'm sure there were only six used and none were missing. Let me see.

Water. No, there's no tap here. There was no water in the flower vases because Miss Fielding had all the flowers thrown out the day before she died. She was going to do them that very afternoon, the poor soul."

Ellen seemed suddenly to be struck with an idea.

"I wonder, Mr. Beef," she said excitedly, "whether that was what it was with the goldfish?"

"Goldfish!" Beef almost shouted. "Was there a bowl of goldfish here?"

"Yes, I found them all dead a day or two after Miss Fielding died. I thought it was because no one had fed them. I felt so guilty about it that I threw them all away."

"Pity," Beef said. "But that's about the answer. Thank you, Ellen. You've been very helpful. Very clever of you to think of that."

"Have I really helped, Mr. Beef?" Ellen said, as she started towards the door. "Oh, I'm so glad. If it helps to find who killed the poor mistress, I shall have had my reward."

"That was a bit of luck," Beef said, as Ellen closed the door behind her. "Pity we can't prove it, but I'm pretty sure I'm right. Well, I must be getting back now." Beef consulted his watch, and as I looked at the clock I was not surprised to see that it had just turned opening time. "See you in the morning. I've just one or two enquiries to make here and then I must get back to my case in the Cotswolds."

"But, Beef," I exclaimed hotly, "you can't leave us in the air like that. Why, we'll all be under suspicion until the whole thing's cleared up."

"Nothing much more to be done here," Beef replied gruffly. "But don't think I shan't clear it all up . . . eventually. Good night."

The house, after Beef had gone, seemed very empty. My brother Vincent had left immediately after the inquest for

Penshurst School. Hilton Gupp, too, had gone back to London. Dinner alone with Edith was a miserable meal, and I felt glad that I need only stay a little while longer. I could not bear the thought of spending much more time in Camber Lodge with only Edith for company. As I wandered aimlessly about after dinner I realised how much of everything in Camber Lodge had depended on Aunt Aurora and what an atmosphere of peace and restful comfort she had unwittingly created. I knew now why my brother and I had come down to stay with her so often, he after a long worrying term at school, I after one of Beef's more sordid cases. It was the perfect antidote. Again I wondered who on earth could have brought themselves to kill so kind, so quiet a person as Aunt Aurora.

Having finished my own novel that morning, I picked up the first book I could find. It was lying with a pile of others on a side table in the morning-room. It was typical of a lot of books of my aunt's. I smiled as I read the title—*Tales of Missionary Work in North China*—and began idly to turn the pages. As I did so, a small square of paper fell out. I stooped to pick it up and glanced at it. Only a receipt for a guinea, I noted, for some charity, and then something suddenly struck me and I looked more closely. 10th, September, I saw. Why, of course, that was the day of Aunt's death. This must be, then, the receipt for the contribution my aunt had made the very morning she was poisoned. She had probably got the book out to show her visitor and slipped the receipt in without thinking. I put it carefully in my pocket. This would clear up another of the small points that Beef was worrying about.

7

Next morning when I told Beef of my discovery of the receipt, he was quite excited.

"Here, let me have a look at it," he said, and taking the paper he spread it on the table.

"CHURCH MISSIONS SOCIETY" it ran

"Received from *Miss A. Fielding* the sum of *one guinea* (£1 1s. 0d.).

Dated 10th Sept. 19—

Signed
(on behalf of the
Church Missions Society)"

"Yes," Beef said, "that's obviously the one the lady gave your aunt that morning. I can't make out the signature. Well, we can soon check up on that. I suppose we may as well let Inspector Arnold do that for us. He ought to see it, anyhow. I'll drop it in at dinner-time. Better take a copy of it first."

I was just copying the paper out when Ellen came to tell me that Mr. Moneypenny was on the telephone and wished to speak to me. Moneypenny, I remembered, was Aunt Aurora's solicitor, who had read the Will after her funeral. When I answered the phone he asked if Beef was still in Hastings and, if so, whether we could spare him a few minutes at his office in Lewes. He had something he thought we ought to know. Beef readily agreed, and I arranged to call about eleven-thirty that morning.

"Tell you what," Beef said, when I had put down the receiver, "that fits in nice. Lewes Races are on today. We'll have a look in there this afternoon. Chap in the pub I'm staying at gave me two horses last night . . . ."

"Beef," I remonstrated, "I hardly think this is the time to go betting on horses. I thought you were down here to try and find out about my aunt's death."

Beef waited. "Remember a fellow who didn't turn up at a certain pub, a bookie's clerk called Tom Raikes. Well, I understand he'll be there in the five-bob ring. I shouldn't mind a word with him."

"Oh well, of course," I replied. "That's different." Now that I knew it was part of the job, I was quite keen to go to the races. The last few days had not been much fun. Though I did not follow horses in the papers and only had a bet on the Derby and the National, I loved to attend an actual meeting. I had not been to many, but I loved going down to the paddock, watching the horses parade, making my choice and betting and then watching them canter off to the starting-post. It was the colour and the crowd that got me. Well, if Beef thought it was part of our job, that was good enough for me.

It was now half-past ten and, as Lewes was nearly thirty miles away, it was time to set off to see Moneypenny, especially as we had to look in and leave the receipt form for Inspector Arnold.

It was one of those days that you get in September, settled and calm with an unbroken blue sky and faint golden haze over the countryside. Our route lay behind the downs and, as the road was good, I kept the accelerator well pressed down. We passed Ringmer and pulled up in front of Messrs. Moneypenny and Moneypenny in High Street, Lewes, just as the clock in the street showed half-past eleven.

Moneypenny did not keep us waiting long, and having seated us in his private office he began:

"I'm sorry to have dragged you over, but I feel I should inform someone and I did not wish at this stage to approach the police. You see, Sergeant Beef," he went on, turning to Beef, "I had an extraordinary visit yesterday. Quite upset me. The two Misses Graves turned up here without any appointment and demanded to see me. I managed to fit in time to see them, but it was most inconvenient. When they came into my office they were quite overwrought. They wanted me to advance them five hundred pounds there and then out of the money 'due to them' as they put it. I pointed out politely that the Will had not been proved yet, and, until police investigations were over, nothing could be done. I had an awful scene with them then."

The old solicitor took out his handkerchief and mopped his brow. Even the memory of it seemed to upset him. "They wept and ranted and then almost threatened me. They practically accused me of keeping Miss Fielding's money for my own use. Of course I didn't take legal notice of that. They were obviously not in their right mind. However, at last I managed to calm them down a little and learn that they were and had been for some time, living above their income. Well, that's a little harsh, perhaps. Their income had always been small, but before the war it had been, with care, just enough. During the war, with prices rising, in order to live as they had always done, they had spent what little savings they had just to keep up appearances. It was a sad tale. During these last few years they had been getting into debt with all the local tradesmen. At first it had been all right. They had always paid their bills promptly for thirty years and their name was good. Now, I suppose, businesses had changed hands, new managers had come back from the war, and they had been pressed. They produced one court order, two county-court summonses and, to crown it all, two bailiffs had taken up residence that very morning. Oh, it was pitiable, but you see, Beef, what was I to do? I could not advance them a penny."

"I know that, Mr. Moneypenny. You mean, if they had a hand in the poisoning business they weren't entitled to a farthing."

"Exactly. I should have liked to have helped them out of respect to Miss Fielding, but there you are."

Beef then told Moneypenny of our visit to them and of the painters already at work. "With those old girls keeping up appearances means everything. They'd rather go without food than sack their maid," he said, and brought out his large pipe. There was a pause while Beef and Moneypenny filled their pipes and I lit a cigarette.

"Don't think they will do anything silly, do you?" Beef asked.

"Suicide, you mean?" Moneypenny replied. "I trust not. I gave them all the advice I could. I told them to go to each of their creditors and explain the position fully. I even gave them a letter, saying that if Miss Fielding's Will was proved in its present state they would inherit a thousand pounds. I also undertook to deal with the summonses and the court order. I told them I thought I could have the bailiffs dispensed with . . . ."

"Yes." Beef smiled. "It was those bums that put the lid on it and sent them scuttling over here. Poor old things. I didn't like them much, but you can't help feeling sorry for them. Well, Mr. Moneypenny, you did quite right in asking us to come over here, and I must thank you for your information. Perhaps we'll meet again."

"Goodbye, Beef. By the way, how's the investigation going? I do hope we can get the Will cleared up soon. There's so much to settle."

"I hope so too, Mr. Moneypenny," Beef replied. "Don't you worry, I'll have it all sorted out for you, but it takes time. By the way, what made Miss Fielding cut her nephew, Gupp, right out of her Will? He told Mr. Townsend here that it was because he had tried to touch her for a loan, but I feel there must have been more than that behind it."

Moneypenny's face almost lightened into a thin smile. "Well, I shouldn't really betray confidences. The facts are that he did try to borrow a large sum from Miss Fielding. This was bad enough, but he then broke into her private desk with a skeleton key where she kept her Will, just to make certain he was included. He didn't know, but she saw him through the glass door. She'd heard a noise in the night and came down to see what it was. That's why he was so dumbfounded when I read the clauses of the Will. As he said, he'd seen that he was one of the legatees. What he didn't know was that Miss Fielding called me next day and told me about it and made a codicil excluding Hilton Gupp altogether. Most upset about it she was, but *quite* adamant."

"Thank you again, Mr. Moneypenny," Beef said, rising and taking his hat. "That was it, was it? I thought it must have been something like that."

"I hope we shall soon be able to settle up everything with you and your brother, Mr. Townsend," Moneypenny said, as he was seeing us out.

After leaving Moneypenny's office, we drove straight up onto the downs to the racecourse. We parked the car, paid our

entrance fee and entered the five-shilling ring. Beef, as soon
as we were inside, made straight for the bar. While we were
drinking our beer and eating a sandwich I heard a little group
of people next to us discussing the latest murder, which was
splashed across the evening papers that they were studying.
An elderly woman had been battered to death in her shop
for the sake of five pounds.

"They haven't caught the one who poisoned that poor old
lady in Hastings yet, have they?" one was saying.

"Oh, it was one of those nephews. Clear as daylight. The
police know what they are doing. They'll catch up with them."

"Never could abide murderers who go in for poison.
Remember Armstrong . . ."

"That's your town, Edie, Hastings, isn't it?" I heard a voice
saying.

"Oh yes. I went to the inquest too. I saw them all. The
one I didn't like the look of was the younger nephew, the one
they never called. Nasty quiet sly-looking fellow, I thought.
Shouldn't be surprised if he was the one."

I looked at Beef to see if he had heard and saw his red
face almost apoplectic with laughter. "Got you nicely weighed
up," he said as we moved away.

"That's why I asked you to come to Hastings in the first
place, Beef," I replied. "I knew the sort of beastly gossip that
would go on till the case was solved. It's about time you
produced some results."

"Well, we're trying, aren't we?" he answered, in a grieved
voice. "What else have we come all this way for? Oh, I mustn't
forget those two horses." He dug a dirty piece of paper from
his waistcoat pocket and showed it to me.

"There you are, see? Silver Fox three o'clock and Maid of
the Mountains for the three-thirty."

Beef spoke with an air of finality as if they were both already past the post, which annoyed me.

"I always watch the horses and pick my own," I answered.

Beef laughed. "What do you know about horses? I don't believe you can even ride."

The horses were just going up to the starting-post for the first race as we came out.

"We'll pass this one up," Beef said, "and see if we can find that chap Raikes. He must be working for one of the bookies along the front here. You know him by sight. Don't let him see you if you can help it. Just walk along the line and come back and tell me which bookie it is and what's he dressed in."

It was easy to locate Raikes without being noticed, as the bookies were busy with the last-minute rush. People were hurrying to and fro, watching the prices quickly changing on each bookie's board, and hastening to place their bets before the off.

I moved back to higher ground and watched the race and then walked to the place where I had left Beef. He was nowhere to be seen. I was looking vaguely round when I suddenly saw him outside the fencing of the ring, making weird signs that I gathered meant he wanted me to follow.

"Didn't you see him?" Beef asked impatiently, as I joined him on the open down outside the rings. "Gupp. Mr. Hilton Gupp, your cousin, as large as life. There in the five-bob ring. I don't think he spotted us. I watched him come in, and then he went away to the back and spoke to someone. No, I don't think he knows we're here and I particularly don't want him to. What's that big stand over there? We can watch fine from there."

"That's the Members' Stand. Tattersalls. Cost us thirty-bob each," I said.

"Well, it will all come out of my expenses," Beef replied
with a laugh. "You and your brother will have to cough up.
I haven't had much fun out of this case yet. Besides, I've got
those two horses. They'll pay for everything and more besides."

Beef, I thought, for all his experience of crime, still retained
some of the ingenuous qualities of the country bobby. He
had a childlike faith in the tip that had been given him in
his pub. I could imagine the scene—Beef buying some tout
drinks and the tout telling Beef about stables and jockeys and
probably tapping him for a dollar at the end.

When we entered the Members' Stand, Beef proudly
attached the round disc to his buttonhole. He then climbed
high up in the stand. "This will do nicely," he said. "Now
I want you to keep those glasses"—I had brought a pair of
binoculars—"trained on the five-bob ring. See if you can see
Raikes from here."

It was an interval between the first race at two o'clock and
the two-thirty, consequently the view of the lines of bookies
was more or less unimpeded. I soon picked up the sign "Alf
Silverman", which was the name of the bookie Raikes was
clerking for, and could see Raikes with his big ledger quite
clearly.

"Beef," I said excitedly, "Gupp's with them, too. The
bookie, Raikes and Gupp are all standing together."

"Good," replied Beef. "Now we can concentrate on this
racing business and have a drink or two in peace and quiet.
Nice little set-up they have here," he added, looking round
the ring appreciatively. A group of county people were next
to us, quiet check caps, regimental ties and enormous binoculars in heavy leather cases. They looked amused at Beef
clad in his blue suit, a bit shiny and covered with pipe ash
and his bowler hat slightly askew, but Beef returned their

curious glances with a smile. I left him for a moment to put a small bet on the two-thirty, and when I returned I found Beef deep in conversation with the whole party.

"Silver Fox, eh?" I heard a man say who was wearing an old Etonian tie and a somewhat different kind of bowler from Beef's. "Well, I must say I hadn't thought of that horse. Let's have a look at his form."

He got out his form book and muttered to himself. "Yes, might have a chance. Amanda, we'd better have a saver on Silver Fox. This gentleman has the tip from a very good source."

Once again I was astonished at Beef. If anyone had been able to converse on friendly terms with this crowd, I should have thought, being an old public school fellow myself, it would have been I, but they seemed to ignore my few words of warning about the reliability of Beef's tips, and listened attentively to every word the Sergeant said.

"I don't often come racing, madam," Beef was saying to the horsy lady in grey who had been addressed as Amanda, "but, when I do, I like to do the thing properly. Come in the best seats. Find one or two good horses and put a real bet on. No street-corner two bobs for me. Just a waste of money."

The horses of the two-thirty flashed by in a colourful stampede, but the one which I had backed was not in the first three.

"Well, sir," Beef was saying, "we'll just go and put on our bets. See you in the bar when Silver Fox is home."

"Oh, rather," the Old Etonian replied affably. "We'll owe you a drink if he pulls it off."

As soon as we were out of earshot on our way to the paddock I began to remonstrate with Beef.

"Beef, you shouldn't mislead those people with your tuppenny-ha'penny tips. They'll probably put a tenner or so on."

"What do you mean 'mislead'?" Beef answered, quite angrily. "I very much fancy Silver Fox, and the fellow told me . . ."

I could bear no more. "Let's have a look at them. All the papers give Dolabella. Betting forecast six to four."

"There he is," Beef shouted. "See. No. 4. That little grey one. I like him. Come on. We'll go and get our money on."

Beef almost ran to where the bookies were standing. "What are you giving for Silver Fox?" he asked one bookie fiercely.

"Seven to one," the bookie replied, without looking up.

"Well, here's five pounds," Beef said, producing five rather dirty notes from his pocket.

"To win or each way?" the bookie asked wearily.

"Win, of course," Beef answered, as if the man was a fool not to know. So carried away was I by Beef's confidence that I put a pound each way myself, as well as two pounds to win on Dolabella. I managed to get two to one on Dolabella, which was lucky as it closed at five to four.

Beef's behaviour during the race was conspicuous, to say the least of it. He kept standing up in his seat, shouting encouragement, and every now and then putting my binoculars to his eyes. It was a mile race. Dolabella took up the running from the start in front of a field of about twelve. Silver Fox was running third—very nicely I had to admit. As they came into the last furlong, Silver Fox moved forward without effort and came home by two lengths.

"There you are, you see. What did I tell you? You never seem to think I know anything. Gosh, how much is that? Seven fives is thirty-five. Thirty-five pounds, eh?"

"And your stake money back," I said.

Beef was as excited as a schoolboy. "Coo, it's like shelling peas. Don't know why I worry with detecting. Come on, we'll go and celebrate."

I myself had won, even with the two I lost on Dolabella, six or seven pounds. I followed Beef to the bar, where he was at once surrounded by our county friends who insisted on champagne. Beef was definitely the hero of the moment, as they all seemed to have cleaned up nicely on Silver Fox.

Beef produced his other tip, Maid of the Mountains, but fortunately, as it turned out (for Maid of the Mountains came in nowhere), someone else ordered another bottle of champagne and racing was forgotten for the moment.

"Better collect our winnings and get back to business," Beef said in an aside to me, and we left them to what seemed to me might well develop into quite a party.

Beef explained that having established the fact that Raikes and Gupp seemed to be on close terms—though he realised, of course, that Hilton Gupp, like ourselves, had known Tom Raikes since early days—he only wanted to have a few words with Raikes alone. He thought the best way to effect this was for us to go back to the five-bob ring, and while he kept Gupp out of the way, if necessary, I should approach Raikes, feign surprise at seeing him, ask him where he would be that evening—it must be somewhere near, he said, since there was another day's racing at Lewes still to come—and try and fix to meet him in some pub.

Tom Raikes seemed pleased enough to see me, and, finding that he was staying in Lewes, I arranged to meet him for a drink at the Black Lion at seven o'clock. I did not mention that Beef was with me, but knowing Tom Raikes I felt that he probably guessed the reason I wanted to see him. However, he seemed quite eager to meet me and I left it at that.

Beef was pleased at the arrangement and insisted at six o'clock on our going to the Black Lion "so as to be in plenty of time and not to miss him". He filled in the time of waiting by roping me in to make a four at darts against two race-goers who were, even with Beef handicapped by my inaccurate throws, what he termed "easy meat". Having won several pints off them, we were just finishing the last game when Tom Raikes walked in. I bought him a pint and, as I had left Beef his favourite double top to finish, it was only a matter of seconds before he joined us. I introduced them and we all sat down at a small table.

I did not know what Beef wanted so I began by telling Raikes of our luck over Silver Fox.

In the pause that followed this Beef broke in, "Look here, Raikes, you know who I am and what I'm doing here. I just want to ask you a few questions. I know you needn't answer them, but I think, somehow, you will."

He paused in a heavy dramatic way and then went on.

"You took the odd twenty quid from Miss Fielding's bag the very day she was poisoned, didn't you? When you were fixing the curtain rod."

"Well, I'm not saying I did or I didn't," Raikes replied, looking a bit hangdog but not really worried, I felt. "How was I to know she was going to die that day?"

"That's as may be," Beef answered.

"Stop that," Raikes said, in a voice I had never heard him use before. "You're not going to try and get me mixed up in that."

"I should just like to know," Beef went on evenly, "what game you and Mr. Hilton Gupp are up to. That's what I'd like to know."

This time there was no doubt that the bolt had gone home. Raikes, in spite of all his faults and weaknesses, had often shown shame but never before had I seen fear in his eyes.

"What do you mean?" Raikes asked, more to gain time, it seemed, than information. "I suppose you saw him with me today. Well, why shouldn't he be at the races the same as Mr. Lionel here."

"There's more in it than that," Beef replied. "Why did you tell him about the key of the medicine cupboard being found on the top of Mr. Vincent Townsend's wardrobe?"

Raikes looked pale and shaken. He mumbled something about running into Gupp and casually mentioning what his wife Mary had told him. "Anyway, I must be getting along now, Mr. Lionel," he said to me, and without a word or a glance at Beef he strode out of the pub.

As soon as we were in the car on our way back to Hastings I couldn't help asking Beef the question that was puzzling me.

"The money was stolen, then, after all?" I asked. "I never quite understood about it being overlooked and then turning up again."

"'Course it was," Beef replied. "Why do you think young Charlie sold his motor-bike? He knew his dad too well. He knew where the money had gone and he and his mum weren't happy till it was put back."

"By jove," I said. "Why of course. I'll get the boy the best bike that money can buy as soon as our legacies come through. That depends on you, Beef. It seems to me that we've had a lovely afternoon racing, but we've not got much forrader with the clearing up of the case."

"I call it a very satisfactory day," Beef replied. "In every respect." And he patted his wallet affectionately.

8

It was nine o'clock when we reached Hastings and as it was rather late to ask for a meal either at Camber Lodge or at the pub in which Beef was staying we went into a restaurant. We had not had much to eat all day and we were both hungry, so little was said till we had eaten. As we lit up pipe and cigarette afterwards, Beef began to talk reflectively.

"I've just one or two things to clear up here tomorrow," he said, "and then I'm off back to my other case in the Cotswolds. You'd better come along. Give you a much better story to write up than this one. Real nasty atmosphere down there."

"I've been away a long time already," I protested. "I'm not at all anxious to interest myself in another case before you have solved this one. After all, this has a personal urgency. It was my aunt who was murdered and my brother and I who may be suspected by the police."

"I'll come back to this," said Beef. "But in the other case the scent will be getting cold unless I go ahead at once. There's no reason why this shouldn't be left for a few days. We've done all the immediate things."

I did not like to confess what was in my mind.

"Well, I had thought there might be a novel in this case," I said at last. "And the fact that it was my aunt would give it a more personal and interesting appeal."

"So there ought to be in the other case," said Beef sulkily.

"*Two* novels?" I exclaimed.

"Well, perhaps you could make one book of the two of them," suggested Beef. "Suppose we was to let them run neck and neck? Do a little bit of this one, then a little bit of that, I mean. How would that be?"

"It wouldn't do at all. People don't want to be jerked away from one case to start all over again in another. That's why books of short stories are never successful."

"Don't you be too sure," said Beef. "If I was reading I should like a bit of contrast. Anyone could have too much of your aunt's case—dear old lady though she may have been. This other chap who's got himself murdered is a very different kettle of fish. You have a try at making one book of the two. I think it would turn out all right."

I shrugged.

"If you're determined to take up the Cotswold case again I suppose there is nothing for me to do but come with you. But I shall have to look in at my flat on the way and pick up a suitcase."

"That will suit me nicely," said Beef, with enthusiasm. "I'd like to look in and see my old woman, too. It's just as quick to motor through London, in fact quicker by the time you've mucked around side roads."

"I can see it's the car you really want, Beef," I said, laughing.

"Well, in this case it would come in *very* handy. The place where the murder was done is miles from anywhere. Nearest pub is seven miles. That shows you, doesn't it?"

"What's the case all about, Beef," I asked, "and how did you come into it?"

"It's a funny case," he said ruminatively, sending up enormous waves of smoke from his pipe. "A wealthy old chap was found hanging from a beam in his house. At first it was thought to be suicide. That's how I came to be called in, see? His brother is a clergyman with a large family. The old boy who's dead was a widower. Though he hadn't left his brother the money, which all goes to a niece, he'd taken out a huge insurance of about thirty thousand pounds, and that went to his clergyman brother in trust for his children. But of course the clergyman realised quick when he heard that his brother had been found hanging that if it was suicide he wouldn't get a penny from the insurance. So he comes along to me the very same day as he heard—that was the day after the murder—and employs me to find out if there's any chance of foul play, as they say. There's a bit more to it than that. The clergyman knew that his brother was hated by pretty well everyone and that more than once he'd been threatened with violence."

"And was it murder?" I asked.

"Oh yes, clear as daylight, but that's about all that is clear, same as in your aunt's case. You see, it looks like money again being the motive, though there's other motives too in this case. He was a nasty, mean, miserly old man and a lot of people would like to have bumped him off, whereas I can't think of anyone wanting to do in your aunt. As nice an old lady as you could meet, I'm sure. You can see that from the house and the servants. You wait till you see this barn of a place in the Cotswolds. Gives you a nasty turn every time you look round. Well, you'll soon be seeing it for yourself. You ought to be able to make something up about the atmosphere of a place like that."

The first surprise I had the next morning was to find no Edith Payne and only one place laid.

"Miss Edith went off to London as soon as you'd gone yesterday," Ellen told me. "She's only taken a suitcase and says she'll be back in a few days, Mr. Lionel," Ellen went on, becoming almost human as excitement crept into her voice. "You know how she's been since your aunt died? Like a death's head you might say. Well, yesterday she calls me up to her room and there she was packing. She looked ten years younger, her face all flushed and *that* excited I didn't know what to make of it. 'I'm going to London today,' she says. 'I'll be back in a few days and I'll have a great big surprise for you'."

"Was there a letter for me from my brother?" I asked casually.

"No, sir," Ellen replied. "But there's been one the last two mornings from him for Miss Edith. She'll show you them, I daresay, when she gets back."

I was a bit worried about this news. Was it possible that Vincent and Edith had cleared out? I turned to the paper and finished my breakfast. It was no use worrying until I had more facts. I was just going out to smoke in the garden when Ellen reappeared and I could tell by her manner that she had more to tell me.

"Have you heard about the vicar, sir?" she asked. "Terrible it is. I don't know what Miss Fielding would have said if she'd been alive. Perhaps it's as well she's spared it."

"What is all this about the vicar, Ellen?" I asked rather impatiently.

"Gone right off his head. Loopy, sir, they say. He was taking a christening yesterday afternoon when he was suddenly took queer. Nearly drowned the poor little thing, so I hear. Overwork, they say. It's all that restoration he's having done. Been working day and night and practically not a bite to eat, so his housekeeper tells me. They've taken him to a private mental home."

I could stand no more shocks just after breakfast and went out into the garden to wait for Beef, who said he would be up about half-past ten. Before I went out I had told Ellen I was leaving and asked her to pack my things.

When Beef arrived, I told him first about the vicar, but he didn't make any comment. Then I gave him Ellen's story of Edith Payne going to London.

"She's gone to meet my brother Vincent, I'm sure. You don't think they are doing a bunk, Beef?" I asked anxiously, feeling almost a traitor to my brother in suggesting it.

"More like wedding bells, I should say," Beef replied.

"I hope so," I said, though I didn't fancy Edith as a sister-in-law. At that moment Ellen came out with a silver tray in her hand. It was a telegram from Vincent.

"Married to Edith by special licence today. Love from us both, Vincent," I read, and showed it to Beef.

"I wasn't far out, was I?" was all he said. "It's time we had a talk with the police."

Inspector Arnold greeted Beef and myself in his usual impersonal way.

"I'm afraid I haven't had any luck with that receipt form you left with me," he said to Beef. "None of the local people know anything about the Church Missions Society, but I've sent it up to the Yard. They'll be able to give us an answer, but I don't think I shall worry very much about it."

Beef mentioned that we had seen Gupp yesterday, but again he showed little interest. "There's no breaking his alibi. We've tried everything," was his only comment.

"Well, I'm off back to that case in the Cotswolds," Beef told him.

"Oh, you're interested in that fellow who was found strangled and then hung up on a rope, are you?" Arnold commented. "Looks interesting."

When Beef told the Inspector that I was going with him, he made no remark. My brother Vincent's name came up, just as we were leaving, and I mentioned that he was being married that very morning.

"Yes, we know all about that," Arnold said, rather grimly, I thought.

"I expect he found running a House at Penshurst all by himself rather too much. All the housekeeping, you know," I said to the Inspector.

"Possibly," he said. "There's also a very convenient law that a wife can't give evidence against a husband, and vice versa. Good day."

I was a good deal worried by the Inspector's remark. After a while I could not help asking Beef if he really thought that the Inspector suspected my brother and Edith, but got little comfort from him.

"Well, you're all bound to be under suspicion till it's cleared up," he said. "There are not many flies on Inspector Arnold. Very little goes on that he doesn't know about."

We collected Beef's things from the pub where he had been staying and drove to Camber Lodge.

"It will feel strange," Mary said, when I went to say goodbye. "Nobody in the house, not even Miss Edith. I don't know what we shall do with ourselves."

"Oh, we'll all be back soon for one of your real dinners, Mary," I answered.

Charlie had put my bag in the car and we set off for London.

We stopped for the usual ill-cooked meal that hotels on main roads still serve as lunch and arrived at my flat about tea-time. Beef had never seen the small flat near Marble Arch where I lived, so I asked him in.

"So this is where you write up my cases, is it?" he said, looking around. "Very comfortable, too. Be able to afford something a bit bigger if this case turns out all right," he added.

There had been no further police activity concerning me as far as I could gather, and after putting together some clean underclothing, a tweed suit, and, on Beef's advice, my thickest overcoat ("The nearest village is called Cold Slaughter," Beef explained, "and when the weather's nasty I should think it could be about the coldest and bleakest place in England"), we drove to the drab little house that Beef had taken when he first set up as a private detective. It was as near Baker Street as he had been able to manage. Mrs. Beef, a kindly countrywoman whom Beef had married in his early days as a constable in a small village, gave us tea. She obviously thought the world of her husband and sent him off with solicitous instructions about looking after himself.

I took the High Wycombe road, followed the bypass leaving Oxford, a crown of spires in the gathering dusk, passed through Witney, caught a passing glimpse of the beauty of Minster Lovel and Burford, and then, leaving Oxfordshire as evening was beginning to close in, entered the long high bleak stretch of road that leads into Gloucestershire.

9

After some twenty miles or so of the main windswept road, we turned off to the right. A signpost gave several names, none of which I had ever heard before, but among them I could see *Cold Slaughter 16 miles*. This, Beef told me, was a village some five miles from the house where Edwin Ridley had been murdered. "There's quite a nice little pub there where I stayed before," he added. "I've sent them a telegram, so they'll be expecting us."

We were driving now down quite a narrow lane. The country had become more hilly and wooded. I could see little but the walls of grey Cotswold stone on either side. Occasionally we passed a cluster of farm buildings, but for the most part the countryside looked wild and deserted. Once we came on a small village at the bottom of a steep hill, but before we had time to see anything the lane swerved abruptly and we were climbing again.

The wind had risen, with night coming on, and a fine rain had begun to settle on the windscreen. I was glad when at last at the top of a hill I saw some lights below and knew that we must be close to our destination.

"This looks like it," Beef said, as we passed a cottage or two. The road opened up after the first few houses into an open space and I could see that Cold Slaughter was quite a small village.

"The Shaven Crown. There's our pub," Beef said, pointing out to me a building that in our headlights looked cold and austere. There were lights shining inside, however, and I was glad the journey was over. I had not made any further protest at Beef's dropping my aunt's case to continue his investigation of this one because I realised that it would be useless. Once a resolve had formed in his thick head, nothing could shift it. He had promised faithfully to return to Hastings, and I had to admit that the Cotswold murder sounded a promising one from the literary point of view. Besides, although I would not admit it, I had rather come round to Beef's suggestion about running the two stories in harness. Why not? Two murders on the same day being investigated by the same detective at the same time . . . they were linked securely enough to make a single novel. At any rate, I had decided to try them like that.

I drove the car under an old arch into a large courtyard, where we left it and entered the bar. Half an hour later, with the car safely parked in a garage, our bags in our rooms, a large whisky in my hand and the smell of a meal being prepared for us, I began to feel more cheerful. After an excellent supper of veal cutlets and Welsh rarebit, Beef told me what he had discovered so far about the death of Edwin Ridley.

I was to learn much about Edwin Ridley, his early life and his business as publisher, from his brother, Alfred, the clergyman, and from an old friend of mine, who was also my literary agent, Michael Thorogood. What I gathered from Beef that evening were the facts about Ridley's murder so far as Beef had managed to learn them in the few days he was down here, before he received my letter about Aunt Aurora's death and left for Hastings.

"Well," Beef began, "as I told you, the morning after Edwin Ridley was found dead the police naturally got in touch with his nearest relative. That was his brother, the clergyman. He's the one I told you about. He was in a nice state, thinking his children might lose all the insurance, the whole thirty thousand quid, if it turned out to be suicide. All he knew was that his brother had been found dead with a rope round his neck. He had heard about me by chance—I'd once helped some friends of his wife over a little matter of retrieving a stolen necklace—and he hops in a taxi and comes rushing round to me. We have a little argument over the fee. He was nearly as close with money as his brother must have been. You could see he was torn between parting with a few quid and losing the chance of a fortune. All he wanted me to do was to see that the coroner's verdict wasn't suicide. 'If I take up the investigation,' I said to him very dignified, 'I shall probe it to the depths. One hundred quid,' I said, 'and expenses limited to fifty. That's my last word.' He tried to beat me down on expenses, but he saw it was no good and eventually agreed. I came down here that very day, landed up at the nearest station, hired a car, and reached the house. I was lucky to catch the Superintendent in charge there and get in right with him. I showed him a letter from the Rev. Alfred Ridley, authorising me to act for the family, and he became quite pally. I think he was glad of a bit of support. He hadn't had many big cases round here."

Beef paused to lower half his tankard.

"You'll see the house tomorrow, so I won't go into that," he went on. "Gloomy great place. Ridley lived there with only two servants, a man and his wife. I wouldn't trust either further than I could see. Then there's a young secretary, young fellow of about twenty-five. A bit nancified, he seemed to me. That's all the household. Ridley was found by the manservant hanging from a beam in the large room which he used as a study and for his books. That was about six o'clock in the morning. The body was quite stiff and cold then. He rushed out and roused the secretary. He took one glance at the body and phoned the police. Death must have occurred about six hours before the body was found, so all this took place around midnight of the tenth of September. That, if you remember, was the day your aunt was poisoned."

Beef paused. Then slowly that expression of amusement came into his face that I knew so well—amusement at some piece of human pretention or frailty.

"And the joke of it is," he said, "that if the Reverend Alfred Ridley hadn't been quite so eager, he would have saved his hundred and fifty quid because by the next day it had been established on medical evidence that Edwin Ridley was already dead, strangled, before he was strung up on a rope. Suicide never came into it, and as far as the reverend was concerned I never had to lift a finger. 'Course he was wild as soon as he heard. He wrote me at once, apologising for giving me the unnecessary trouble of a journey to Gloucestershire and saying that he was sure I would agree that my services were no longer required in view of the doctor's decision. Fortunately, seeing what sort of bird he was, I'd made him sign one of my contract forms, so he can't get out of it. Funny, wasn't it?"

I suggested moving into the bar now, as the green-plush tablecloth, the bronze bowls of ferns, and the fading photographs of early relations of the innkeeper were beginning to depress me. There Beef continued.

"It looked like an outside job. Ridley kept some valuable books in his library and there was some nice stuff in the house. Two people benefited by his Will. First there was the clergyman, but apart from his calling me in he had his alibi vouched for that night by a dozen people apart from his family. Then his niece. She gets the bulk of the money—which is quite a lot, I believe. She, I understand, is a frail little thing nearly forty who spent that night with the Dean of Fulham and, anyway, hadn't the strength to string Ridley up from a beam."

"What I can't understand, Beef," I said, "is why you are going on with this case now."

"I told the Reverend Alfred I was going to probe it to the depths, and probe it I will. Besides, there are one or two strange things in this case that interest me. Interest me *very much indeed.*"

"Also," he had added with a twinkle, "there's that fifty quid expenses. I'm going to spend every penny of it."

Next morning we set out after breakfast for Bampton Court, which was the name of Ridley's house.

The rain that had begun to fall the night before still persisted, and the country looked cold and colourless. We came to some rather fine wrought-iron gates and drove in. The drive was little more than a rutted cart-track overgrown with weeds, and the fields on either side looked equally untended. We passed through a small wood, and round a bend we came on the house. Even to my untutored eye it was obviously a beauty—as fine a piece of seventeenth-century architecture as you could meet. Yet curiously, as Beef had said, it was a great gloomy place. As I looked around I realised why it should seem to be so. The garden had been allowed to grow quite wild, the grey Cotswold stone was covered with moss where it was visible at all, for trees and creepers had invaded terrace, lawn and drive, all around the house entirely unchecked and seemed to be eager to overwhelm and strangle the shapely beauty of window and eave. Only the tall slim Tudor chimneys rose still free from those green, engulfing tentacles.

"Gloomy, isn't it?" Beef said. "Can't understand anyone living in a place like that."

I nodded. Yes, I thought, but the gloom was due to decay and neglect, and must to a certain extent reveal something of the man who had lived here. I could imagine the house a hundred and fifty years ago in the time of Jane Austen, the home of a large family, the gardens laid out, and the stables full of horses and carriages. It would not have been gloomy then.

Beef went up to the front door, a fine piece of old oak, and pulled at the bell. An unprepossessing figure of a man of about forty-five appeared, untidy and dirty and looking as if he could do with a shave.

"Oh, it's you back, is it?" he said to Beef morosely.

Beef paid no attention but pushed into the house, saying he wanted to speak to Mr. Lovelace, the secretary. "That's the manservant I told you about," Beef said, as the man stumped off to find the secretary. We were standing in a large hall and I could see that, although everything seemed worn and undusted, there was some valuable furniture there, rugs and chairs and a particularly fine gate-legged table. I had little time to observe everything before a tall willowy figure appeared.

"I'm so glad to see you, Mr. Beef. I'm going positively crazy in this house alone. Well, alone except for those two revolting servants, who are quite out of hand now that there's no master in the house. We haven't met," he said pleasantly enough, but I was conscious of two very blue, very shrewd eyes fixed on me.

"This is Mr. Lionel Townsend," Beef said. "He helps me with most of my cases and then writes them up. This is the late Mr. Ridley's secretary, Mr. Lovelace."

"Yes. I'm Adrian Lovelace. How do you do? So you're the Doctor Watson, are you, or is it the Captain Hastings, of the ménage? I've always wanted to meet one of those faithful recorders. Such nice, dependable men, so loyal and not too fashionably subtle. We must have a long talk about the writing of detective stories. I'm an absolute glutton for them, and I've some wonderful theories."

I could see that Beef was getting impatient while the young man prattled on in a pleasant but rather high-pitched voice. Though too thin and pale, his features were arrestingly well-formed, but there was something displeasing to me about him. Whether it was the slightly petulant mouth or the closeness of his very pale-blue eyes, I could not decide. His clothes, too—the pale-grey suit, lavender tie and grey suede shoes—though all expensive and beautifully made, did not seem right in this house. They were more suited to Maidenhead or a theatrical garden party.

"I'd like to have another look at the room where the old boy was found dead," Beef said, and Lovelace led the way down a long stone corridor at the end of which was a stout oak door set in a stone arch.

"This room was built on much later," Lovelace said, turning a huge key. "It's less than a hundred years old. It was used as a private chapel by the family who lived here. They died out in the 1914 war and the house was empty until Edwin Ridley bought it about 1930. It's an ugly barn of a place, as you see."

I gazed around and wondered how anyone could so mis-use the stone of the Cotswolds. There were tall Victorian gothic windows with clear leaden panes, except at the far end where stained-glass windows in hideous garish colours gave a ghoulish nineteenth-century version of Abraham preparing to sacrifice Isaac. There was a lot of fumed oak and a door leading out into the garden crowned with the inevitable gothic arch. The roof was open and beams ran from side to side. Everywhere the plain dignity of the stone had been spoilt by a fussy foliated design. Most of the walls were lined with bookshelves, and books of every kind and shape filled them.

"Yes," Lovelace said, as he saw me looking at them, "he was a bibliophile. A real honest-to-god collector—about the only honest thing about him, I'm afraid."

I looked around at the old calf folios and quartos, at the sets in seventeenth- and eighteenth-century morocco, and at the rows of three-volume novels, the gilt lettering still bright even in this dim-lit room.

"Must be a valuable collection," I said.

"Valued at about twenty thousand for probate a few years ago, but he's added quite a bit since."

Beef showed me the beam from which Edwin Ridley had been found hanging.

"How did the murderer get him up there?" I asked.

"He must have used one of the ladders we keep for fruit-picking," Lovelace replied. "But would you like to hear the whole story? I almost know it by heart now, I've told it so often."

Beef had opened the door into the garden and was busy examining both inside and out, so I agreed.

"Well, the last time I saw my employer alive," he began, "was at dinner that night. We dined together, as usual. Perhaps the only slightly strange thing was that he sent Fagg—that's the unshaven creature who let you in—for a bottle of red wine. We were having duck, I remember, and he particularly wanted a bottle of Burgundy. It wasn't unheard of for him to open a bottle, though he was as mean as hell, but it was almost always when he had some guest who was useful to him or when he had picked up cheap some unusual bargain for his collection."

Lovelace noticed that Beef had joined us. "Oh, Mr. Beef, you don't want to hear all my story over again, do you?" he said, but he seemed pleased at the addition to his audience.

"I was always free after dinner, as Ridley invariably took his cigar into this room and spent the evenings with his beloved books. I would sometimes hear him go to bed about twelve, but often the whole household was asleep before he retired. Fagg used to leave a glass and a siphon of soda for him on the side there. He had his own bottle of whisky locked in a cabinet after he had found the bottle an inch and a half lower than he had left it, so he said. Quite a fuss there was. It must have been Fagg, because I wouldn't touch the beastly stuff. I don't mind an occasional gin and lime, but whisky. Eugh!"

I caught Beef's eye, and it was all I could do to suppress a chuckle.

"So you see he was never disturbed at night. I went off on my motor-cycle to play bridge with the doctor at Cold Slaughter. I got back about twelve. The lights were still on in this room, I could see as I put my bike away. There was nothing unusual inside the house. I drank my glass of hot milk and went straight to bed. The next thing I knew was a fearful banging at my door. There was the creature Fagg, looking even more dishevelled and repulsive than ever, shouting that the master had hanged himself and screeching to me to come down quickly. I threw on a few clothes and followed Fagg to this room. Oh, it was *quite* awful. It was still not yet light and there was that thing dangling on the end of a rope. I nearly fainted. However, the Fagg creature seemed to have quite lost his head so I had to do everything myself. There was a chair upset below the body. I picked it up and stood on it. I could touch the body from there. It was quite cold and stiff. I went straight to the hall and telephoned the police. Then I was sick."

He paused and looked round at us both as if he expected a round of applause.

"What I want to know," Beef said, "is why Fagg was up and about the house at six o'clock. That was when he found him, I think. I'm sure it's not usual for either of them to get up at that hour."

"I asked him that," Lovelace replied. "He said he couldn't sleep and got up to make a cup of tea. Then he thought he'd have a look at the paper. Of course the paper of the day before. We don't get a paper delivered in this place before midday. He knew that his master always took the papers into his book-room after dinner so he came down to that door." He pointed to the door leading from the corridor. "It was locked and he could see the key was inside. This really surprised him, as he knew his master was always in the habit of turning the key from the corridor side on his way to bed. He went into the garden and round the side of the house to see if the garden door was open by any chance. Well, it was, and that's how he came to be banging and shouting at my door."

"Do you do the cataloguing of these books?" I asked Lovelace.

"For my sins," he said, showing me a large cabinet full of cards. "Here they all are, neatly typed. A4," he quoted.

"That's the shelf. Milton, John . . . . You see there's a separate card for each book. Every time he got a new lot, he used to dictate to me a description of each book and I'd type a card."

"Then you'd know if anything was missing?" I asked.

"You are a Doctor Watson," he replied impatiently. "That was one of the first questions your friend Beef and the Superintendent asked me. Well, as I told them, I couldn't check the whole library, but he kept his really valuable books locked in a special case. That one over there. The cards were also in a tray of their own. It was easy to go through them, and I soon found that none of his really valuable books had disappeared."

He paused and turned to Beef.

"One rather curious thing I noticed. You see that bundle of books over there. About half a dozen of them. The paper they were wrapped in is still there. I've never seen them before and I'm pretty sure they weren't here the afternoon before Ridley was murdered. I would have noticed them."

10

Beef did not show any great interest in the books, saying, "We'll have another look at them presently. I'm more interested in the packing. The books are more in your line," he said, turning to me.

"Now, Mr. Lovelace, I want to get some real idea about the late Mr. Edwin Ridley. We're all agreed that he was murdered, that the murder took place about midnight, that he was strangled by hand first and then strung up with a new piece of rope. If it wasn't you or Fagg, it must have been the work of someone outside. Do you know any likely reason anyone had for bumping him off? Any special enemies?"

Lovelace thought for a moment.

"It's like this, Sergeant. While he was alive and my employer, I never said anything against him, but now he's dead I feel free to speak. I think he was the hardest and meanest man I've ever met. Mind you, it didn't affect me. He paid me a good salary. We lived well and, though he worked me hard, I had entire freedom to do what I liked when he didn't want me.

"I should think in an area of fifteen miles there are a dozen people who hated the sight of him for one reason or another, but I can't say that any of them would take their dislike as far as murder. It's been one long series of local rows since I've been here, and that's over two years. Would you like to hear the local gossip? If you would I suggest we move out of here into my sitting-room. This place gives me the shivers. I'll make you some coffee."

He led the way on to a half-landing and showed us into his room. After the cold bleakness of the rest of the house it was pleasant to find this bright little oasis. A fire was burning in a Queen Anne grate, there were bright curtains and rugs, and on the walls well-framed prints of the French impressionists. Rows of modern books of the more esoteric type lined his bookshelves, and the whole effect rather reminded me of the room of a female student at Oxford in the early 'thirties.

"Do you like it?" he asked me, as he began to toy with a percolator and a coffee grinder.

"I must say it's very different from the rest of the house," I replied, noncommittally. "It's pleasant to see a fire."

Beef was making violent signs behind Lovelace's back, which I gathered meant that he was not keen on the idea of coffee, but wanted a drink.

"Beef doesn't care for coffee," I said to Lovelace. "What he'd really like is a glass of beer, if you have one in the house?"

"You'd like my coffee, Sergeant," he replied. "But if you prefer beer I'll go and get a bottle or two from the cellar."

As soon as the door had shut behind him, Beef said in a hoarse whisper:

"See what I mean when I said 'a bit nancified'. But he's no fool and we may get something from him. I don't think much went on here that he didn't know about. Regular old woman for his gossip, I should say."

He came back with a few bottles of beer and poured out one for Beef.

"I don't really know where to begin," he said, as he busied himself with preparing the coffee. "I think the first row he had was when he stopped the village cricket team playing their matches on five-acre. The Cold Slaughter team had played there for years and it was the only decent flat piece of ground in the district. But it was his ground, and though they offered to pay rent he wouldn't alter his decision. Some of the lads had annoyed him, and the local grocer, he considered, had overcharged him. That led to a lot of unpleasantness. Some of the chaps even came up here one Saturday night and covered everything with green paint. The next trouble I think was with the Hunt. Old Colonel Lethbridge is the M.F.H. He lives about seven miles away. Nice old boy, but a bit eccentric and irascible. Ridley claimed five pounds from the Hunt for the loss of some chickens, which he said a fox had had. The Hunt sent him two guineas, saying they were very short of funds, so Ridley closed his grounds to the Hunt. There are about six hundred acres belonging to Bampton Court. The old colonel came to see him, thinking he could settle the whole dispute with a few words. Ridley threatened to have him thrown out, and the colonel, whose temper was never very good, called him a usurious ill-mannered paper-merchant. Ridley was a publisher, you know. I thought the colonel was going to strike Ridley with his riding-crop, but he managed to control himself. He jumped on his horse and rode off, uttering the most blood-curdling threats and oaths I've ever heard."

I dare say the result may be worth the trouble, but I am afraid I would never have the patience that some people have over making coffee. All this business of grinding beans and heating and cooling in percolators, it may be worth it. I don't know. There only seems to me to be one essential thing about making coffee and that is to put in enough coffee. I must say, when I did eventually receive a cup from Lovelace, it was good and strong. However, I, too, should have preferred beer.

"I gathered he wasn't very popular around here," Beef said, pouring himself out another bottle of beer, "but I didn't know it was as bad as all that. Any other quarrels?"

Lovelace gave a little snigger.

"Dozens, my dear Sergeant," he replied, losing his stiff, rather prim manner as I had seen so many people do after Beef had been in their company a short time.

"He prosecuted poor old Tom and Harry Purkis. Two old brothers. They had always spent Sunday mornings ferreting for rabbits down by the old quarry. It did no harm. In fact the place is overrun with rabbits. Ridley had them up before the local bench and they were fined. That caused a lot of bad blood. The old boys hadn't a bean, but everyone in the village liked them. They were always willing to help with any odd job. Oh, there were a lot more. There was some trouble with the doctor, and then the two families who live in the cottages down by five-acre. He wanted to turn them out. He was still fighting about that up to the time of his death. As for the rows in the house . . ."

"With the Faggs?" Beef queried.

"Yes, two or three weeks I'd hear them go at it hammer and tongs, but I think they all had too much on the other one to come into the open, though they gave each other notice time and again."

"And what about you?" Beef asked. "Did you never quarrel with him?"

Lovelace smiled. "No," he said. "I'm sorry to disappoint you. I'm afraid you'll really have to dismiss me as a suspect. Much as I disliked the old boy, the job suited me. I adore the Cotswolds and I'm just in the middle of my book on modern poetry—Auden and Spender and all those, you know. I'm making a final and definitive anthology from Eliot onwards and I'm writing the most *explosive* preface."

"So his death doesn't suit you, then," Beef said, rather brutally ignoring the poor fellow's literary aspirations. "Apart from people round here, did he have trouble with anyone else, do you know?" Beef went on.

"There was always trouble with people in his business, but I saw very little of that. One or two of his authors threatened to sue him, I believe, and we had that young fellow down here who tried to commit suicide in the grounds, saying Ridley had robbed his mother of her life's savings. You may remember the case, possibly, about six months ago. Young fellow called Greenleaf, who'd written a novel. I don't really know the rights and wrongs of it, but apparently Ridley had made him pay towards the publishing and it never sold more than a few copies. The young man came down here and forced his way into Ridley's study. Ridley had him thrown out, and he took poison in the grounds, leaving a letter blaming Ridley for his action. He had not taken enough poison, and recovered. However, Ridley proved the transaction was perfectly legal. The fellow was obviously a bit nuts, anyway. He was bound over. But I can't give you the details of the business side of his life. I knew there were quite a few threatening letters and some cases settled out of court, but you'll have to get all that from someone else. By the way, curiously enough I heard that that young fellow Greenleaf had been seen in the village a few days before Ridley's death, but I really can't think there's any connection. He was an untidy, rough fellow. Not a bit like a writer, I thought, but I shouldn't have imagined he'd go in for murder."

Beef took out his watch. "I think I've just got time to have another word with Fagg before I go for my dinner. I shall be back this afternoon. I've arranged to meet the Superintendent here about three o'clock."

We found Fagg and his wife in the huge stone kitchen. She was a little thin-lipped waspish woman who had nothing to say. Fagg repeated his story of finding Ridley dead at six o'clock and, though Beef tried to suggest it was very unusual for him to rise so early, the only answer he got from Fagg was, "Well, it's not every day you find your master dangling on a rope, is it?"

"You said no visitors came to the front door that night. If someone outside did it, that person must have got in somehow," Beef said.

"I don't know anything about that," Fagg replied. "I've said all along it was a burglar, and I still think so."

When Beef began to question him about Ridley's unpopularity in the district and about other visitors who had been here, Fagg closed up like a clam, and, though we both felt he could have told us a lot more, it was obviously useless trying further at the moment.

"The only thing that would make him talk," Beef said, as we left the house, after telling Lovelace we would be back to see the Superintendent after lunch, "is if we could get something on him. I don't think he had a hand in the murder, but I reckon he and that old witch of a wife of his know something."

We lunched at the Shaven Crown, and when we drove up to the house again we could see a police car was already there. We found the Superintendent in the room where the crime had been committed. He was a big jovial man and seemed pleased to see Beef.

"My chief constable has decided to call in Scotland Yard," he said, after greeting Beef and being introduced to me. "I said in my report that I didn't think it was a local job. I can't say I'm sorry. It's a devil of a case."

"If Fagg is telling the truth," Beef said, "the murderer must have either broken in somewhere or else Ridley let him in."

"Looks as if he let him in. The old boy was very keen on having everything locked up, and there's no sign anywhere of windows being forced. But, whoever it was, he hasn't left a clue anywhere. Not even a fingerprint."

"There's that little bundle of books," Beef said: "the secretary fellow doesn't think they were here before the night Ridley was murdered."

"There are so many blasted books around here I don't see how he can tell. Anyway, they are old ones and there are no names in them, except in two. Then it's the name of some old josser who died a couple of hundred years ago. Even the brown paper's got no marks on it, and the newspapers are a month old. No, I've the inquest tomorrow, and after that the Yard fellow can have it all. Pity it wasn't suicide—nobody would miss him; but it seems to me when you start trying to find out which of his enemies did him in you might as well look for one particular pebble on the beach at Brighton."

"Or Hastings," Beef said, turning to me for the first time. "Go and have a look at those books. See what you make of them, and don't forget what I said about the packing."

I picked up the small bundle and glanced at the titles. There was a two-volume edition of Gray's Poems, Butler's *Hudibras*, *The Vicar of Wakefield*, and some bound volumes of eighteenth-century plays. Not a valuable lot, I thought, but pleasant early editions and clean calf bindings. Some pencil price markings had been carefully erased and, as the Superintendent had said, the only names on the fly-leaves belonged to the eighteenth century. Then, remembering Beef's words, I had a look at the packing. The brown paper was new and bore no marks except for the string, but when I unfolded the two

sheets of newspaper which formed an inner wrapping I saw
they were headed *The Sussex Gazette,* and dated 16th August.

"We might be able to trace where these books came from,"
I said, not mentioning the newspaper, but determining to
tackle Beef about that later. "If they were bought from a
shop, I expect we could find out where."

"Shouldn't be surprised if they were pinched," the Superintendent said. "The late Mr. Ridley wasn't above doing a
little quiet receiving, so I've heard, when it came to books. I
shouldn't be surprised if it didn't turn out that he had fixed
to see someone that night who was bringing some books for
him to buy. Ridley lets him in. They have a row over prices.
Ridley threatens to hand him over for stealing, and to shut
his mouth the visitor throttles him. Then he gets the wind
up and tries to make it look like suicide."

"What about the rope?" Beef asked. "If it happened as you
say, how did he come to have on him a nice long new piece
of rope, just the right thickness—and length?"

"We don't really know there wasn't some in the gardener's
shed where he found the ladder. We've only Fagg's word for
that. Mr. Lovelace wouldn't notice a thing like that."

I was not so sure. I did not think there was much that
escaped that young man's pale-blue eyes.

"By the way, Beef, I have found one thing I must show
you." He produced a piece of plain folded notepaper. "I found
this among Ridley's letters. It looks like a childish threat and
probably has nothing to do with the murder. One of the
locals sent it, I expect. Unfortunately there's no envelope.
Lovelace says he saw most of Ridley's correspondence, but
he was never shown this."

Beef took the paper and spread it out flat. It was dated
6th September, four days before the murder. Then followed

large heavy print, "Don't think you'll get away with it, you little rat. The day of reckoning is drawing near."

"Looks like some kid's prank," I said, as I read the puerile threat and noted the roughly formed letters. It was good notepaper, I noticed, but the top had been torn off.

Beef smiled and handed it back to the Superintendent. "Thanks," he said. "One more thing to bear in mind. When's the fellow from Scotland Yard arriving?"

"He's coming to see me in my office tonight," the Superintendent replied. "I've got to put him in the picture so that he can follow all the points at the inquest tomorrow. He'll be attending that so you can see him there."

"Not me, I shan't," Beef said. "I reckon I've seen all I want to down here for the moment. It'll be London for me tomorrow."

We said goodbye to the Superintendent, and were just leaving when Lovelace came out. "I hear you're going," he said as we went towards the car. "I am disappointed. I did so want to have a long talk about crime and detection. Shall you be down again?"

Beef mumbled something about possibly, and we drove off. "I wonder what he's up to," Beef said. "Something I don't quite trust there, and I'm usually not far out."

"So it's London tomorrow, Beef," I said, as we drove to Cold Slaughter.

"Yes," Beef replied, lighting his pipe. "I want to learn a bit more about Mr. Edwin Ridley. We'll see that brother of his. He should be able to tell us a bit. Then there's this publishing business of his. Sounds a bit fishy with threatening letters and authors trying to commit suicide."

"I've been thinking about that," I said. "I know who'll give us the whole story. My literary agent, Michael Thorogood. He knows all the publishers. But have you given up the idea that it might be someone local?" I asked.

"Not necessarily," Beef said. "From what I hear I can understand quite a few people round here wanting to wring his neck, but there's a big step between wishing someone was out of the way and actually doing them in."

"What about a row?" I said. "Supposing someone like the M.F.H., Colonel Lethbridge, or the captain of the cricket team or any of the people he'd quarrelled with—supposing one of them called that night. Ridley may have let them in. They have a row, lose their tempers, start fighting, and whoever it was suddenly finds he's throttled Ridley. Could easily be done. After all, Ridley was only a little rat of a man, I hear."

Beef did not say anything but went on puffing away at his pipe.

"Well, it's possible, isn't it?" I said. "Then, finding out what he's done, the murderer fakes a suicide. If it was a local man, he could easily go and fetch the rope. After all, the coast was completely clear from dinner-time till six the next morning."

"Well, we'll see," Beef said, in a rather pompous voice. "You and the Superintendent have both made out a good case and I dare say we'll find it happened something like that. I still think I'd like to know a bit more about Ridley. By the way," he said, "in your theory how do you account for those books?"

"Oh, that's easy," I said. "If they were brought by the murderer, they were probably his excuse to get an interview. I expect whoever it was flattered Ridley to see him and get his opinion on some books."

"And the newspaper from Sussex?" Beef asked. "How does that fit in?"

"Do you really think it might have something to do with our other case?" I asked eagerly.

"It's a funny coincidence."

"But there are a hundred explanations," I could not help saying. "If these books were bought at a shop, that may have been the packing which the bookseller used. He'd have books coming in from all over the place."

We were entering Cold Slaughter now.

"What did you think of Ridley's household?" I asked. "Lovelace and the Faggs? Do you think they had anything to do with the murder?"

"I don't say I'm not interested in who did it and how it was done," Beef replied, "but I'm much more interested to know why it was done. You remember what the Inspector down at Hastings said. Motive. That's the key to every murder. And that's why we're off to London tomorrow to find out a bit more about Ridley. Even if Ridley was murdered in a fit of temper, there must have been something pretty powerful behind it all to make a man get in such a rage."

I drove the car into the courtyard of the Shaven Grown, and went up to my room. I had a bath and sat down and made a few notes. I thought I might possibly be able to use this case as a story. It was a good setting. It rather depended on how it was going to turn out. What should I call it, I wondered. *Corpse in the Cotswolds?* . . . *Body of a Bibliophile?* Well, some title would come when I had written it. I was sorry, in a way, to be leaving Cold Slaughter. The weather had cleared and it looked as if it might be fine in the morning. The Shaven Crown was comfortable enough, and when we had gone into the public bar the evening before, we had soon got on friendly terms with the locals, regulars mostly, and for once I had really enjoyed an evening's darts. There was none of the slick play of the pubs in a town. It was a pleasant leisurely game where a man would pause in the middle of his throw to answer some question that had been asked. And when each game was over and the beer bought—or in many cases it was rough cider—there was a friendly pause and a chat.

"Let Arthur play," one would say. "He hasn't had a game all the evening. I'll stand down for a bit."

Beef, I was pleased to see, was at home among these countrymen. He suited his play to the company—a very different game from the one he played against the two racing touts at Lewes, who were only out to win a couple of cheap pints.

When I came down I found Beef alone in an empty bar. "We don't get many in before eight these days," the landlord said. "They can't afford it, you know. Ruinous these prices to the working man, especially in the country. That's really where the pub is most needed. It's a club and everything to these chaps. Are you ready for your supper?"

Once again an excellent little meal was produced. The landlord's wife had been cook at one of the big houses in the district and everything was beautifully served.

"Pity we've got to leave this," I said to Beef, when we were lighting up after supper.

"We'll probably be back," he replied. "I must get my revenge on that postman who beat me last night. He only comes on Wednesdays and Saturdays, so he won't be in tonight."

While we were drinking a pint before joining the players round the board, the landlord called Beef aside.

"There's a chap here would like a word with you. Of course they all know what you're down here for. Shall I bring him up?"

Beef agreed, and a young fellow was introduced to us as Bob Chapman. "He's chauffeur to Sir Henry Woodhouse, the local M.P." After Beef had bought him a drink and I had produced my cigarette-case, he seemed more at ease. "I don't know whether this is any good to you. It may be nothing at all. I haven't mentioned anything to the police, because it really didn't seem important enough. Well, the night the gentleman at Bampton Court was done in, I was driving back with Sir Henry and his wife about midnight. They'd been to a Conservative Dinner in Cheltenham. I had to pass Bampton Court on the way. A bit further on there's a small lane that leads to the back of the house. As I passed it I noticed a car parked about twenty yards down. My boss and his wife wouldn't see anything as they were sitting behind and had the small roof light on. I thought it was funny at the time, but you know how these things are. Sir Henry wanted to drive to London the following day and it went clean out of my mind till I heard about you gentlemen making enquiries about his death."

Beef thanked him. "You never know how these things work out. 'Course, it may have nothing to do with the murder. On the other hand it may. You didn't notice a number or anything?"

"It was too dark, I'm afraid, and there was no light on, but it looked like an old saloon Austin by the shape of it. One thing I did see. There was a star-shaped crack on the left of the rear window. My headlight just caught it as I turned. I hear you throw a pretty dart. Shall we make up a four?"

"I will in a minute," Beef replied. "There's just one more thing I want to enquire about. Do you know anything about a chap called Greenleaf, who tried to commit suicide in Ridley's grounds?"

"Yes, I know him. He was supposed to have been seen near the village the day of the murder. One of the women thought she recognised him. This fellow was hiking, it seems. He had a great rucksack on his back, but you know what some women are. I shouldn't stake too much on that story. We never heard about it till after the murder. You usually find stories like that cropping up after anything happens. Look, they're just finishing now," he added, pointing to the score. "What about it?"

11

The Reverend Alfred Ridley was vicar of St. John's, a parish in a respectable suburb south of the Thames. Beef had warned him that we were coming to see him in the afternoon and it was about half-past two, after an uneventful drive to London, that we drew up at a large Victorian redbrick house that was the vicarage. Alfred Ridley belonged neither to the type of clergyman typified by the vicar down at Hastings—extremely devout, impractical, usually tall, emaciated and untidy, and almost invariably a bachelor—nor to his extreme opposite—the round-faced tubby cleric, often a rowing man at Oxford or Cambridge, hearty, well-fed, with a large family, who prides himself on no nonsense and meeting his parishioners as man to man. He was of the type who become deans and bishops, having something of the fanatical faith of the former but combined with a practical grip of Church politics. He had read deeply and had written several treatises which were held in high esteem. In addition, he had a deeper worldly wisdom than the latter type and conducted the business side of his job with cold efficiency. All this I was soon to learn.

We were shown into a large airy room. "This is my workroom," Alfred Ridley said, after greeting Beef and being introduced to me, and, as I looked round, I could appreciate his description. On a large flat desk was a typewriter, calendar, diary with numerous neat entries, a row of reference books—I noted *Crockford's, Who's Who,* and an *Oxford Dictionary* as well as many clerical books with which I was not familiar—a telephone with a filed list of numerous numbers as well as several directories, private notepaper and envelopes and a large fat wad of foolscap. The walls were lined with books, not the kind which his late brother would have housed, but what seemed to me a pretty comprehensive collection—English literature, the classics, a good deal of the more serious modern stuff, and a whole wall packed with theological books.

"I've just had a wire from Gloucestershire," he went on. "I arranged for them to let me know the result of the inquest held this morning. Wilful Murder by Person or Persons Unknown. Well now, Sergeant, much as I wish to see the culprit apprehended, I think we can safely leave that in the hands of the police, don't you? You got my letter, I hope?"

"I'm afraid, sir," Beef replied, "once I've started on a case I must see it through. It's my reputation, you see, I have to think of. I told you that, you remember, the morning you came to see me and signed my contract..."

"My dear fellow, of course I realise that legally you are in the right, but I thought that naturally you'd be reasonable. You wouldn't care to take a sum of money, I'm sure, without—what shall we say—earning it honestly."

"Oh, I shall earn it, all right," Beef replied. "You'll see. I shall get to the bottom of this business before I've finished. The sooner I do that the better. That's why I've come to see you. I want your help. I want to know as much about your brother as you can tell me. At the moment it would appear that his murder was without any motive, though, if I may say so, there seem to be quite a few people with whom he wasn't very popular."

"As I said," the vicar replied, "I naturally wish this unpleasant affair to be cleared up and I will of course give you all the help I can. Let me see now what I have on this afternoon." He consulted his diary. "Nothing very much till five o'clock. Then two appointments for which my curate can deputise. If you'll excuse me, I'll just phone him.

"Now," he said, as he put down the receiver, "I'm at your service. You want some account of my brother as I knew him. I can't pretend, even though he is dead, that he was a likeable man in every respect. Though he was a successful business man, he was, I'm afraid, very close with money. In my early days, when I was struggling with a family—before our father died and left us both comfortably off—he could so easily have helped me. A few hundred would have meant so much then. However, I must not dwell on that side of his character. He made amends in the end and, as you know, my children benefit from a very generous life insurance policy which he took out on their behalf."

He paused to light a cigarette and, as an afterthought, handed round his case. I took one and Beef produced his enormous pipe.

"Perhaps I should go back to our early days. Our father, who died many years ago, was a merchant in Mincing Lane, dealing with India and the East and was modestly successful. He sent us both to a good school"—he named a well known public school—"and as I was going into the Church, he sent me on to Oxford. Edwin was at first a bitter disappointment to my father. He would not go into the family business but wanted to become a writer. In those days he was a shy self-contained young man, a year older than I. My father sent him abroad on the continent for two years. He lived with a family, a French family, at Tours and a German family in Hanover. My father's view was that if his attempt at writing failed, the knowledge of the best French and German would be a help commercially. When he came back, he seemed little changed. Still very sensitive and wrapped up in himself. I was surprised, therefore, when one day he called me to his room, swore me to secrecy and then produced the manuscript of a novel he had written a year before. He had already submitted it to two or three publishers, who had turned it down, and he showed me the rejection slips. Then he took a letter from his pocket and gave it to me to read. It was from a publisher of whom I had never heard. The publisher, apparently, was very taken with my brother's book, thought it showed much talent and promise of great things in the future. He would count it an honour to be allowed to sponsor the publication. Unfortunately, as things were, he could not undertake the whole financial risk himself, but if my brother would care to share with him the expense he would be delighted to launch what he hoped and believed would be a new star in the literary firmament, or words to that extent."

A thin smile appeared for a moment as he said this, and then he went on. "My brother, of course, was thrilled at this eulogy, and I too caught his excitement. We were very young. I persuaded him to allow me to speak to our father about this. The result was that my father, proud of a son who could do something quite beyond his own comprehension, agreed at once to put up the money. The book was published."

The vicar paused, and I looked at Beef, wondering whether he was still interested in this apparently irrelevant story. He was puffing contentedly away at his pipe and I could see he was carefully following the vicar's words.

"Ordinarily, of course, the book would have passed by unnoticed. It was a terribly bad book, of course—a silly historical romance. One or two provincial papers dismissed it in half a line, and then the unfortunate—or fortunate—thing happened. A weekly paper got hold of it and tore it to pieces in a long article, asking how such rubbish came to be foisted on the public and casting a few very nasty innuendoes at the firm of publishers.

"This had a most curious result. It cured my brother of ever writing another word and turned him into the—I must say avaricious, I'm afraid—misanthrope you have heard about. At his express wish my father bought him a partnership in the very firm which had published his book. The senior partner was an old man, who died some ten years later. My brother carried on the business. Curious, if it hadn't been for that vicious criticism of his novel he might have remained an unknown impecunious writer. As it is, he has died a wealthy and successful man."

"He was a widower, wasn't he?" Beef asked.

"Yes. His wife died over ten years ago."

"No children?" Beef queried.

"None of his own," the vicar replied. "There is a stepson. My brother married a widow, you see. Her married name was Howard, and she had a son, Roger Howard, who would be about the middle thirties now. He never got on, unfortunately, with his stepfather, and when he was twenty-one and came into a thousand or so from his mother, he quarrelled violently with my brother Edwin and left home. I've never heard my brother speak of him since. I know he cut him right out of his Will. Everything goes now to our elder sister's girl, Estelle Pinkerton. My brother was more fond of his sister than anyone else in the world, and when she and her husband were killed in an air crash he told me what he had decided to do with his money. Estelle and Roger were to have equal shares of everything, but he increased his life insurance heavily and left my children to benefit from that. He knew I was comfortable enough with what had come to us from the family business. Estelle has been living on her mother's share of that, which was not very large, but I daresay as an unmarried young woman—she's about thirty-eight now—it was sufficient for her needs."

"Owing to this quarrel with his stepson Roger," Beef said, "his niece Estelle Pinkerton, you say, comes into the lot. Where does she live? I understand she was staying in London at the time of her uncle's death."

"Yes, she was up for a few days from Cheltenham, where she settled after her parents' death. She was staying with some old family friends, the Remingtons. He's dean of Fulham, you know."

"Her address, in case I have to get in touch with her," Beef asked, producing his large notebook.

"Fairy Glen, 10 Puesdown Road, Cheltenham," the vicar said, and Beef wrote it down slowly.

"Thank you very much," Beef said, rising and refusing the offer of tea. "I think I've got all I want from you of his family life. Just one more question. I'm not going to beat about the bush. You know that a lot of people didn't like him. That's putting it mildly. You know also that he was always having rows. Can you think of anything like that which might have been serious enough to turn to murder?"

The vicar was silent for a moment or two. His eyes were fixed on a window and he seemed oblivious of us. Then he turned quickly to Beef.

"No, I can't think of anything that could possibly have led to murder. Well, if you can't stay for a cup of tea, I must be getting on. A hundred and one things to do. We parsons work nowadays, you know. Now what about your fee . . . ."

Beef interrupted him. "We'll see about that later when I've cleared up the case. Well, sir, goodbye. By the way, you've no idea how I could get in touch with Roger Howard, the stepson?"

"None at all, I'm afraid. I heard he went to South America after the quarrel. My niece Estelle may know something. They were friendly at one time."

We motored back to town and I dropped Beef at his home, after arranging to meet him on the following day for lunch. I had already fixed for Michael Thorogood, my literary agent, to be there, and he had promised to tell Beef all he could about the notorious firm of Thomas Thayer, of which for many years Ridley had been sole proprietor.

First I thought I would drive straight back to my flat, but the thought of a solitary dinner did not seem attractive, so I parked the car in Waterloo Place and strolled up Hay-market. Someone had taken me a little time before into a new restaurant called The Flying Dutchman which was being run by an alleged member of the resistance movement in Holland and was plentifully splashed with orange. The meal had been good, so I thought I would try it again. As I entered and walked towards the little semi-circular bar on the left, I noticed that a special table was being laid for about ten people. Waiters were fussing round with flowers and buckets of ice and I noticed an expensive-looking menu at every place.

I ordered a dry martini and, for something to say, I asked the barman what all the fuss was about. "Oh, it is for a gentleman who comes here very often. He is giving a special dinner-party to a few friends from the Dutch East Indies. Ah, here he is. Good evening, sir." The barman's voice achieved that special timbre of intimate flattery that seems never to fail with clients whose money only equals their pretension.

I looked round to see who this potentate from the East might be, and nearly spilt my drink as I recognised Gupp coming towards the bar. For a moment he seemed equally taken aback at seeing me, but he recovered himself quickly and held out his hand.

"Hullo, Lionel," he greeted me heartily. "Have a drink."

"No thanks," I replied, without very much enthusiasm. "I've got a full one here."

"Oh, Lionel," he went on, drawing me out of earshot of the barman. "I suppose you think it's rather strange to find me here, splashing money around. Especially after that weekend at Hastings."

I made some noncommittal reply about it being none of my business, but he did not seem satisfied with that.

"Tell you the truth I've had a bit of luck since then," he said. "I can't tell you now, but forget all I said to you and your brother. I was a bit worried at the time."

I finished my drink, and left Hilton Gupp greeting the firstcomers to his party and showering drinks on them. I could not help wondering who had suffered for what he called his "bit of luck".

I left The Flying Dutchman, not wishing to witness cousin Gupp spending what I thought were probably ill-gotten gains, and had a quick snack elsewhere. Then, picking up my car, I returned to my flat.

It was pleasant to be back again, even if it were only for a night or two. I poured out a whisky and soda and lit a cigarette. So much had happened since the morning I had heard of Aunt Aurora's death. There had been the realisation that I should in future be comparatively well-off. Then there was my brother's marriage to Edith Payne. I wondered how she would fit into the atmosphere of a public school. There was something about her of the hospital nurse, a sort of aseptic impersonality, that would guarantee the cleanliness of the dormitories, but would not, I feared, endear her to the boys in my brother's House.

A hundred different ideas came to me when I began to think about my share of Aunt Aurora's money. A house in the country? Somehow I did not feel I would want to be so far away from the interest and excitement of Beef's cases. Travel? To begin with I did not think one could travel nowadays, as people did once, going from place to place in a leisurely way without a plan and turning up in England a year later bronzed and with a fund of improbable stories. Not with Treasury restrictions, visas, and a thousand other forms. Besides, most of the world that one wanted to see was either behind the Iron Curtain or in a zone where war was only just round the corner.

Perhaps I would get married instead.

12

I had arranged to meet Beef and Michael Thorogood at one o'clock in the Café Royal. It seemed the right sort of place for them to meet each other for the first time, but I need not have worried about the setting.

I had known Michael Thorogood since we were thirteen. We had been new boys together at our public school and, since our names both began with the letter T, we had friendship more or less thrust upon us. Curiously enough it had flourished on this forced incubation and had lasted for nearly twenty years. It had been really due to him that I had turned what had been a chance encounter with Sergeant Beef in his first big case, a murder case which he had successfully solved, into my first story. I had been having dinner with Michael, I remember, and telling him of that curious case when he turned to me and said, "Put it on paper, Lionel. I'll get you a publisher if it's any good." I was looking round for a job at the time and was glad of something to do. Michael had given me a few hints—what to avoid in the telling of it, the rough length, and lots of other useful advice, but, even so, I found it was no easy task, however simply one attempted to tell a straight-forward story. It was finished at last and Michael approved. He found a publisher, and Beef duly had the gratification of seeing himself in print.

As I have said, I need not have worried about where or how Michael and Beef met.

"I'm delighted to meet you, Beef," Michael Thorogood said as I introduced them. "Knowing your character from our friend Townsend's books, I suppose I should really get you a tankard of beer, but somehow I think you'd like to join me in a whisky and soda."

After that they were off. Michael had a pretty good knowledge of my books about Beef—I suspect he had spent the evening before glancing through them. He did not, like so many people, under-rate the ex-policeman or suppose that his rubicund exterior hid a plethoric intelligence. He had arranged for us to have a table well on its own, and after I had ordered I let Michael talk.

"You want to know something about Ridley's firm, Thomas Thayer. Well, before I start I must say that it will be highly slanderous, so don't quote me, Lionel, in your book. Personally I would never have any dealings with them at all. It's a wicked blood-sucking business. They advertise all over the place for new writers, and such is the vanity of the human race that hundreds fall for it. In would come the manuscripts, novels, short stories, poems, family histories, accounts of sport, books on shooting, hunting and fishing, belles lettres. The whole lot. The wonderful line in their advertisement that scored a bull every time was, 'Every man or woman has the material for at least one book. Why don't you write yours?' And they did. In thousands. Then there were those who had had manuscripts turned down by agents or publishers for years. To each of these aspiring authors went the same sort of letter, praising the work, saying that it showed every sign of promise of future success, and varying the bait according to the writer and his particular form of literary pretension. They were clever letters. I've seen some of them."

I interrupted Michael to tell him of our interview with Ridley's brother. "Oh, that's interesting," he said. "Edwin Ridley got caught the same way himself, did he? That's what started him off. I often wondered. Well, all I can say is that the firm in the old days did the thing fairly respectably. It wasn't until Ridley himself took a hand that the ramp really began in earnest.

"He found that many of his victims would come a second and third time. Then he branched out into songs and music. It was a lovely racket. He couldn't lose. He had hundreds out of some of them. You see, once he'd got in touch with a would-be author, in nine cases out of ten he landed him and his money. The next letter would say that, good though the work was, and though success seemed assured, the demand from an illiterate public with no real taste for this particular book, essays or poems, or whatever it was, might be limited and the publishers would have to ask the writer to share in the risk of publication. A figure would be quoted, enough in prewar days to show a handsome profit for printing a few hundred copies. Only a dozen or so were ever bound up. The writer would hesitate, but only for a second. The lure of having his name on the cover of a printed book proved in almost every case too strong. The wretched writer would think of the glowing tributes from some fictitious reader to whom Ridley had supposedly submitted the manuscript for criticism. 'The beauty of the prose' or 'this writer has the rare and happy knack of telling a story', tingled in his ears as he wrote out a cheque. In due course the volume would appear cheaply printed and badly bound, a few copies would be bought by an admiring family and a small circle of friends, and that was the end."

Michael paused while the waiter produced another course. "Wonderful ramp, don't you think so, Beef?" Michael asked.

"I can well understand it," he replied. "I'm never surprised, after some of my cases, at anything that human beings can get up to."

"It was harmless enough in most cases," Michael went on. "It didn't really matter whether a young man or woman spent eighty pounds in having a small booklet of poems printed for their own benefit. The trouble arose when the writer was not quite normal. Most of them had some sort of kink. Ridley had some nasty rows with some of his authors. There were threats of suing him for obtaining money under false pretences. There were one or two violent scenes in his office, I believe, when it almost came to a set battle. Ridley managed to keep most of them quiet. No one likes to admit being the victim of a confidence trick, especially after having boasted to their friends about their writing."

Michael sat back and sipped his coffee and brandy.

"Did you ever hear anything about that young fellow who tried to commit suicide in Ridley's grounds? Chap called Greenleaf?" Beef asked.

"Yes," Michael replied. "As a matter of fact, though a bit cranky, the fellow can write. Fortunately, after that business someone got hold of him, read some of his stuff, found it was good and brought him along to me. He told me the whole story after I'd given him a meal. The wretched chap was literally starving. Have another brandy, Beef," Michael said, calling the waiter, "and I'll tell you about him. Lionel's paying. I've no conscience now that he's come into a fortune. That is, unless you're waiting to pinch him for murdering his aunt. I wouldn't put it past him. I remember at school once he lost his temper and nearly killed a science master with a retort. A glass one. Verbal cleverness was always a bit beyond him."

I managed to smile at these reminiscent sallies, and we all had another brandy and Michael continued about Greenleaf.

"Ridley had had nearly two hundred quid from Greenleaf. Most of it a widowed mother's savings, I understood. They were absolutely broke when he went down to Ridley's house in Gloucestershire to try and recover something. Ridley had him thrown out, but what was worse, laughed at his writing. Now Greenleaf was an absolute fool, but one thing he did believe and that was that he could write. That laughter was one of Ridley's worst crimes, a much more serious one than doing him out of his money. He nearly killed a damned good writer. I'm looking after his affairs now. I've managed to get him the promise of a fairly decent contract on his second novel. Trouble is he's still tied to Ridley's firm for his next two books. I tried to get Ridley to tear up the old agreement, but he wouldn't. By Jove, I suppose the silly fool didn't . . . ."

"Didn't what, Mr. Thorogood?" Beef asked.

"Oh, nothing . . . only where Ridley was concerned, friend Greenleaf was *not* normal," Michael replied, but we all knew what he was going to say. "Ridley was like a red rag to a bull to him, I'm afraid. I thought Greenleaf was going to throw a fit or something when I last mentioned Ridley's name to him."

"When I tell you, then," said Beef, sinking his whole glass of brandy in one gulp, "that Greenleaf is thought to have been seen near Ridley's house in the Cotswolds the very night the murder was committed, you would include him among your suspects."

"My dear Beef," Michael answered, "whoever murdered Ridley did the world a good turn. Personally, I'd like to shake his hand. I don't particularly care who did it, but if you want my serious opinion I would say that Greenleaf certainly has a curious complex about Ridley. I don't think he would plot a cold-blooded murder, but he may have gone down there to try and get some of his money back from Ridley. He may even only have wanted Ridley to release him from his contract. But I'd be afraid of the consequences if he once got into Ridley's company. He'd be bound to go off the deep end. What would happen after that, who can say? Greenleaf crazy with fury. A scuffle. Then perhaps"—Michael shrugged his shoulders—"a little *too* much pressure on the windpipe. Et voilà."

Michael lit a cigarette.

"Personally, I should be very sorry. I think I shall earn a lot of money out of Greenleaf before I've done. So don't arrest him right away, Beef. Give the chap the benefit of the doubt. I don't care much about him personally, but I tell you he can write."

I asked for the bill and began to thank Michael for his help. Beef joined in. "Very interesting indeed. As I said to Townsend here, I'm trying to find the real motive and you've helped me a lot. I think we might have one more brandy," Beef said, and I noticed that face was slightly more rubicund than usual. "I must live up to my character in front of Townsend's literary pals." He winked broadly at Michael, who had never refused a drink in his life.

"If only people who write would trust their stuff to reputable publishers—preferably through my agency!—blood suckers like Ridley and Co wouldn't have a chance," Michael said, preparing to go.

"Just one more thing," Beef said, as we came out into Regent Street. "Could you let me have that fellow Greenleaf's address?"

Michael thought for a moment. "I can't remember it. I know it's Bayswater way somewhere. If you ring my office, Lionel, they'll give it to you."

"By the way, Michael," I asked, "you say you found Greenleaf more or less starving. What's he been living on? He can't have got an advance on his second novel till he's free of Ridley's contract."

Michael laughed, and in rather a shamefaced way admitted that he had lent Greenleaf enough to get on with. "I'll get it back, all right," he said. "Besides, since then I've sold a few short stories of his. He'll be a good investment, you see."

"Not if he were to hang," I replied

"Think of the publicity," Michael said, and turned to leave.

"Just one moment, Mr. Thorogood," Beef said. "When was it you first lent him some money?"

Michael paused thoughtfully. "Let me see. Oh, yes, I remember. He came in to see me one afternoon. He looked very down and out. In fact he looked so starved that I asked him to dine with me that night. Over dinner I got him to accept a cheque. I may have the date here."

He flicked back the counterfoils of his cheque-book.

"Here we are. Greenleaf, 11th September. Twenty pounds. That was the first money I ever lent him."

Beef made a note, and Michael disappeared into the crowd.

Three o'clock found us ringing the bell of a drab house in an equally drab street in Bayswater. A tall, gaunt rather formidable woman answered the bell.

"Mrs. Greenleaf?" I asked.

She nodded.

"I'm a friend of Mr. Thorogood, your son's literary agent. I wonder if I could see him for a few minutes."

"I'll see if he's in," she replied tonelessly. I was a little ashamed of the subterfuge, but, from what I had heard, I felt this was the only possible way of getting an interview with Greenleaf.

In a few moments she returned and showed us into an untidy room at the back of the house. A young man of about twenty-eight was sitting at a table strewn with papers. There were a number of books around on shelves, on the table, on the floor, anywhere, but they were for the most part cheap editions or very much second-hand. He rose as we came in, and I saw an obvious younger edition of the mother. He was equally tall, with a strong face and a powerful body. His clothes were old and shoddy, and no attempt had been made to make the best of them. His collar was dirty and his suit unbrushed and unpressed. His hair was wild, and a dark stubble showed that he had not shaved for a couple of days. Only something about the forehead and the intense look in his eyes under the shaggy eyebrows upheld in any way Michael's belief that the fellow might have something unusual in him.

I introduced Beef without disclosing who he was, and chatted for some minutes about Michael Thorogood. I asked him about the second novel Michael had mentioned and made a few general remarks about publishers. He answered politely enough, but was obviously so accustomed to bottle everything up in himself that he found it difficult to speak to anyone about his work. I could see he was puzzled about my reason for coming to see him, and he kept casting suspicious glances at Beef, who, I must say, did look more like a policeman in those surroundings than I had ever noticed before. I decided I must take the plunge.

"Talking of publishers, what I really came to see you about is the death of Edwin Ridley." Even as I mentioned the name I could see his muscles tauten and his face grow pale and set in a hard mask. "I know it's a painful subject for you. He treated you very badly in the past, I believe, but Beef here is trying to solve the mystery of his death and we felt you might be able to help us."

"The only thing I know about his death was that it was the best thing that could happen. The man ought never to have been allowed to live."

His voice, as he spoke, was cold and hard, and behind it such an intensity of hate that I was almost frightened.

"Do you object to answering a few questions, Mr. Greenleaf? You know it's every citizen's duty to help uncover a crime, however much we may dislike the victim."

"I don't know who you are or why you've come here interrupting my work. You're not the police?"

I explained that Beef was acting for Ridley's family. "Well, I don't want anything to do with the matter at all. I thought you came here about my writing, or I'd never have seen you; I think you'd better go."

"One thing I'd like to know before we go," Beef said. "Did you leave a parcel of books when you were down at Ridley's house on the night he was murdered?"

"Get out!" he shouted. "Get out, both of you, or I'll throw you out!" The door burst open at that moment and his mother entered.

"Arthur, you mustn't get so excited. You know what the doctor said. He never knows what he's saying when he's like this," she said, turning to us. "You'd better leave him," she went on. "I don't know how you've upset him, but I wish you'd all leave him in peace after what he's been through."

We took up our hats and left. She stood for some moments, a motionless figure at the front door, watching us as we walked down that ugly street towards the lights of the main road.

I did not return to my flat until about seven o'clock. Beef had agreed to dine with me there. I had asked him because I wanted to know what he was really after. I was worried that he seemed to have left my aunt's murder completely in the air, which was unlike him. Even though he was engaged on the Cotswold crime before I had asked for his help, I felt that the time had come for him to return to investigation at Hastings. Instead he appeared to be quite taken up by this other murder.

A good service flat I had found the best method of living for one like myself who was always being called away unexpectedly and who never knew when he would return or for how long. I was pleased to see a bright fire burning in the grate. It was cold these September nights, and a fire gave to this modern flat a more permanent and lived-in appearance. There was a letter with an Essex postmark that I knew was from my brother Vincent.

> "My dear Lionel," it ran,
> "Edith and I are now fairly comfortably settled in the new House. The boys seem a pleasant lot and my assistant master *very* manageable. Edith and matron don't seem to get on very well yet. There was quite a row over a case of suspected measles, but I hope it will all blow over. To tell you the truth, I'm very worried about Edith. She is still very pale and nervy—not at all like her, as you know. I'm afraid she has taken Aunt Aurora's death very much to heart. To cap it all that fellow Arnold, the Hastings Inspector, was up here the other day. He had a long interview with Edith. She seemed very upset after it, so I didn't

question her. He also asked me a lot of questions and brought up the old question of the medicine cupboard.

"What is your friend Beef doing? I wish they'd let the whole matter drop. After all, they can't bring Aunt Aurora back to life now. If she died of poison, it must all have been some awful mistake. No one would murder poor Aunt Aurora in cold blood—it's unthinkable.

"Do write and tell me the latest news and what Beef is doing and what his views are. Any assurance I can give Edith at the moment would be most welcome.

"Fortunately no gossip about Aunt Aurora's death has spread here among the boys, though one or two of the other masters and their wives seem to have heard about the inquest. Matron, too, I believe, made an unpleasant innuendo to Edith when they had a row about the measles. Something about bowing before her superior knowledge of patent medicines. Quite upset her.

"Well, I must go round the House now. It's nearly lights-out time, and Simpson, a new prefect, is on duty. I don't *quite* know whether I've made a mistake there. He's perhaps a little too friendly with some of the juniors.

"Your affectionate brother,

"Vincent."

Beef arrived just as I had finished reading the letter and, thinking it might be a good way to open the subject of what he was up to, I handed him the letter to read while I got out something to drink. He finished reading.

"Your brother seems very keen to know what I think," he said, handing back the letter.

"It's only natural, isn't it?" I replied. "I'm pretty anxious to know myself. You've kept everything to yourself, and, after all, she was our aunt."

"Yes," Beef said, "I realise you're both upset about her death. Then, of course, there's the money. I expect you'd both like to get your hands on a bit of that . . ."

"Really, Beef," I said rather crossly, "you don't seem to realise that Vincent and I were both very fond of our aunt. We've known for a long time that we should come into something on her death, and we're very grateful that she felt like leaving it to us. But we would have happily waited for many years for that."

"Well," Beef replied, "all I can say is that the money has come in very handy for both of you just now. Your brother has been able to spend what he wanted in doing up his new House and in getting married, and you . . ."

"Yes," I said rather coldly, "what about me?"

"Well, there's the young lady who lives on the Thames near Wargrave. The one you visited the day your aunt was murdered. You had dinner with her, too, that time you drove me up to town from Hastings. I suppose you're thinking of getting married too, now. I mean, you couldn't before on what you made out of writing about me, could you now? As I've said before, hardly anybody seems to have heard the name Beef. Now take Hercule Poirot . . ."

I had been too taken aback by what Beef had said to stop him running on.

"Look here, Beef, my brother and I are not paying you to spy on us. We hired you to find our aunt's murderer . . ."

"That's what I'm going to do. Make no mistake," Beef replied. "That's why I have to look into everything. As a matter of fact, Inspector Arnold gave me all the information about your visiting Miss Rutherford. Clever fellow Arnold, as I've always said."

"Well, I wish you'd concentrate on my aunt's murder and leave this other business down in the Cotswolds," I said. I was still angry with Beef.

"Now look here," Beef answered in a more conciliatory manner. "Just pour me a little drink. You'd better have one yourself, too, and I'll tell you something." He paused while I poured a whisky for him and a sherry for myself.

"Do you think I'd leave a case like the Cotswold one after being on it only a day or two to come all the way to Hastings unless I had a very good reason? I know. You'd say that it was enough that you and your brother wanted a bit of help. Well, I agree that was partly it, but there was something else. You remember that newspaper that the books were wrapped in—*The Sussex Gazette*—I told you to look at it carefully. You didn't notice, I suppose, the pencil mark which the newsagent had made. It was 'Camber. Highfield'. That paper was obviously delivered to your aunt's house Camber Lodge, Highfield Road, on the sixteenth of August. When I got your letter saying about the death of your aunt, Miss Fielding, and with the address at the top, Camber Lodge, Highfield Road, I thought it was time I had a look at Hastings. Bit of luck, I must say. Not that I wouldn't have found out in a day or two anyhow about the other murder, and anyone could have traced the address. Another funny coincidence was the two murders taking place the same day."

"But, Beef," I replied, "I don't see how there can be any connection. Anyhow, the paper was nearly a month old. My aunt didn't die till September."

"I know," Beef replied. "But you must admit it would be a very funny coincidence. Two rich old people bumped off at the same time and a paper from one house found in the other."

Dinner was brought in at this point, and it was not until we had finished and were sitting smoking in front of the fire that it was possible to reopen the subject. Beef, however, seemed singularly unwilling to discuss the case further.

"I'm going to have a look at that niece of Edwin Ridley's. What's her name. Estelle something . . ." He took out his notebook and found her name and address in Cheltenham that Rev. Alfred Ridley had given him. "Ah yes, Estelle Pinkerton. She's the one who gets the dead man's money."

"But she was staying with the dean of Fulham in London the night her uncle was murdered," I said. "Anyway, a woman couldn't have done it."

"I'd like to have a look at her just the same," Beef replied. "As I've said before, I owe a lot to the old routine I learnt in the police. Besides, there's that stepson Roger Howard. She may be able to tell us something of him. But don't think, after what I've told you, that I'm neglecting your aunt's death altogether."

"You still seriously think, Beef," I asked, "that there may be some kind of link between the two?"

"I don't put a lot of trust in funny coincidences, but we'll see. You'll call for me in the morning, then? It's not as if Cheltenham is very far out of our way. We'll be able to make Cold Slaughter in time for a game of darts."

13

Fairy Glen, the home of Estelle Pinkerton, we found when we called to see her that afternoon, was a diminutive white house on the outskirts of Cheltenham. The path from the front gate was of crazy pavement, and, though only some fifteen yards long, had been made to curve to and fro on its way to the front door. The lawn on either side was encumbered with little coloured china ornaments, pixies and mushrooms. There was a miniature pool about the size of a hand basin, no doubt with gold fish in it, and a bridge like a bit of rustic Meccano spanning it. Dwarf shrubs grew around the house, while the gate and all the paintwork of the house was painted yellow and blue. A small wooden windmill about three feet high and a teeny weeny dovecote filled what was left of the garden.

I lifted a brass ring on the door, on which was inscribed "Knock, Friend", to beat a tattoo, but before I had time to do so the door opened.

"Are you Mr. Beef?" were the opening words of a woman who could only be Miss Pinkerton herself. "Do come in. I got your telegram this morning. I've heard all about you from my Uncle Alfred. The vicar of St. John's, you know. Such a clever man."

Estelle Pinkerton was a perfect blend with her house. Small, with a pink and white complexion she wore gaily coloured clothes, a woollen jumper festooned with little balls of wool that she had obviously made herself, and a skirt that seemed to me to have lots of unnecessary bits and frills.

The inside of the house, too, matched the outside. Coloured calendars, pictures of pets and flowers on the bright walls, books by A. A. Milne and Michael Fairless in limp leather enclosed by china book-rests. The chair on which Beef sat looked as if it would collapse under his weight at any moment.

"I don't often have men visitors to my little home. Quite a rare pleasure." A flush of colour had come into her pink cheeks as she prattled on, and she seemed quite breathless at this unusual excitement.

"Mr. Beef, you don't look very comfortable," she went on. "Let me get you another cushion. Perhaps you'd both like a nice cup of tea after your journey."

We declined tea, and Beef cleared his throat.

"I've come to see you about your uncle's death," he began, but Miss Pinkerton interrupted him.

"Oh, I know all about you. My uncle told me in his letter I was to answer all your questions. He hoped you'd soon have the horrid business all cleared up. So nice to have a man like Uncle Alfred to advise a lonely spinster like me in these difficult days. I don't know what I should have done without him."

"You were staying with the dean of Fulham at the time of the murder, I think?" Beef went on.

"Oh yes. The Remingtons are very old family friends. Whenever I go to London, I always stay with them."

"Do you often go to London, Miss Pinkerton?" Beef asked.

"No, indeed, Mr. Beef," she replied. "I only go once or twice a year usually. It's so expensive. Besides, Cheltenham is so good for shopping. Our shops are quite as good as the London ones, I always say."

"Did your friends invite you or did you have some special reason for going this time?" Beef queried, breaking into her garrulous flow as politely as he could.

"I felt I must see Uncle Alfred and my cousins before the winter. I hate travelling in the cold weather. When winter comes I shut myself up here like a little dormouse." She beamed round at us. "So I wrote to Ethel Remington, and she replied she'd be delighted to have me for a few days."

"I'm sorry to ask you, but would you repeat what you told the police about your visit. The dates and what you did."

"Of course, Mr. Beef. Let me see now. I went up on the eighth of September by the morning train. It's such a good one and you get quite a nice lunch. Sometimes one meets such nice people. I always book a seat at a table for two, and I've made many friends that way. Where was I now? Oh, yes, I arrived at the Remingtons for tea. We went to the theatre that night."

"It's the day of the murder I'd like you to tell us about again," Beef said, a little impatiently. "That was the tenth of September."

"Oh, you want to know where I was when poor Uncle Edwin was being done to death. As I told the police, I spent the entire evening at their house with the dean and his wife. They had a small dinner-party for me and we played games after. It was quite gay. I remember the last guests didn't leave till eleven. Then the three of us sat talking and drinking Ovaltine till past midnight. It was my last night, you see, and we really hadn't had a chance for a good chat about the past and all our friends. We'd been out to the theatre and to a recital the other two nights. I used to go out after breakfast and do my shopping. I knew they were busy all day so I used to have my lunch at the Army and Navy Stores. Rations are so difficult nowadays, and I didn't want to put them out, especially as I'd asked myself."

I was getting bored with her long recital and began to look at the numerous water colours that covered the walls. Miss Pinkerton saw this.

"Ah, Mr. Townsend, I see you're looking at my poor little pictures. The arts, I'm afraid, now are my only pleasure. I don't know what I'd do without my easel, my piano and my acting in our little dramatic society. Such an inspiration I find them all. Those two water colours over the mantelpiece are of my grandfather's château in Normandy. I often go over and stay there. Such lovely sketching country. Those over by the window are souvenirs of last summer in Cornwall. Those three next to you I'm rather proud of. They're my latest. The beach and casino at Estoril. I felt quite brave going all the way to Portugal by myself, but I had a lovely time. There was no trouble about language. Everyone in Estoril seemed to speak English. I must show you my portfolio. I've some I'm very fond of that I did of the lakes. My one little extravagance. I take a month's holiday every year and go somewhere and paint, even, if I have to save up all the year for it."

"Well, you won't have to do that now," I said. "Your uncle has made you a rich woman, Miss Pinkerton. You'd have quite a fortune when this unpleasant business is cleared up. I'm sure my friend Beef will find the criminal pretty soon. You'll be able to make life one long painting holiday . . . ."

"Unless you've any other plans," Beef broke in. "Perhaps you're thinking of getting married. You should, you know, an attractive young woman like you."

Miss Pinkerton had turned a deep scarlet. It was most embarrassing. I thought it was too bad of Beef to tease the poor gushing little thing.

"Mister Beef, you shouldn't flatter me like that. Who would want to marry someone like me?"

"I should have thought you'd have had lots of eligible bachelors after you in a place like Cheltenham. There must be plenty of nice comfortable parties who'd need a wife like you to look after them."

"I wouldn't say I haven't had offers, you know, Mr. Beef, but I could only marry someone I really loved." She sat back with closed rapt eyes, a flush still in her cheeks. "Someone young and strong. Someone who would tear me away from this comfortable life. Someone who would look after me. But there I go. Forgive me, Mister Beef, we artists, you know, we have our dreams."

I found all this very painful, but Beef showed no sign of irritation. I was glad, however, when he brought Miss Pinkerton back to the object of our visit and enquired about Roger Howard, her Uncle Edwin Ridley's stepson.

"I've not heard of Roger since the war finished," she said. "He did very well in the army, and I believe he's still in it. I could get his address for you from his mother's family. I still hear occasionally from them. Dear Roger, such an impetuous boy and, I'm afraid, always in debt. And that wife of his, so extravagant. He was stationed here during the war and I saw them once or twice. I tried to get him to go and see his stepfather, but he never would, after that terrible quarrel they had. And now it's too late."

Beef gave Miss Pinkerton his address and asked her to let him know Roger Howard's whereabouts as soon as she could. She led us out through the little hall. "Such a sad time of year," she said. "All my poor flowers are nearly finished. But, as the poet says, Mr. Beef, 'If winter comes can spring be far behind'."

"Didn't ought to, did it?" Beef replied. "Well, thank you, madam. Don't forget to let me have that address."

We strolled down the crazy pavement and out through the yellow and blue gate.

"I should have thought it would have been quicker to get Roger Howard's address through the police," I said, as we got into the car.

"I have my reasons," he replied, in what I called to myself his policeman voice.

As we drove back through the September dusk I could not help thinking about Estelle Pinkerton, her fussy little house and arty-crafty garden.

"I wonder what she'll do, Beef," I said, voicing my thoughts. "I mean when she gets the money."

"Get a man, that's what she'll try and do. Couldn't you see? Why, it stands out a mile. She's just the sort that that chap would go for who drowned his wives in a bath. He'd have had her money in no time, and there are plenty more like him about. I don't mean to say that they'd all go as far as murder, but they'd have her money before you could say Jack Robinson. All that business of meeting people in trains. Why, she'd fall for any fairly good-looking chap who paid her attention. She'd probably go and stay in some foreign hotel, and the fact that she'd just come into a tidy fortune would soon spread. She could never keep her mouth shut. Clear as day."

What a difference, I thought, between this gushing, vain, empty-headed little spinster, with her water colours and self-interest, from my aunt, whose only similarity to Miss Pinkerton was that she had never married. I thought of Aunt Aurora, upright, dignified, unselfish and unself-centred, who pretended to no cleverness, but who had by the kindly simplicity of her life left a pattern that could still be seen. If it had been Miss Pinkerton who had been murdered she would have been erased from life, leaving nothing behind; but when Aunt Aurora died, the whole life at Camber Lodge, for us, for her servants, for her friends, had changed, and one realised that it was Aunt Aurora who had unconsciously created that small corner of life.

14

When we arrived at Bampton Court the next morning we found the Police Superintendent talking to a tall thin grey-haired man with a hatchet face.

"Come in, Beef," the Superintendent said. "This is Mr. Potter, the Oxford bookseller, with whom Edwin Ridley did a lot of business. I found some accounts of his among Ridley's papers and asked him if he'd kindly come over and have a look at the bundle of books that Lovelace, the secretary, said he'd never seen before. He's made rather a curious discovery. Perhaps you'd repeat what you were telling me, Mr. Potter. Mr. Beef is looking into Ridley's death on behalf of the family so he'll be most interested."

"I'm afraid I can't help you about those few books that seemed to have recently appeared. They're just ordinary stuff that Ridley wouldn't have bothered with. They might have been bought anywhere for a few shillings each. Even if you circulated the antiquarian booksellers, I fear you wouldn't have any success. Although they've got nice old calf jackets, they're too unimportant to be remembered." Potter spoke in a quiet, precise voice and gave the impression that he knew what he was talking about.

"No," he continued, "I can't help you there, I'm afraid, but I have found something rather interesting. Two at least of Ridley's real prizes have disappeared and inferior copies have been substituted. Come over here and I'll show you."

He led the way to a large glass-fronted bookcase which the Superintendent unlocked.

"Now in this case he used to keep all his real treasures. Books worth up to a thousand pounds or more. He often asked me over to look at some new purchase, and I knew his library fairly well. As you see, he had a cardboard container made for each one with the title on the back."

He picked out one of these containers.

"I can't say for certain about the rest, but from what I know of his collection he wouldn't have bothered to have cases made for some of these, nor would he have kept these later issues in his special bookcase."

"Looks as if someone, might be himself even, has been taking away the valuable copies and putting these others in their place," the Superintendent said. "Anyway, it's been done in two cases. We know that for certain from Mr. Potter. Could you tell us, Mr. Potter, your opinion about this. After all, it was your discovery. Do you think there has been some funny business here?"

"I certainly do, Superintendent," Potter replied. "Whoever substituted those two copies for the originals knew what he was about. Ridley himself would never have parted with his *Gulliver*. I should say it happened like this. Someone who knew the collection well decided to do a little skilful robbery. He must have had some knowledge of books. Anyway, he knew why these particular books were valuable. He goes to London and buys those two later issues from Maggs or Quaritch or some other big bookseller. He could get them for under fifty pounds. He chooses them chiefly for their size and binding, as being as nearly identical to the original copy as possible. Take the *Gulliver*, for instance. It's an ordinary eighteenth-century calf with red labels. So was the copy I sold Ridley. Mine was a taller copy, if I remember, but you wouldn't notice that at a casual glance. He's even transferred the bookplate from the original. I remember this one. A particularly fine one from the Duke of Albany's library. If I hadn't happened to have sold him the original first issue, the substitution would never have been noted. You see after all this copy that's here now is a first edition of *Gulliver's Travels*. Quite a nice book, but not to a man like Ridley who had to have the rare first issue. It's only a small difference in the frontispiece. That portrait in front. The whole library would have been sent up to Sotheby's, probably, and this copy would be sold as it is. After all it's not a fake, remember. It's a real sound first edition. The only thing is that I happened to know that Ridley's copy was the rare first issue. It was a clever idea as long as Ridley himself never found out, and he wasn't likely to examine these special ones of his very often. It would only happen if he wanted to show them to a fellow bibliophile."

A sudden idea had struck me while Potter was talking.

"Wouldn't the catalogue list that Lovelace kept of the library show the difference?" I asked. "He showed me a few entries when we were here before and they seemed to be very detailed."

I saw Beef and the Superintendent exchange glances. "We'll go into that later," the Superintendent said. "Well, Mr. Potter, we're most obliged to you for coming over and giving us the benefit of your knowledge and experience. I don't know yet whether it has any bearing on Ridley's murder. After all, he might have done the substitution himself. Wanted to have his cake and eat it. Got the cash for the original copies and still was able to pose as the possessor of them, knowing all the time that his cardboard cases only held inferior copies. We shall probably have to come to you again. In the meantime, the less said the better."

"I shan't say anything, of course," Potter replied. "It's no business of mine. I'm only sorry that I've lost a very good customer. They're not so easy to find these days. There isn't the money about. I'll be glad to help you if you want any more information."

After Potter had gone, the Superintendent turned to Beef. "Of course, it's obvious who did the substituting if Ridley himself didn't. Knowledge, opportunity, everything."

"Stands out a mile," Beef agreed, and I must say that I too had thought at once of Lovelace as soon as Potter began to speak of a possible theft. I remembered the suspicious, rather furtive look in those pale-blue eyes.

"I thought it was better not to speak of our suspicious in front of Potter," the Superintendent went on, "and I could see Beef thought the same. That's why I didn't go into your suggestion about the catalogue then, but we'll have a look now. Perhaps you'd help us there, Mr. Townsend."

I was pleased at the Superintendent's words, glad that for once I was able to take a part in one of Beef's cases. Beef himself did not seem enthusiastic as I began to investigate the cabinet in which he kept a catalogue of the books. It was a simple card index arranged alphabetically under authors' names, and I soon found the card which showed *Swift, Jonathan*, as all the cards of the really valuable books were together. There was no mention of it being a rare first issue, but when I checked on one or two of the other books which were kept in the special case, there was a much more detailed description, a little note on the book's rarity and how and where he had obtained it.

"Whoever took the original must have typed a new card," the Superintendent said, after examining the entry for a minute or two. "If Lovelace did it, he must have typed the new card after Ridley's death. Ridley might have seen it, otherwise. What do you think, Beef?"

Beef had wandered away while the Superintendent and I had been looking at the cards.

"I expect he did it all right. I said there was something fishy about him from the start. I'm still more interested in that other parcel of books that Potter turned up his nose at."

The Superintendent smiled. "Quite," he said. "But I think we ought to have a word or two with Lovelace. After all, he's the first person we've found who could have done the murder, and seems to have had a motive. I mean, if Ridley had suddenly discovered that Lovelace had been stealing his treasured books, there'd have been hell to pay. I somehow don't think he'll take a lot of breaking down."

But the Superintendent got nowhere with Lovelace, whom he had at once sent for.

"Oh, those old books," Lovelace said, in a rather impatient tone. "It's no good you asking me any more about *them*. I'm sick and tired of them. First editions, first issues, misprints, watermarks, that's all I've had for months. I only typed what Ridley dictated. That's all my job was. I shouldn't know any more about them than you do."

Though the Superintendent persevered, he got no forrader. He hinted at possible theft, emphasised the gravity in a murder case of suppressing evidence, and even voiced a few suggested threats, but Lovelace continued to deny any further knowledge.

"I only know that I checked the valuable books in the special case just as you asked me, Superintendent," he finished by saying. "According to the cards they were all there. When you start talking about different copies and issues and things—I suppose you got all that from Potter of Oxford—I'm just as much at sea as you are."

I could see the Superintendent was not satisfied.

"I see in Ridley's engagement book that a man called Steinberg was due to come and stay for a couple of nights. The day before Steinberg's visit Ridley gets murdered. Steinberg wouldn't be that big American book dealer who's always cropping up in the papers, would he?"

Lovelace this time certainly did seem a bit shaken, but he smiled boldly.

"I expect it was," he replied. "Nearly all the people who visited here came to see Ridley's books. After all, as you know, he never had any real friends."

"Never mind about that," the Superintendent went on. "If Steinberg had come here, Ridley would have got out his copy of *Gulliver's Travels*, wouldn't he, and there'd have been a nice how-do-you-do. Ridley's murder happened very providentially for the person who had been monkeying with one or two of the more valuable books, don't you think, Mr. Lovelace?"

The brittle smile had gone from the Secretary's face. "I've told you all I know," he said sulkily. "I'd never have come here if I'd known all this was going to happen. Unless you've got anything more to ask me, I must go and take some aspirin. You've given me quite a headache."

The Superintendent let him go.

Beef seemed disinclined to discuss this new development with the Superintendent, and said all he wanted was a drink. When I reopened the subject on our way back to the Shaven Crown he was equally unresponsive.

"Even though you can't appreciate the finer points about Ridley's books," I could not help saying, "there was no need to be rude to the poor Superintendent. I thought he showed a lot of intelligence."

"I dare say," Beef replied, without bothering to remove his pipe. Billows of smoke were surrounding me as I drove, and I was peeved that Beef showed no appreciation of my help in the matter.

"You're thinking more about beer than bibliography," I said testily, slamming on the brakes to avoid a heifer that came suddenly out of a break in the stone wall.

"Careful with the car," Beef said. "We shall need her this afternoon. Don't you worry your head about those books. I know pretty well all I want to know about them," Beef said, in his most infuriatingly self-satisfied manner.

After lunch Beef asked me to drive him to Long Alton, a village some seven or eight miles away. He wanted to call and see Colonel Lethbridge, the Master of the local Hunt. I remembered what Lovelace had said about the M.F.H.'s quarrel with Ridley, how Ridley had claimed for the loss of some chickens and, when his claim was not fully met, Ridley had closed his estate to the local Hunt. Nice old boy, Lovelace had called him, but a bit irascible and eccentric. The publican of the Shaven Crown laughed when we enquired how to find Colonel Lethbridge's house in Long Alton. "You just ask anyone. They all know him," he said. "Hope you get back safe," he added, but he would not explain the joke.

When we came to the village of Long Alton, Beef asked me to stop at the small village post office while he got out to enquire the way.

"First big gates on the left," Beef said, as he climbed back into the car. He was smiling and seemed pleased with himself.

"Another good guess," was all he would say.

When we came to the gates the first thing we saw was a large board on which was printed in large letters. *All trespassers will be shot.* As I turned the car into the drive another notice caught our eyes, *Beware of bloodhounds,* and a little further yet another, *Danger. Mantraps.* A pleasant well-kept Cotswold house soon appeared round a curve of the drive. We went up to the front door and rang. A butler appeared and Beef asked to see Colonel Lethbridge.

"The Colonel never sees anyone unknown to him, I'm afraid. Perhaps if you wrote to him . . ."

Beef took one of his printed cards from his pocket-case and, moistening a pencil with his tongue, wrote a few words.

In a few minutes there were loud sounds of barking and two enormous Harlequin Great Danes bounded through the front door followed by a red-faced figure with a bristly grey moustache, clad in a pair of loud tweed plus-fours. In one hand he brandished a riding crop, in the other he held Beef's card.

"Who the devil is Mr. William Beef, private investigator? Go away, both of you. Get out of my grounds. Can't you read? Haven't you seen my notices? I'll get my gun. The only thing I don't shoot on sight are foxes, sir. All vermin here shot, human or otherwise . . ."

"Now then, sir," Beef replied, and I could see the old training as a constable standing him in good stead, "just calm yourself. You won't do yourself or anyone else any good if you get all worked up like that."

While Beef was speaking wild noises that sounded like "Bah" came from the Colonel's throat, but Beef's policeman-like manner was having its effect.

"I just wanted a word or two with you about that letter you wrote to Ridley three days before he was murdered."

"So that's your business," the Colonel barked. "But who's this?" he asked, pointing at me with his crop. "One of these blasted reporters? If he is, if he dares to print one word about me, I'll flog him first and then sue his paper."

Beef explained, and we were at last silently ushered into a comfortable study where a warm log fire was burning. The walls were hung with every sort of animal trophy. I half expected to see a human head or two among the antlers.

"You may sit down," conceded the Colonel. He was address-ing Beef. "What's it you want? Are you from the police, or what?"

The bluster was still there, but a little of the confidence seemed to be shaken by Beef's stolid manner.

Beef explained that he was acting for Ridley's relations.

"Mean little paper merchant," the Colonel snapped.

"That may be so, sir," Beef went on evenly. "But why did you send Ridley that threatening card?"

I thought the Colonel was really going to explode this time.

"What are you talking about, threatening card?" he shouted.

Beef produced the piece of paper which the Superinten-dent had found in Ridley's pocket and read out the puerile threat.

"This is dated three days before Ridley was murdered," Beef went on imperturbably. "I want to know why you sent it."

I thought at first we should have another wild outburst, but I was surprised, as I watched his face, to see a sudden rather guilty smile appear.

"How did you know it was me?" he asked.

"I thought when I first saw it it might have come from you," Beef replied. "They'd told me about the row you'd had with Ridley, you see, and this card sounded very much of a piece. Just to make sure I showed the blank part of the paper to the local postmistress. She recognised your brand of note-paper at once. Then when I saw your notices, I could see with half an eye it had the same literary style."

The Colonel seemed delighted with this piece of elementary detection of Beef's. "We must have a drink on this," he said, and poured out enormous pegs of whisky into three beautiful heavy cut-glass tumblers.

"I've been worried about that foolish card," the Colonel began as he sat down. "Ever since I heard of Ridley's death, I could have kicked myself for such a silly prank. I only sent it as a joke to frighten the little rat. The police don't know I sent it, do they?"

"Not yet," said Beef, emptying his glass and pushing it forward in a marked manner.

"I'd scarcely be able to show my face on the Bench if the story got round. Not because I told him what I thought of him but because I made it anonymous. Can't *think* what can have possessed me. I ought to have thrashed the little bounder, not written to him."

"And you see how awkward it would be," Beef replied, "if they started connecting you and your threats with Ridley's death. However, as far as I'm concerned you needn't worry. The police won't hear anything of this from me. To be quite frank with you, sir, it's not your sort of crime. You might strangle a man in a fit of temper. You might even choke yourself. But everything points to this murder being planned beforehand. I can't see you prowling round Ridley's house in the dark."

"Thank you," the Colonel said, and wisely left it at that. "Now is there anything I can do for you?"

Beef questioned him closely about the various other rows that Ridley had had. The Colonel seemed to know the details of them all, the quarrel about the cricket pitch, the two brothers whom Ridley had prosecuted for poaching and who had in fact appeared when he was on the Bench ("Should have liked to have let the fellows off, but I couldn't"), the trouble with the doctor, and the case of the cottages from which he was trying to evict two families. He even told us of a few more. "I know all these people," he said. "I've lived among them all my life. None of them would dream of that kind of violence, however ill-used they may have felt. I can assure you of that."

Beef finished his drink and rose to go.

"A little more progress," he said to me, as we drove back to Cold Slaughter. "I reckon it won't be long before I have got this all straightened out."

"What about my aunt's murderer, Beef?" I asked. "That's what's worrying me. All this rushing round Gloucestershire may be necessary, but it doesn't help Vincent or myself."

"You'll be surprised when it all comes out in the end," Beef answered. "It won't take long now."

15

We had just finished breakfast the next morning when the Superintendent arrived.

"Good morning, Beef," he said cheerily. "I've just got a line on that car that was seen parked near Bampton Court on the night of the murder. I was very grateful to you for the tip, and of course at once circulated the description of it to all the constabulary around. I've just had an answer from Oxford and I'm going over this morning to have a look at it. It belongs to a garage there that does a hire service. They've been notified, so the car will be held for me to see today."

Beef thanked him and accepted, and we were soon in the police car on the way to Oxford.

On the way over neither Beef nor the Superintendent mentioned the murder but chatted agreeably about conditions in the Force, pay and promotion, and exchanged reminiscences happily about the old days. They both agreed that the young chaps of today were not a patch on the recruits of their time, and how slack and easy in comparison was the life of the newcomers, and they both had a few hard words about university chaps from Hendon.

The car drew up presently in front of a large garage near the station. The Superintendent led the way and we were soon ushered into the office of the manager.

After greeting the Superintendent and being introduced to Beef and myself he sat us down and offered his cigarette-case.

"Yes," he said, "I know what you want to see. We had one of your chaps round here yesterday. We've got several cars we let out on a drive-yourself hire system. The one that the constable yesterday was interested in was a little blue Austin saloon. I'll show it to you. It's only just at the back."

He led the way into a large open space at the back of the garage where a number of cars were parked.

"This is the one," he said. Beef and the Superintendent walked round to the back and examined the rear window. The glass, which was of the unbreakable type, had at some time been badly splintered by some hard object. The Superintendent took out his notebook.

"Yes," he said to Beef, "this corresponds with what that young chauffeur told us. A crack like a star on the left of the rear window."

Beef agreed and turned to the manager. "I wonder if you've got a lock-up garage with no windows?" he asked.

The manager looked a little taken aback. "It will be quite safe locked up here, I assure you," he said. "We're open all night, and there are always several men on duty."

When Beef explained that he wanted to make a test in the dark and told the story of a car similar to this being seen parked at night near the scene of an important crime, the manager entered at once into the spirit of the thing. He soon had the car put into a long dark building that had a complete black-out left over from the days of the war. As soon as we got the car parked as nearly as possible as it was that night the manager switched on the headlights of a motor cycle from the other end of the long building. He focused them on the car, and at once the crack in the glass became visible. As it reflected the light of the headlamp it certainly shone in the shape of a star.

"Thank you," the Superintendent said to the manager. "That's all we need. Perhaps we could come into your office a minute and have a look at your records."

We went back to the room we had come from and the manager produced a large folio.

"Here are the details of the various hirings we've had. Let me see. The car you're interested in is Austin Saloon XYZ 56789. What dates do you want to know about?"

"The tenth of this month," the Superintendent replied. "And perhaps a day or so each side," Beef put in.

The manager turned over the pages till he came to the entry.

"Ah yes, here we are," he said. "That car was hired for three days from 9 a.m. on the ninth of September. Hired in the name of William Hawker. Fee and deposit paid in advance. Hawker gave his address as R.A.C. Club, Pall Mall. Car was returned early on the evening of the eleventh of September. Yes, I remember the case now. As the fellow could not give a local address, he was brought into my office. I asked to see his driving licence, but he said he had left it at his club in town. He seemed all right and offered to pay in advance. So I let it go."

"Would you know him again?" the Superintendent queried. "What was he like?"

"Nothing special, I remember. Perhaps I'd recognize him if I saw him again. I don't know. I didn't pay much attention to his appearance. All I remember was that he was a biggish chap. Oh yes, there was something else. This chap Hawker was a bit tight when he brought the car back. I'll call Charlie. He told me about it."

Charlie, a middle-aged man in a greasy mechanic's overall, came in, and the manager explained what we wanted to know.

"Yes, I remember," Charlie said. "Struck me funny at the time. This chap drives the car straight into our yard and parks it right the other side."

"'Hi, sir,' I shouted, 'will you bring it over here?' He turns out all the lights of the car and walks over. I could see that he could hardly stand. I remembered then that I had seen the car parked outside the Randolph just after six that evening. If you're in this business, you get used to noticing your own cars anywhere. I'd had to go out on the Banbury road to a breakdown.

"'Are you handing the car back for good?' I asked him. He mumbled that he'd finished with the car, but when I tried to get him to come to the office to get his deposit back, he asked me to go and fetch it, saying he wasn't feeling too good. All the time he kept away from any light. I thought that was because of the drink. Well, I gave him his money and he made a kind of signature on our form and lurched off. Tell you the truth I thought we were lucky to have the car back without a crash, the way he was."

"Can you be sure it was the same chap as the one who hired it?" Beef asked.

"Oh yes," Charlie replied. "Even in the dark I could see that."

The Superintendent asked Beef if there was anything more he wanted to know, and then, thanking the manager and Charlie for their information and assuring them that it would prove useful, we left.

"Must be the one, don't you think, Beef?" the Superintendent asked as soon as we were back in the police car.

"Yes, but I suppose you'll just check up with that young chauffeur to make certain," Beef answered. "I've one or two things to do here," Beef went on. "What about you, Super?"

"I'd like to join in what I think you're going to do," the Superintendent replied with a smile. "I can't, though, you see. I'm on duty in uniform. I must get back, but I tell you what I'll do. I'll send the car back for you this afternoon."

Beef thanked him and we fixed to be picked up at the main station at four o'clock.

As soon as the Superintendent had gone we boarded a bus. "Didn't want him hanging around," Beef said, as we took our seats. "Where's this place the Randolph?" he asked.

Presently I led Beef up the Turl, past Balliol and into St. Giles.

"That's it," I said, pointing out the Randolph.

"Ugly great place, isn't it?" Beef said. "Now one or two of these buildings are all right. I'd like to have a look round if we've time."

Beef walked straight in and asked to see the manager. When he appeared, Beef produced his card and told some story about investigating a divorce case.

"I don't think they stayed here," Beef went on, "but I'd just like to look at your register."

"I trust not. We're very particular," the manager replied, and told the receptionist to give Beef any information.

Beef opened the register and looked at the entries in the early part of the month.

"See," he said to me, "that's what I'm looking for. Remember Gupp said he was staying here at the time your aunt was murdered. I thought I'd check it up. 'H. Gupp,' it ran,

'British. East Indian Club. Room 42'. I say, look here. There was another friend of ours staying here at that time, though he seems to have arrived well before Gupp. 'Roger Howard (Maj.) British. 10th Loamshires. Aldershot. Room 50.' So Ridley's stepson was here, too. You know the one. That niece of his told us about him. I didn't think to find his name here. That complicates things a bit. Hm . . . m, Miss," Beef said, addressing the girl at the reception desk. "Could you tell how long these two stayed?" and he pointed at the two entries.

"Gupp. Oh yes," she replied. "Here we are. He came on the eighth of September and left on the twelfth. Major Howard. I remember him well. Such a nice man. He was going to stay for a week, but he had such a good day at Abingford races that he rushed back to London on the tenth. He was full of his good luck, and tipped all the staff. Most handsomely, I believe. Everyone was sorry to see him go."

"He never said anything about having relations nearby, did he?" Beef asked. "Didn't ask about hiring a car for instance?"

"No," the girl answered in a long slow thoughtful voice. "He never asked me about hiring a car, but he did keep saying he must go and try and borrow some money from someone. Uncle or something. Quite a joke it was between us. He kept joking about not having enough to settle his bill. I noticed he used to book everything he could. That's why we were all so glad when he had a good day at the races."

"You're sure it was on the tenth of September that he won the money?" Beef asked.

"Oh yes," the girl replied. "Positive. He left in the early evening. Said he was going to have a night in town."

Beef tried then to steer the conversation back to Hilton Gupp, but he apparently left no impression.

Beef was silent and thoughtful as we walked from the hotel. It was only half-past two, and as the car was not returning until four I suggested to Beef that, unless we had any other calls to make, we should stroll round one of the colleges. My brother Vincent had been up at St. John's, and as it lay in St. Giles, where we were, I took him there. It was September still, so term had not yet begun.

"What," Beef said as we walked towards the lodge, "still on their summer holidays? How long do they get, then?"

I told him the summer vacation was four months and that undergraduates spent more time on vacation than they did term time at Oxford.

"Nice job these professors have got," he said. "I thought your brother did pretty well schoolmastering at Penshurst, but this is a picnic compared with that."

The head porter was standing in the lodge and I pointed him out to Beef.

"Not a patch on the porter at Penshurst," Beef commented. "Why, he hasn't even got a uniform, let alone a top hat." Beef's thoughts were back on a previous case when for a glorious week he deputised for the school porter at Penshurst, the public school where my brother Vincent had become a housemaster, dressed up in the traditional garb. For that week he had appeared with a silk hat with gold braid on it, a yellow and black waistcoat and a coat with gilt buttons.

I showed him the gardens and pointed out the rooms that my brother had been lucky enough to occupy. They were the only undergraduate rooms that looked out on the gardens, but Beef's thoughts seemed to be elsewhere. We walked back across the great expanse of lawn in silence. I recalled that my last sight of all this was one summer when Vincent was up and the Archery Club was having a luncheon. I remembered the targets on the lawn and Vincent and those other figures looking so much in tune with the setting with their green blazers with gilt buttons and white trousers. All at once Beef broke the silence.

"It's no good. I can't ignore it, try as I will. I'll have to go and see him."

"Who? Gupp?" I asked.

"No, of course not," Beef replied rather impatiently. "We know Gupp was staying at the Randolph. He said so in his first statement to the police down at Hastings. That was all enquired into. Try as they would the police couldn't break his alibi. We know that he wasn't down at Hastings the day your aunt died. No, not him. It's that stepson of Ridley's. Major Howard. Well, we've got his address without any trouble. Looks as if we'll have to drive to Aldershot tomorrow."

"Do you think Major Howard was the one who hired that car?" I asked.

"Or it could be Gupp, couldn't it?" Beef answered. "He's a big chap."

"That's nothing. So is Greenleaf," I said. "We know he was supposed to be down this way at that time. After all, he had some sort of motive. Gupp wasn't even connected with Ridley. He had no possible motive."

Beef continued to puff at his pipe but made no reply.

"Beef," I went on, "you can't imagine that Gupp had anything to do with Ridley's death? It was from Aunt Aurora that he thought he was going to get some money. He couldn't even have known Ridley. After all, he'd been abroad those years and he'd only just come back. He hardly left London. Just because he happened to be staying in Oxford. Why, it's ridiculous."

Beef looked at his watch.

"Time we were getting down to the station to meet that car," he said. "Shouldn't care to have to walk all that way for the baths and lavatories on a cold morning," he remarked, as we left the college. "Why, it's not sanitary. No running water in the rooms. Even the secondary schools do better than that!"

I was glad that we were out of earshot of two dons who had just passed us on their way into the college, and before he could say any more about the life of an undergraduate I steered him towards a bus stop.

We arrived next morning about half-past eleven outside Balaclava Barracks in Aldershot. A sentry on the gate directed us to a company office where he told us Major Howard could be found. We soon found ourselves being shown by a sergeant into a private office, on which was printed, "Major R. Howard. O.C. B. Coy. 10th Loamshires".

A cheerful, good-looking man of about thirty-eight was seated at a desk. With his fair hair and moustache, both meticulously brushed and clipped, he looked a typical regular officer of the better type. He had an open expression on his unlined face, and at the sight of Beef, who had sent in in advance his professional card, he rose with a smile.

"Private investigator, eh?" he said. "That's a new one here. Get the police often enough, but you're the first private detective we've had. Which of our brutal and licentious soldiery are you enquiring about? Not that old case of Private Dunn, surely. I thought we'd killed that. After all, he only married three women."

"No, sir," Beef replied, "I'm afraid it's not one of your soldiers. I've come to ask *you* a few questions."

"Me?" the Major said. "Whatever do you want to ask me about?"

The light bantering tone had gone. He seemed quite taken aback.

"Well, go on. Don't say one of my cheques has bounced?"

"No, it's not that, sir," Beef answered. "It's about the death of your stepfather. The verdict at the inquest was murder by person or persons unknown. I have learnt that around the time he was murdered you were staying at the Randolph Hotel in Oxford. Is that correct?"

"Yes, I was staying at the Randolph about that time. Took some leave and went there for the Abingford race meeting." Major Howard paused. "Before we go any further you'd better tell me, Mr. Beef, who you are. I see by your card that you call yourself a private investigator. What are you doing in this case? Who's paying you?"

Beef explained about Ridley's clergyman brother and how he had been engaged to look into the matter.

"Sounds all right," Major Howard said, lighting a cigarette. "But why come to me? I've not seen the old skinflint for close on twenty years. Anyway, I don't get any of his money. All I get out of it is what my mother left to come to me after his death. It's only about three thousand."

"Major Howard," Beef said quietly, "you went to Oxford, saying you were going to stay for a week. You tell me now that you went there to attend the Abingford race meeting. You were very hard up when you went there. You told someone in the hotel that you were hoping to borrow some money from a relation who lived nearby. On the day your stepfather was murdered you came back to the hotel, obviously flush again, saying that you'd won a lot of money at the races. That evening, the evening of the tenth of September you left the hotel, not waiting to complete your week. That was the night Edwin Ridley was murdered. Would you like to tell me what

you did that night? You needn't, of course, but if you refuse
to tell me it will be my duty to inform the police about all
this. Then you'll have to give them your story. Think it over.
I want the truth, though."

Major Howard was silent for some moments. He seemed
worried and thoughtful. Then suddenly he looked up at Beef.

"I suppose I'll have to tell you everything," he began. "One
thing I must ask you. What I'm going to tell you has nothing
to do with Ridley's death. If you're satisfied about that, will
you keep it to yourself?"

"I'll do all I can," Beef replied. "Until I hear your story, I
cannot say more."

"I'll lose my commission if this comes out," he said. "Well,
it's quite true that I had another reason for going to stay that
week in Oxford. But it was because of the Abingford races
that I chose that particular week. The truth was that I was
devilishly hard up. I'm always that, but this time it was more
serious than usual. I hadn't even the money to pay my mess-
bill. I'm pretty extravagant myself, but, between ourselves,
my wife is a hundred times worse. I don't mind telling you
that because it's common knowledge in the regiment. What
wasn't known was how much we owed, and there was nothing left to pay with."

I remembered what Estelle Pinkerton, Ridley's niece, had
said about Howard's wife's extravagance.

"You see, she was always used to a lot of money," he went
on. "Her father crashed financially just after we were married and she can't get used to living on a major's pay. I knew
there was a few thousand still to come from my mother's
estate, but that Ridley, my stepfather, had the use of it till
he died. I hated the thought of asking him, but it was a case
of absolute necessity. Either that or I should be cashiered.

You've probably heard of how I quarrelled with him when I was twenty-one. I hadn't seen or heard from him since, but, curiously enough, about a week before I went to Oxford I had a letter from Ridley's niece, a funny, arty-crafty spinster called Miss Pinkerton . . ."

He saw that Beef and I were smiling.

"Oh, you've met L'Estrella, have you?" he went on. "Well, she and I were distantly related by marriage, but, being about the same age, we had known one another quite well in the old days. I had vaguely kept up with her after her parents' death. You know the way one does with relations. Christmas cards and a letter every other year. As I was saying, I had a letter from her the week before I went to Oxford, forwarded from my club. I think she really put the idea into my head. I was surprised to hear from her at all. I'm afraid I hadn't answered her last letter, which I received over a year ago. I did get a card at Christmas, all snow and robins, but that was the last I had heard from her. It was her usual sentimental stuff, but this time she seemed very keen that I should make it up with my stepfather. So sad, she said, I remember, if he were to pass away without a reconciliation. Couldn't I sink my pride and all that? She was sure he was lonely and would welcome the prodigal son. He would be deeply touched if I wrote or went to see him. I thought if I could 'touch' him deeply, it would be the first time it had ever been done. Anyway, it was a case of needs must. My wife was away, staying with her sister, so I fixed a week's leave and went to the Randolph. As I said, I was also keen to attend Abingford meeting and thought I might pull off something there. Beef, do smoke if you want to. And you too," he said, turning to me and offering a thin gold Asprey cigarette-case. "Just out of pawn," he said, smiling, when he noticed my gaze. "But we're coming to that. I arrived in Oxford on the seventh and the meeting was on the eighth, ninth and tenth. In for a penny in for a pound, I thought. I'll have a fling here first. If I win, all's well. If I lose, I'll be forced to go and see my stepfather in order to pay my hotel bill. My credit was good with the bookies, so I only needed entrance fees. The first two days nothing much happened. I was a quid or two down, but on the last day I couldn't go wrong. For the first time in my life, and I expect the last, I literally went through the card. What's more, of course, I pulled off the tote double. It was a corker, too, because the second horse was a complete outsider, but one I had been watching for a long time. Backing only in fivers and tenners, I was six hundred and forty quid up. The tote alone brought me in over four hundred. Well, you can imagine how I felt. Devil take stepfather Ridley, I said to myself. I don't need any favours from anyone. I went back to the hotel. Paid my cheque. I'd told the girl behind the desk she'd be lucky if she saw the colour of my money, but she only laughed. Little did she know how nearly it came true. Oh, I suppose you got onto me through her. Anyway, I couldn't stand Oxford any more. I felt like a celebration. So I beetled up to town and was back here for dinner in mess the next night. That's the lot." He breathed a sigh of relief. "Thank heavens that's off my chest. Come and have a drink in the mess."

"Just a minute, Major," Beef said. "I'm very grateful to you for telling me all that. If you could just tell me where you stayed or where you went, I don't think I need trouble you further."

Major Howard paused and looked carefully at Beef.

"Can't do that, I'm afraid," he said, a little uneasily. "It's not my secret, you see. I told you my wife was away. Come and have a drink. Even if I'm a murderer, it won't hurt you. I shan't put arsenic in your glass."

"I think we ought to get back, Major. Thank you very much, all the same," I said hurriedly. I had visions of Beef hobnobbing with the Colonel.

"You'd like a drink, Beef, I'm sure," Major Howard pressed.

"I think I should," Beef replied, rising impatiently.

I ought by now to have known better. When we reached the mess, Beef became at once a centre of attraction. His highly coloured accounts of the seamy side of his job went down so well, and so did his drinks, that I had difficulty in dragging him away.

The only conversation I had was with a rather elderly captain. "You in the Services?" he asked.

"No," I replied.

"Oh," he said, and moved away.

We left soon after, though the Colonel eagerly pressed Beef to stay to lunch.

16

It was late in the afternoon when we arrived back at the Shaven Crown in Cold Slaughter. Beef had insisted on a number of stops on the way back. His reception in the officers' mess seemed to have gone rather to his head.

As I went up to my room, I felt how pleasant it was to be back here again. Soon, I thought, as I turned on a bath in the bare clean bathroom, I would go down and join Beef in the bar for a beer or two, then we would sit down to one of these excellent meals of steak or chops and home-grown vegetables, and after that a quiet evening in the big public bar. Then to bed. But I did not know then how long it would be before I saw my comfortable bed again.

I had become accustomed to these stone Cotswold houses that had at first seemed to me so bare, so drained of colour and warmth after the rich red brick of the south. Now I felt a kind of comfort in the thick solidity of the walls and began to feel something of the beauty of this bit of England—a beauty that seemed to have guided man's hand for centuries unconsciously and without apparent effort into shaping every building so that it conformed in simplicity of line and in the subdued hue of the stone with these very hills themselves.

Again I congratulated myself on the lucky chance of my accidental meeting with Beef that in turn had led me to this way of life. The freedom and variety of the job of being Beef's biographer never failed to please me. We never knew where the next case would take us nor what strange collection of human beings we should meet. The worst I had to look forward to was a long period in my flat recording the case. Even then there was always the chance of a few days' excitement on some new venture.

Beef was alone in the bar when I got down, and I joined him in a beer. We were just thinking of throwing a few darts before our meal when a young fellow entered and came up to us.

"Got some news for you," he said rather excitedly. "I've just seen that fellow Greenleaf."

I recognised the speaker as the young chauffeur who had told us about the car standing in the lane near Bampton Court on the night Ridley was murdered. Dressed in his dark-blue uniform, he looked a handsome young rascal. Chapman, Bob Chapman, that was the name, I remembered. The older men in the bar had told us quite a lot about him after they had seen him talking to us. He had been, apparently, pretty wild in his early days—he was only twenty-two or three now—and though he seemed to have settled down to a steady job as chauffeur to the local M.P. he was still counted as rather an irresponsible character. No local dance or cricket dinner, apparently, was complete unless he was there. They spoke of him, however, with a kind of indulgent affection and I could tell that, with his open laughing face and neat figure, he was a favourite in these parts.

Just then two or three strangers entered the bar. Beckoning us to follow him, Beef picked up his tankard and led the way into the room where we used to have our meals.

"Now, young fellow, what's all this excitement? You say you've seen Greenleaf? Where?"

Chapman blew a couple of rings from the smoke of his cigarette.

"I thought you might be interested so I came in here special, just to tell you. I've just come back from Long Alton station. I had to take my boss and his wife down to catch the five-forty. They're off to London for a day or two. I don't expect you know, but the evening up-train and the down-train arrive about the same time at Long Alton. Well, I'd got Sir Henry and his missus nicely settled in an empty first-class carriage and I was just off, when she suddenly said, 'Oh, Bob, I completely forgot. There's a parcel for me from Fortnum and Mason at the station. It came by passenger train this morning. They phoned about it. Collect it before you go, will you, and take it back to the house.' So, instead of going straight back to the car I go into the office at the back of the booking-window. They do everything there. The first thing I notice as I go in is that there's a chap there whose face is familiar. Yet, I thought, he's not a local. Gracious, I said to myself, I know who that is. That's that chap Greenleaf who tried to do himself in."

He had recognized Greenleaf so easily, it appeared, because he had attended the court when Greenleaf was up for attempted suicide. "The boss had to go," he said, "and as I had to drive him there I thought I might as well look in. Never know when you're going to be up in court yourself, do you? Not that I'd ever try *that* game. I felt like it once when I was seventeen and a skirt turned me down, but I've learnt a bit since then, see. Always more fish in the sea, eh?"

"You aren't half spinning this yarn out, young Bob," Beef said.

He paused for another cigarette, lighting the match negligently with a finger-nail, and then continued his story.

"As soon as I see him, I think of you two and what I told you about some folks saying they'd seen him in the neighbourhood around the time old Ridley was done in. I said to myself, 'Bob, this is where you do a bit of Sherlock Holmes.' You wouldn't know, but at Long Alton station there isn't any public telephone. If you want to phone you use the one in the office. As I come in, this fellow Greenleaf goes up to old Jim, the clerk there, and asks if he can phone. I stay well in the background, but, anyway, he wouldn't know me. 'Certainly,' Jim says. 'Is it local?' Greenleaf says yes, and Jim says, 'Well put tuppence in and dial. You know the number, I suppose.' Greenleaf says yes again and turns towards the phone. It was a bit dark in the office, but as he goes towards the phone I can see his face properly for the first time. Gosh, he looked terrible! Ten times worse than when he was in the dock."

"Piling it on a bit, aren't you?" Beef said, but I could see he was smiling. "I bet you don't half think you're a Dick Barton . . ."

"No, honest, he did. Real wild he looked. First I thought I'd try and get near enough to see what number he was phoning, but then I thought that might make him suspicious of me so I stayed in the background, but near enough to hear what he was saying. I heard him say 'This is Greenleaf here,' and then poor old Jim the clerk has to turn round and see me there, and of course he must go and interrupt. He asks me what I want and I tell him about the parcel. Thank God it took a little while to find, but he keeps chattering all the time. However, I got the most important part. I heard him say, 'I don't know anywhere else round here,' and then he suddenly said, 'What about the Druids' Stones? I know them. I could find them any time, day or night', and then just as he rang off I heard the real bit I wanted. 'Very well, I'll see you by the stones some time after eleven. Yes, I realise you may be late. I'll wait, and mind you turn up.' He slammed down the receiver and stalked out without even a glance at me. He seemed really worked up. I collect my parcel and hurry out to the car, but it was dark then and he'd vanished. This is a job for Beef and me, I say to myself . . . ."

"What d'you mean by 'Beef and me', eh?"

"Let's come with you," he pleaded. "You'll go out tonight, won't you, and see who he's meeting at the Druids' Stones? I know the place well. Quite a landmark round here. On the hill nearly a mile from Cold Slaughter. Let me come along. I know every inch of the country. I used to play among those stones as a kid. I promise not to say a word."

Beef rubbed his chin. "What about your job?"

Bob laughed. "Didn't I tell you the boss and his wife have gone away. I'm free as air. I'll just take the car back and drop her ladyship's parcel. Bet there's a nice large pot or two of caviare in that. I'll have to get round the cook again, I can see. I must pass the word to Doris—she's my latest—that I can't meet her tonight. She'll be wild. Can't be helped. I'll come back here on my motor-bike. How's that?"

Beef nodded. "All right, Bob me lad, but don't you go saying anything to nobody about this. It might be dangerous."

"I say, do you think so?" Bob said, his voice full of excitement. "Shall I borrow the old man's revolver?"

"None of that, now," Beef said ponderously. "This is not a kid's game nor one of your Hollywood crook films. I'm just a hard-working detective."

"Bet you're good, though."

"What are these stones you keep talking about?" Beef asked.

"Haven't you heard of the Druids' Stones?" Bob replied. "They're about a mile away. Up on a hill. They're like Stonehenge only much smaller. I don't think many people know about them except folk round here. A few old chaps, professors and so on, come and look occasionally, but mostly they're allowed to become overgrown. You'll see 'em tonight. Supposed to be haunted, so you'd better look out, Beef. Well, cheerio."

"Nice young fellow that," Beef said, when he had gone.

"He certainly knows how to manage you, Beef," I said. "A heavy dose of flattery . . . ."

"He can see I'm good," Beef replied, making for the bar. "Pity a few others don't realise it."

17

The church bell was striking the quarter hour after ten as we stepped out of the Shaven Crown. We had purposely waited until after closing time so that our going out at that time would arouse no comment among the few who had just left the bars. We had arranged to pick up Bob Chapman at the far end of the village. It seemed very dark at first, until our eyes became accustomed to the September night. There was a heavy wind blowing and dark clouds hid the moon for the most part, but every now and then a shaft of light would appear as a rift appeared in the scudding bank of cloud. When we had passed beyond the last house of the village and had come into the open country, I soon became aware of a dark shadow motionless against the stone wall. As we approached the shadow became recognisable as the slim figure of Bob Chapman.

I had found an old history of Gloucestershire in the inn parlour, and while waiting for our evening meal I had looked up the Druids' Stones. I could only find one short paragraph about them. A curious irregular circle of stones, the book said, near Cold Slaughter. They are thought to date back to prehistoric times and probably belong to the same period as Stonehenge on Salisbury Plain. There was a comparison between the two, quite a bit about the early customs of that period and a steel engraving of the stones themselves. Then followed a typically Victorian sentence. "Many strange beliefs are still held concerning these stones in the villages around and it would be difficult to persuade any of the local inhabitants to go near them after nightfall."

Very comforting, I thought, as we walked forward in silence, with Bob leading, and I was glad of the company of these two. The warmth and confidence that I had felt earlier in the evening as I drank a few pints of beer before the bar fire seemed to vanish when the wind went whistling across the open fields and the rare gleams of moonlight lit now and then the desolate landscape and revealed for a moment or two the strange twisted shape of a tree or barn.

Presently we came to an old five-barred gate and I could see beyond the darker shadows of a wood. Bob climbed over and tried to open it, but it was covered with lichen and overgrown and would not budge. It had obviously not been used for a long time. Beef followed, climbing over the gate. With all his bulk, he showed an agility that surprised me. When we had advanced some twenty yards up what had been a ride through the wood, but was now only wide enough to allow us to walk in single file, Bob stopped in a small clearing.

"This is not the usual way up to the stones," he said, as Beef and I came close. "I'm taking you up a back way. It's a bit further round, but I thought it would be better. We might have run into Greenleaf the other way in the dark, but we're quite safe here. He can't possibly know this path through the wood."

"What about the person he's meeting?" Beef asked. "He must be a local."

"Even if he lives round here, I don't suppose he could find his way through this wood in the dark. Anyway, there'd be no point in going a long way round."

"How much farther is it?" I asked. It was a stiff climb through the wood and I was not in training.

"Oh, not far," Bob replied. "We'll be there in twenty minutes."

Beef looked at his watch.

"We should be there just after a quarter to eleven. That should be all right. Can we get pretty close without being seen?" he asked.

"I've got all that worked out," Bob replied, and I could tell from his voice that he was thoroughly enjoying himself. There was a note of confident pride arising, I suspected, from the fact that he was acting as leader to a real detective. Without him, he felt, we should be lost among these trees. "On this side, you see, the wood stretches right up to the stones." He went on, "The moon will be on our left so we should be able to see what we want if these clouds break at all. Noise is the only danger. We'll have to go carefully later when we get close. Greenleaf may be there already. Twigs make a hell of a noise at night. Luckily, there's a wind which will cover a lot. We'd better get on now. I'll tell you when we're getting close."

We followed on up the steep path. It was heavy going, for the ground underfoot was wet and soggy and every now and then our clothes would be caught by thorns, or we would trip on a half-hidden log, or a branch would block the way. The old police training seemed to stand Beef in good stead and he again surprised me. I was beginning to pant and blow, but Beef moved silently forward and seemed to avoid instinctively the twigs that continually slapped my face or the coil of a blackberry bush that would wind round my legs.

It seemed a long and wearisome climb before I came upon Beef and Bob Chapman standing motionless under a large beech tree. The path seemed for some time to have become more level and I imagined that we must be reaching the crown of the hill on which Bob had told us the Druids' Stones lay.

"That's the end of the wood," Bob said, in a low voice, pointing to a patch ahead that was lighter than the surrounding shadows. The wood was so thick that it was impossible to see far in any direction.

"I think," Bob went on in a whisper, "it would be best if I went on alone and had a look round. If I'm not back in five minutes you follow with Mr. Townsend."

Beef nodded.

"It's quite easy. There's a well-worn path from here to the edge of the wood. Don't make a noise, though, or we may put them on their guard. If there's nobody there yet it will be easy. Anyone coming to the stones any other way has to approach them across an open field, and we should easily see them in good time. I'll come straight back if anyone's there."

For a time we could see his figure moving among the trees, but it soon disappeared. Apart from the wind in the treetops I could not hear a sound, and I thought that it would be fairly easy for us to follow undetected anyone outside the wood. I could see Beef looking occasionally at the luminous dial of his watch, and I too began to feel some of the excitement of the chase. I wondered whom Greenleaf had arranged to meet and why it had been necessary to choose this outlandish spot. A sudden rather unpleasant thought came to me. Had he chosen this place purposely because it was so far from anywhere? Beef interrupted my thoughts by nudging me and pointing to his watch. Then he, too, disappeared down the pathway towards the edge of the wood. I could not help feeling very much

alone and defenceless once he had gone. Every sound made me
start and every dark shadow assumed human shape. I waited
for some moments, perhaps a minute, and then took the path
down which the other two had gone. I advanced slowly and as
silently as I could. Suddenly I felt a hand on my arm. Stifling
a cry I turned and saw Bob at my side. He led me forward a
few paces and then lay on his stomach, motioning me to do the
same. As I lay down, I became aware of Beef a little way ahead,
also prone on the ground. Bob plucked my sleeve and pointed
ahead. My eyes had become accustomed to the darkness now
and through a thin curtain of branches I could see the open
grassland and the dark shapes that must be the Druids' Stones.
They were not tall, like those at Stonehenge, but formed a more
complete circle. Bob was still attracting my attention, and as
I followed his pointing finger I saw advancing across the grass
towards the circle of stones the tall figure of a man. Beef was
gazing motionless ahead. I looked round at Bob and saw a look
of thrill and triumph lighting up his broad open features. He
nodded to me gaily, as if to say, "What did I tell you?"

As the figure approached it was not difficult to recognise it
as the tall ungainly shape of Greenleaf. When he reached the
circle he looked carefully around and gave a low whistle. It was
an eerie sound in the dark emptiness of the night. He paced up
and down and then sat down on one of the stones that lay hori-
zontal on the ground. I looked at my watch and was surprised
to find it was only just before eleven. Only three quarters of
an hour since we had left the homely warmth of the inn fire,
I thought. Out here we seemed to have passed into a different
life, something more primitive and nearer to nature itself.

Apart from the intermittent soughing of the wind, there was
complete silence, broken only by the hooting of an owl, the distant barking of a fox and every now and then a rustle somewhere

near us in the wood, which I took for a stoat or weasel or some other animal on a predatory prowl. Greenleaf himself was sitting quite still, though every now and then he would turn his head and look around. Though I knew we were completely invisible, it was a curious sensation to watch his head turned towards where we lay and know that his eyes were fixed on the wood.

Just then Beef turned round towards us and beckoned. Bob motioned me to stay still while he crept silently forward. I could just hear a faint whisper and then I saw Bob disappear into the open in the direction opposite to that in which Greenleaf was facing. I watched him slip forward, a black streak against the faint light, and fade into the protecting shadow of one of the biggest of the stones which stood near to where Greenleaf was sitting.

He had no sooner got there than I heard a sharp click, and looking up I saw Greenleaf raise his right hand. The moon shone for a moment and I could see the silhouette of his hand, which seemed strangely distorted. Something glinted in the faint light, and with a shock I realised that he was holding a revolver in his hand. He was pointing it towards the moon and looking down the barrel. I could see that Beef had noticed this and I hoped Bob had too. I felt we were responsible for his safety, anyhow.

Then a new noise broke the silence, and for a paralysing moment I realised that it was coming from within the wood quite close to where we lay. There was a cracking of boughs and a heavy tramp of feet. I looked over my shoulder and saw away to our left a torch shining. Someone else was using the woods that night. I watched as Greenleaf looked up, but was relieved to see that he remained seated. Then not twenty yards to our left a second figure broke out from the woods and made its way towards the stones. Greenleaf made no movement as the newcomer came towards him.

"What a place to choose," the newcomer said, and I was surprised that we were near enough to hear what was said. Beef obviously had been afraid that we might not and had sent Bob nearer. I was just thinking that there was something familiar about the newcomer, his voice and movement, when I heard Greenleaf reply.

"You know very well, Fagg, I couldn't risk coming to Bampton Court. Someone was sure to have seen me. This was the only place around here I knew. Anyhow, have you got it?"

"Not so much of your hurry and bluster, Mr. Greenleaf," Fagg replied, and now I could clearly recognise the unpleasing features of the manservant of Bampton Court. "This is going to cost you a lot of money. I've taken a big risk in getting it. If that blasted private dick gets on to it, it'll be me who'll suffer. A hundred quid is what I want for this bit of paper. I know you can't produce that much now. What I want to know is how much you have brought. Let's not waste time. Here's the papers you want. Where's the dough?"

Greenleaf put his hand in his breast pocket. "Here's thirty pounds," he said. "I'll let you have the rest in a month when I get that money I told you about."

Fagg handed over what looked like an envelope, and for a few minutes they were both silent, while Fagg seemed to be counting the notes, and Greenleaf, producing a small torch from his pocket, was intent on the papers Fagg had given him.

"Only just right," Fagg said unpleasantly. "And I'm not worried about the other seventy. You'll pay that all right. And before a month's out, because you know very well if you don't what'll happen. I'll have to go to the police and tell them about your little visit to Bampton Court on the tenth of September."

"It would only be your word against mine," Greenleaf said.

"That's where you're wrong, Mr. Greenleaf. You don't think I'd trust you with those papers and you still owing me seventy quid if I hadn't something else up my sleeve, do you?"

Greenleaf stared, without replying.

"Do you?" Fagg repeated, in an even nastier tone. "Well, I'll just tell you in case you get any ideas about clearing off and not paying. I've got a newspaper at home," he went on, in a jeering tone. "It's the *Daily Telegraph*. The London edition. It's dated the tenth of September. You bought that paper in London and carelessly left it in the hall at Bampton Court when you called on Ridley that night."

"That paper proves nothing," I heard Greenleaf reply, but his voice was strained and uneasy.

"Doesn't it?" Fagg repeated. "Doesn't it prove anything when it's got a nice little crossword neatly filled? I bet that detective could soon prove it was yours. It's beautifully done in ink with a fountain-pen. Black ink, too. I bet your pen is filled with some now."

"Your dirty blackmailing rascal," Greenleaf shouted as he rose. "I'll show you why I chose this place. See what I've got in my hand . . . ."

At this moment several things happened. Beef leapt to his feet and I saw a figure slide swiftly out of the shadows. There was a sharp cry, a loud report, and on the ground all that could be seen was a dark swirling human mass.

Beef covered the distance that separated us from the mêlée like a born athlete, and when I came up the struggle was over. Greenleaf was on his feet, but I noticed Beef held him in a firm grip. Bob was nursing his hand, from which blood was pouring rather freely, but of Fagg there was no sign.

I had a look at Bob's hand and found it was only a flesh wound. The bullet had fortunately caught the fleshy part of his palm and there was dark discolouration caused by the revolver being fired at such close range. I bound a clean hand-kerchief tightly round the wound and told him to keep it up. Beef was holding the revolver in his right hand, while he gripped Greenleaf with his left.

"You're coming with me, Mr. Greenleaf," Beef was saying. "I'm not a policeman now, but it's my duty as a citizen to keep you under my eye until we've had a word with the local Superintendent. You can tell your story to him."

This time we took the main pathway back to Cold Slaughter.

"Bob, you go and get your hand seen to by the doctor," Beef said, as we came into the village. "Tell him you've been out rabbiting. I'll see him in the morning and explain. We don't want a lot of gossip. Come and see us at the pub tomorrow. In the meantime keep your mouth shut."

"O.K., Beef," Bob replied, as he entered the gate of the doctor's house. "I told you I ought to have brought the old man's gun," and we heard him whistling cheerfully as he walked up the drive.

"I'm taking you along to the pub we're staying at," he said to Greenleaf. "Then I'm going to phone the Superintendent."

Greenleaf just mumbled a reply. He looked utterly dead beat. He certainly showed no sign of resistance and seemed almost glad that all decisions were being made for him.

Beef roused the landlord, when we got back to the inn, and asked for some hot water, a bowl of sugar and a bottle of rum.

"Nice rum punch," Beef said. "That's what we all need," and he went to phone the Superintendent. Half an hour later the latter arrived. Greenleaf had recovered somewhat by now. Beef told the Superintendent how he had come to witness the scene at the Druids' Stones and all that had happened there, and handed over the revolver.

"I think you ought to have informed me about this, Beef," the Superintendent said rather curtly. He was obviously annoyed at being roused in the middle of the night and, in addition, felt probably that Beef had stolen a march on him.

"Now, Mr. Greenleaf, I think we want some explanation from you. Would you like to make a statement?" he asked. "Of course, if you would I shall have to give you the usual warning."

Greenleaf at first became truculent saying that no one could hold him without making a charge, but eventually agreed to explain.

"It's really quite simple," he said. "All I wanted was to get my contract back from that blood-sucking swine Ridley. I admit I called there the night he was murdered, but he was alive when I left him. I'll admit, too, we had words, and I lost my temper. I tried to get hold of the papers I wanted by force. That crook Fagg had told me where to look, but the desk was locked. I couldn't get hold of them. I told Ridley I was going to publish and be damned with another firm. He'd have to sue me and I'd show him up. I left him just before midnight."

"How did you get to Bampton Court?" the Superintendent asked.

"I walked from the station," Greenleaf answered.

"You didn't see a car when you left the house that night?" the Superintendent went on.

Greenleaf seemed uncertain what to reply. "No," he answered at last, "I don't remember one. Well, I'd better just finish my story. Fagg, when I told him I had been unsuccessful in finding the papers I wanted, offered to get hold of them for me if I paid him a hundred quid."

"Wait a minute," the Superintendent said. "When did all this happen? You seem to have been on pretty familiar terms with Fagg."

"We'd exchanged a few letters after my last visit," Green-leaf replied rather sheepishly. "I admit I was a fool. I knew Fagg was crooked, but I was determined to get the better of Ridley by fair means or foul. Fagg wrote to me two days ago and said that he had managed to get hold of the papers I wanted while the police were going through them."

I saw the Superintendent frown, but Greenleaf went on without noticing.

"I came down here tonight, or rather yesterday," he went on, for it was already well past midnight. "I phoned Fagg from the station, I didn't want to be seen in the village so I arranged to meet him at the only other landmark I knew. You heard the rest," he ended, turning to Beef.

"Why did you bring a revolver?" the Superintendent asked.

"I knew Fagg. I thought I might have to frighten him a bit if he tried any funny business. As you heard, he was as good as threatening blackmail. I never meant to fire the gun. It just went off when that chap of yours sprung out on me from behind."

"I'm afraid I shall have to ask you to come along with me."

When they had gone, I felt very sleepy, and, much as I wanted to question Beef, I could hardly keep my eyes open and felt it would be better to leave that until the morning. It had been a long day. Our drive to Aldershot and back, then the long climb up to the Druids' Stones and our vigil there, then Beef's strong rum punches, all seemed to weigh down my eyelids. I had never been so glad to slide into bed, and as I dropped off to sleep I remembered my thoughts of a peaceful evening in the inn and how differently the night had turned out. It was difficult to believe that the scene by the Druids' Stones had really taken place. Like the stones themselves, such passion as Greenleaf had shown seemed to belong to a more primordial state of nature.

18

I was woken the next morning by the sound of bells from the village church. I glanced at my watch and found it was nearly eleven o'clock. I was making an effort to rise when there was a knock at the door and the wife of the landlord appeared with breakfast on a tray.

"Thought I'd let you sleep on, sir," she said, "after all your adventures last night. It's the talk of the village, you know. But you wouldn't have heard the latest, I suppose. They've arrested that Greenleaf fellow. I said to my husband from the first, I said, it's not a local person who did it, you mark my words. Mr. Beef said for you not to hurry. He's not going out this morning, but he wants to drive to London this afternoon. I'm afraid you'll both be leaving us. He's got a private challenge match against George this morning. George is the postman, you know. He doesn't want to leave without playing that off. We shall miss Mr. Beef when he goes. Quite a character he's become in the public bar in these few days. It usually takes our customers a long time before they take to a new customer, but Mr. Beef certainly's got a way with him. He throws quite a good dart, too. Well, I mustn't let your breakfast get cold."

She put the tray on the table beside the bed and departed, leaving, I was pleased to see, the Sunday papers I had ordered.

I can do without papers on a weekday, but a Sunday without my favourite papers would be hell. I can never quite make up my mind whether I prefer the *Observer* to the *Sunday Times*, so I always come back to having them both. About the necessity for taking the *News of the World* I have never had a moment's doubt. The *Sunday Express* completes the quartette, but that, I am afraid, remains rather as a tribute to the Nat Gubbins of the war years.

I love to read them leisurely, as I could that morning, sipping tea, eating a mouthful of bacon and egg or a finger of toast, entirely on my own. It's selfish, perhaps, but I like to have them crisp and unopened and not have to share them with anyone else. For there is an art, I find, in consuming this Sunday fare. One begins with the light hors d'oeuvres, Sayings of the Week in the *Observer*, The Stars and You in the *News of the World*, Nat Gubbins in the *Express* and Henry Longhurst in the *Sunday Times*, and works one's way through the whole menu, the book reviews, Atticus, Scrutator, the savouries in the centre pages of the *News of the World*—always a flavoursome tit-bit and with such endearing titles—and until not a dish remains to which full justice has not been done.

It was, therefore, nearly half-past twelve when I eventually came downstairs. I found Beef enjoying *his* Sunday morning ritual at the bar, a ritual which he would be equally unwilling to forgo. "Have you heard about them arresting Greenleaf?" he asked.

I nodded. "For the murder?" I asked.

"Yes," Beef replied. "I thought they might hold him. He got a pretty good grilling last night, I expect. Well, it simplifies everything. We'll leave here this afternoon. I've learnt all I want in the Cotswolds. The arrest can't be out till Monday's papers, but I want to be in London early this evening, just to be on the safe side. I shall miss this place, you know. Don't always get a decent crowd like the one that comes in here. There's some good players, too. That reminds me. I must play that final challenge against old George. He's over there. Hasn't got his uniform on today. Two All, it is. It'll be anyone's game."

Beef went over to the board, and when I glanced across a few minutes later it was clear that the great match had begun. Quite a crowd had gathered, and Beef, I knew, would be in his element. There was something of the actor in him that brought out the best in his playing when there was a crowd. Young Bob Chapman was among the spectators, his damaged hand heavily bandaged. He was, I noticed, rooting loudly for Beef.

We did not have our Sunday roast beef until after the pub closed at two, so that it was nearly three before we set out.

Beef was silent all the way up, which was unusual with him. I thought at first he might have gone to sleep after the heavy midday lunch, but whenever I looked across at him his eyes were fixed ahead. He looked thoughtful and rather formidable.

It was not until we drew up at his house that he spoke. "I must see that fellow Gupp again. It's more urgent than ever, now they've arrested Greenleaf," he said, as he lifted his bag from the car. "I can't get the police to do it. They won't have any more to do with him. They say they've questioned him till they're blue in the face and can't break his alibi, so we'll have to do it unofficially. It's most important that I see him tomorrow at the latest. I've two questions I must ask him. Will you help me to get hold of him?"

I said I would, but I did not relish the idea. What Beef had in mind I did not know, but I was reluctant to act the pawn if Gupp should be the king Beef was trying to corner.

"I've got his address here. Inspector Arnold gave it to me in Hastings. It's Buckingham Gate. That's where he lives. I want you to go along there now and try and see him. Ask him out for a drink or a meal. If you can't fix anything for tonight, it will have to be tomorrow. But it would be better tonight. When you've got something fixed, phone me and I'll come along casual like. I expect he'll see through it, but he can't avoid me very well if you're there."

"Supposing he's out?" I said.

"Leave a message asking him to phone you tomorrow morning. Say it's very important. You'll have to think up something between now and then to discuss with him till I come along. I tell you, it's really urgent. I shall be waiting to get your call. I shan't even go out to the local tonight, that's how serious I think it is. I'll spend an evening with the old woman. She's very good, seeing how little I'm there. Don't forget, ring me as soon as you can."

Ever since Beef had heard of Greenleaf's arrest I had noticed a change in him. I knew him so well by now that I would see a difference when it would not be apparent to outsiders. Since then he had seemed almost anxious and worried, which he rarely was, and the long silence he had kept all the way up to London struck me as not at all like Beef.

I drove the car through the park and found that the address which Beef had given me as Gupp's was that of a small expensive-looking private hotel. When I enquired for Gupp, they told me that he was away. I asked when he left and was told Friday night.

"Rather unexpected, wasn't it?" I asked casually. "I had arranged to dine with him tonight. He didn't leave a message or his address or anything, did he? I'm his cousin."

The porter said he would make quite sure and rang through to the office, but Gupp had left no address or message.

There was nothing further I could do there so I went to the nearest phone box and rang Beef. He did not say much when I told him, except that he wanted me to get in touch with Gupp at the Asiatic Bank where he worked.

Next morning I telephoned the St. James's branch of the Asiatic Bank, and after being put through to various departments I got into an assistant manager who told me that Mr. Gupp was not in. When I began to ask questions he became very brusque. "Please phone his home address, if you must speak to him. We don't encourage private calls here."

I thought that I had better see Beef, so I drove round to his house. He called me in.

"Seen the papers?" he asked, and put in front of me the midday specials.

I had seen a small paragraph in my morning paper just giving the details of Greenleaf's arrest in what they called the Cotswold murder, but I was not prepared for the publicity that the midday papers gave to the news. There were photos of the Druids' Stones and of Bob Chapman with a bandaged hand and a highly coloured account of our midnight adventures. Beef was termed as "that well-known private investigator, Mr. William Beef". There was no mention of me, but Bob had quite a write-up, and had given an interview which made good reading. I rather thought that the landlord of the Shaven Crown must have had a record Sunday night attendance.

Beef listened rather impatiently to my news about Gupp.

"Well, if we can't get in touch with him, we'll have to do a bit of routine work ourselves. It's office work, so I'd like your help. We must get on to that right away. I must find out on what boat Gupp came back from the East Indies. That's what I wanted to ask him. It says in my notebook that he told us he landed early August. We'll go to all the shipping companies this afternoon and look through their passenger lists till we find it. It must be about that time because he called on your aunt the middle of August."

Just as he finished speaking there was a ring at his front door. A few minutes later Mrs. Beef opened the door.

"Rev. Alfred Ridley," she said, ushering in a figure in a clerical collar, whom we recognised at once.

"Ah, Beef, I see the police have got my brother's murderer. The morning papers state they've arrested a fellow called Greenleaf. I don't like all these headlines in the midday papers. I see you were involved in this rather melodramatic business."

Beef was making some noncommittal reply when the vicar began to speak again.

"I came this morning about an extraordinary coincidence. A rather curious thing has happened. I don't suppose it has any connection with the case but I felt I'd better tell you. You've met my elder sister's daughter, Estelle Pinkerton, I think? You called on her in Cheltenham she told me. Well, I always have a talk with her on Sunday evenings over the phone. She loves to hear about the children, you know. She's godmother to two of them. She has no phone of her own so her neighbours, a retired colonel and his wife, allow her to use theirs."

He paused to light a cigarette. "I got through as usual on Sunday and she was most mysterious. She said she was going away in a few days. She told me she didn't know when she'd

be back, but I wasn't to worry about her. I tried to get her to
tell me more, but she wouldn't and rang off. Knowing that
now an arrest had been made she'd probably be able to draw
on her uncle's money, I was worried. You know what she's
like—most unworldly. I'd met her neighbours, Colonel Fordyce
and his wife, when I'd visited her a few years back. Somehow
I felt I wasn't quite satisfied so I put another call through and
spoke to Mrs. Fordyce. She made the matter seem even worse,
hinting that there was a man in the case. Well, when a woman,
a spinster at that, close on forty comes into a large sum of
money one must be prepared for fortune hunters, but I didn't
anticipate anything like that so soon. I wonder if you could
look into the matter for me? It's very awkward, you know. I
can't interfere with her. She's of age, of course. But all that
money . . ." He shook his head. Then he added, almost in a
whisper, "It should all come to my children when she dies, but
if a man gets hold of her, goodness knows what may happen."

Beef agreed.

"Going away without telling me where or for how long.
It's so unlike Estelle. She's always consulted me. I don't like
it. I should feel much happier if you could find time to go
and see her and reassure me that everything is all right. You
know, she's a wealthy woman now and that colonel's wife
seemed quite perturbed about her."

Beef promised to do what he could, and the vicar left.

"Come on, quick," Beef said, as soon as the front door had
closed behind the Reverend Alfred Ridley. "We'll get down
to those shipping companies. We must work fast now."

It was not until after one o'clock, when the clerks in the
Dutch East Indian Line, where we had come in desperation
after meeting with no success among the English shipping
companies, were showing impatience that I at last came on

Gupp's name in a passenger list. The boat, the *Appeldorn*, on which he had travelled, was a slow one, apparently, and seemed to have called everywhere on its way back. Even after Marseilles I noticed that it had put in at Barcelona, Gibraltar, Lisbon and Cherbourg, before it eventually berthed at Tilbury on 6th August. It was a cheap fare, I could not help noticing, and I thought that that was probably the reason Gupp had been forced to choose that particular line.

I had done most of the checking of the lists while Beef occupied himself in being pleasant to the various officials in these offices and enlisting their help. When I found Gupp's name, Beef got out the glasses which he only used on very special occasions.

"Let me have a look," he said, and I could detect a quiver of excitement in his voice as he eagerly scanned the list.

"It's there all right," I replied. "There's no need to check it."

I was impatient to get away now that we had found Gupp's name, but Beef was in his most irritating mood. He had got out his huge notebook and was busy making copious notes. When he had finished, he thanked the clerk who had helped us and we walked out into Haymarket.

"I must get down to Hastings right away," he said, as we walked towards the Carlton. "There's not a moment to be lost."

"I'm glad now the police have arrested someone for the Cotswold murder," I could not help saying. "Now you can get back to my aunt's case. I suppose you'd like me to drive you down?"

"There isn't time for that," he answered, "but drive me as far as Victoria. I'm only going straight down and back again as quick as I can. I've just got to get two answers. Then I think my case is complete."

When we were in the car he went on:

"I want to ask Raikes, the cook's husband, the fellow we saw at Lewes races, you know, just one thing. I want to know what he saw exactly that morning when he was outside your aunt's room, cleaning the window. That's the first one. Then I want that dressmaker woman, Miss Pinhole, to tell me who she thought she recognised that same morning as she was going in to see your aunt. You remember she told us she could fix the day of the murder, because just as she was coming to your aunt's house she thought she saw someone she knew. I know Raikes is there because I phoned Camber Lodge this morning. I'll have to risk catching Miss Pinhole. She's not the sort to be far away."

I drove into the station yard at Victoria and Beef got out. "I'll catch the first train back I can," he said, as we left the car. "Wait in at your flat until you hear from me, will you? Have the car filled, too. We may have a long run to do before night."

As I waited that evening for Beef in my flat I could not help feeling something of the tenseness, the suppressed excitement that I had detected in his voice and manner during the last two days, and I was glad to have something to keep me occupied until Beef came. I cut some excellent sandwiches, put out a half dozen bottles of beer and, as an afterthought, added a bottle of whisky, which I had been keeping for just such an expedition as this.

Just before six the bell of my flat rang, and I found Beef on the doorstep.

He nodded approvingly at the sandwiches and the beer.

"Just what we need," he said, picking up the whisky bottle: "we've a long cold drive to do tonight," and quarter-filled two large tumblers.

"Nice drop of Scotch," he said, sucking his lips, and began to empty his overcoat pockets. First came his favourite torch.

Then I was surprised to see him bring out a pair of handcuffs. I had never known him use them before.

"I slipped round to tell the old woman," he said. "I collected these while I was there. Got that heavy sword-stick of yours. Bring that along, too. We may see a bit of action before the night's out. We've got to take a chance. I can't get the police to act, not in the time, but I *know* I'm right this time."

His last words were spoken, I thought, more to assure himself than me.

I could see he was anxious to be away, so I put everything together and led the way to the car.

"Keep her going," Beef said, lying back in his seat and lighting his pipe. "It may be a close thing. We must try and get there in time."

"In time for what?" I could not help asking. Beef was being purposely mysterious, I felt.

"That's what I want to know, but I shouldn't like to have another murder on my hands."

It was a cold dark night, but dry, and ideal for driving. At last we were on the last lap to Cheltenham. The road began to fall away down to the valley and I could see the lights of Andoversford below.

"Ahh . . ." said Beef, but whether with anticipation or relief I couldn't decide.

19

Estelle Pinkerton's house showed no lights as we looked towards it from the garden gate. The blinds were drawn, certainly, but not even a faint glow showed anywhere. The chimney was smokeless, though it was late September. The whole place had a cold and deserted look.

"Doesn't look as if anyone was at home," I said to Beef, as we looked across the little lawn whose ornaments were mercifully hidden by the dark.

"I'm not taking any chances from now on. We'll have a scout round after we've tried the bell," Beef replied, and went forward to the front door. I followed. The house was still and silent and I had quite a shock when the silence was broken by the shrill tinkle of a bell until I realised that it was Beef who had rung. Not a sound came from within. Beef then beat a loud tattoo on the knocker, but this was equally without result, though the sounds echoed through the house.

"Enough to wake the dead," I said, and then, suddenly realising the significance of what I had said, I felt a cold shiver run through me.

"We'll go right round the house and see if we can find a way in. Look out for an unlatched window," Beef said. The back of the house was as deserted as the front, but I did notice an open window on the floor above, which I pointed out to Beef.

As we came to the front again, we saw the light of a torch at the front gate. I felt Beef's hand on my arm. It was impossible to see who it was, but a few seconds later the beam of the torch was focused on us as we stood by the porch.

"Were you looking for Miss Pinkerton?" we heard a woman's voice saying. Beef said that we were, and for a minute the light of the torch moved over us, up and down.

"You must excuse me," the voice continued, "but I'm terrified of burglars. I'm Miss Pinkerton's next-door neighbour. I heard someone knocking at her door so I thought I'd better come and see who it was. I'm afraid you won't find her in. She's gone away, I think."

"Are you Mrs. Fordyce, madam?" Beef asked.

"Yes. How did you know?" she replied. Beef then told her of the vicar's visit that morning. She seemed amply reassured about us after that.

"You'd better come along to my house. It's only just a few yards," she said leading the way.

We were introduced to a rather ancient representative of the Army, who sat motionless in a leather armchair. The only contribution he made to the whole scene was to lower his Blackwood's for a moment when Mrs. Fordyce said, "My husband, Colonel Fordyce."

No encouragement was necessary, however, to make Mrs. Fordyce speak. She was obviously dying to tell us her story.

"I'm really very worried about Estelle Pinkerton," she began. "It's all so strange and so unlike her. If I hadn't known her all these years, I should be tempted to put the very worst construction on the whole thing."

"Perhaps you'd tell us everything from the beginning, Mrs. Fordyce?" Beef said.

"Yes, that would be best," she said, "or else I shall go running on and you won't know what I'm talking about, will you?"

She beamed across at Beef. "It all really began on Friday. I'd just gone in to ask her about a recipe of hers. We were having some people to dinner that night and Estelle was so clever with her soufflés. It was after lunch, I remember, and she was just seeing me off at the front gate when a telegraph boy came up and gave her a telegram. 'Oh dear,' she exclaimed when she'd read it, 'now I'll have to go back to the town and do some more shopping.' But all the same she seemed pleased and excited. There was no answer to send so the boy cycled off, but I waited expecting that Estelle would tell me her news. She had always confided in me. Well, that is until recently, but that's another story. I asked if she'd had bad news, trying to win her confidence, but she wouldn't say any more."

"You say that recently, Mrs. Fordyce, you've noticed some change in Miss Pinkerton. She didn't confide in you as she used to. Did she behave at all differently with other people? Did you think there was anything on her mind?"

Mrs. Fordyce thought for a moment.

"Yes, I think there was a difference," she replied slowly, weighing her words. "I've noticed it for over a month now, ever since her holidays. She seemed—oh, how shall I put it? I know it sounds silly, but she seemed to have grown up. Before she would be round here asking our advice on every tiny little thing. Recently she seems to have taken her own decisions. Why, when she heard she had inherited all that money by her uncle's death, she took it so calmly. Not a bit as I expected. Well, I must get on with my story. Friday evening a taxi drew up outside her house, but I was cooking dinner and only just had time to see someone going towards, her front door with a suitcase. Believe it or not, I wouldn't like to swear it in a court of law, but I'm convinced it was a man. A youngish man at that. Next morning I saw nothing of Estelle or her visitor, though I was in the garden for an hour or two. After lunch I thought I'd just drop in and see her."

I saw a look of understanding pass between Beef and Mrs. Fordyce.

"Yes," she went on with a smile, "I just had to try and satisfy my curiosity, but, I'm sorry to say, I had no luck. When I rang, Estelle came to the door, but for the first time since we've known each other she didn't ask me in. I knew something funny was going on then. We chatted for a few minutes and then Estelle said she had something in the oven and asked me to excuse her. Well, all that Saturday I kept my eyes open, but it wasn't until the evening, just after the news, that I saw anything. Even then I only managed just to catch a glimpse of Estelle going out of her gate. She went hurriedly down the road the other way. All I could see was that she wasn't alone and her companion was a man. You know about the telephone call on Sunday, and how her *other* uncle, the vicar, called me again. Well, after he'd called I was so worried I thought I'd try and have a talk with Estelle. I went round to the house, but, though I rang and knocked as you did just now, I couldn't get any answer, and that's the last I've heard or seen of Estelle Pinkerton. I tried again this morning, but there was still no answer. That's why I ran out when I heard a noise at her door tonight. It's such a relief to confide in someone. It hardly seemed a case for the police. If she wants to go away and not tell us where she's going, that's her business, but I must say I felt hurt after being such friends all these years."

Beef handled her beautifully, and assured her she could safely leave everything to him.

"I feel better already," she said, and I could see that Beef had made another conquest. "Mr. Beef, do let me get you something. I'm afraid I can't ask you to a meal. We only picnic on Sunday night. Perhaps a glass of sherry or a whisky?"

"Well, madam, it's very kind of you," Beef said, smiling and rising to his feet. "Perhaps a whisky would go down nicely, but I mustn't be long. I'm going to have a look at that house next door, if I have to break in. I don't like the sound of your story."

Whether it was Beef rising to his feet or the word whisky, I do not know, but the silent figure of Colonel Fordyce came suddenly to life. With a swiftness and dexterity surprising for his years, he whipped out a decanter of whisky and some glasses. I noticed, however, that it was Mrs. Fordyce who had unlocked the corner cupboard where the whisky was kept.

"Excuse me for a few minutes," she said. "Henry, look after them, but remember what the doctor told you."

"Jolly glad you chaps came along tonight," he said, looking carefully at the closed door. "My wife, excellent woman, keeps me very short on rations. I can't get out on Sunday nights. Come on, put that down and we'll have another."

When we had finished our drinks we said good night to the Colonel and his wife and made our way back to the house next door. It was very dark now and we were glad of Beef's torch. There was no change. No light had appeared anywhere in Miss Pinkerton's house, and no sound could be heard. Beef rang again. The sound of the bell ringing in that empty house gave me the shivers. There was something eerie about it.

"Well," said Beef, "there's only one thing for it. You'll have to climb in that open window. I'm too big. We're breaking the law, I know, but I must get in that house somehow. It's a matter of life and death."

Something about that empty house filled me with apprehension, and as I looked at the darkened windows I felt a strange reluctance to face the task of penetrating the inside alone in the darkness, but, as Beef had said, there was nothing else for it. We found a small ladder in a toolshed and I climbed up slowly, rung by rung. I came level with the window and peered in rather nervously, shining Beef's torch around inside. The window was only on a landing and I clambered in. As I made my way to an electric-light switch, which I had located with the torch, I tried to overcome my nervousness by saying to myself that there could not be anyone inside, but I was glad when I turned the switch and the light came on. I hurried down the stairs and quickly opened the front door and let Beef in.

Slowly and methodically Beef went from room to room, examining cupboards and even looking under the beds and in trunks.

"Well," he said, as we finished investigating a small attic, "there doesn't appear to be anything here."

I had by this time fully expected to find a corpse, and I felt sure that Beef himself was slightly relieved that our search had revealed nothing so gruesome.

Everything in the house was in perfect order. Every plate and dish was neatly arranged. Saucepans hung from their hooks clean and polished and the beds were made and covered with coloured counterpanes. The only sign of recent habitation was the ashes of the fire. Beef bent down and felt the fire-bricks.

"That's not been out many hours," he said. "It looks as if we're just too late. I must go through this place and see if I can find anything that'll tell us where she's gone. Go and get that grub from the car. We may as well make ourselves comfortable. You can get a meal ready while I'm looking round."

He went towards a rather nice-looking bureau, which was unlocked and full of papers. "This may give some clue," he said, as he began to go through the various pigeon-holes. I left him to it and, after collecting the food and drink from the car, went into Estelle Pinkerton's neat little kitchen.

When I brought the meal I had prepared into the living-room, Beef was still busy at the desk. "Shan't be long," he said. "She keeps everything nice and tidy."

In a few minutes he closed the last drawer and came and sat down.

"Nothing much to go on here," he said, as he helped himself to a sandwich. "I can't find her cheque book, but if she's gone away that would explain it. Her paying-in book's there. There's an entry there I don't much like. She paid in a cheque today, Monday, for two thousand pounds. An advance from the solicitor, I expect. If she paid that in today, it looks as if she's been to the bank and probably drawn something out. After this I'm going through the house from top to bottom and then we'll have another word with Mrs. Fordyce. I bet she'd know, if she came over here, whether any of Miss Pinkerton's clothes are gone, or whether any suit-cases are missing. Women living as close as they did would be able to tell you down to the last nylon what the other had. That would help. Anyhow it'll tell us for certain whether she's gone away or not."

When he had finished his meal and lit his pipe, Beef wandered out of the room. Presently I heard his footsteps overhead.

When he finally came back, he had a copy of *Dalton's Advertiser* in his hand, which he added to the few papers he had taken from the bureau.

"We'll go and see Mrs. Fordyce again," he announced, and led the way out of the house.

Mrs. Fordyce seemed pleased to see us again and agreed at once to coming across to the empty house and seeing if she could tell us what was missing.

"I expect she's wearing her green tweeds," Mrs. Fordyce said as we entered Fairy Glen. "She would this cold weather. Especially if she were going by train."

We left her to examine Estelle Pinkerton's bedroom and the small box-room, and I could tell from her manner the task was not altogether unwelcome.

"She's taken the two big adjustable suitcases that she bought this summer for her trip," Mrs. Fordyce said, as she rejoined us.

"I can tell you that for certain. The little brown one she used to use for her London visits is not there, but she did talk of giving that away. Her tweeds are not there either, as I suspected, and her new evening dress isn't hanging in the wardrobe, but it might be at the cleaners. There's another coat and skirt I can't find. It looks as if she's taken quite a bit. There are practically no stockings or handkerchiefs left and all the brushes and things from her dressing-table are gone."

Beef thanked her.

"Gone for quite a time, I should say," Mrs. Fordyce went on. "I do think it strange of her not to come and tell me."

"Madam, you can't think of anything that would help us to trace where she's gone, can you? Any little thing she's said or done."

Mrs. Fordyce looked across thoughtfully at Beef.

"Well, there is just one curious thing I forgot to mention. While she was waiting on Sunday night for a call from her uncle—she always comes in and has coffee with us you know on Sunday evenings—she asked if she might put a call through herself. Our phone, you know, is in the morning-room. While she was there, I strolled through to the library. Quite by chance, you know," she added with an innocent smile. Beef smiled too. They knew. "Well, there's only a thin partition between the morning-room and the library, but you don't notice it. The morning-room has been papered over and the books cover the library wall. I did just manage to hear her say. 'Thank you, Mrs. White, I'll sign the agreement and pay a month in advance when I see you.' I didn't catch any more, because she seemed to be finishing her conversation and I thought I'd better hurry back. I was quite surprised when she came in a few minutes later and opened her purse. 'I owe you this for a trunk call,' she said, and handed me some silver. 'I checked with the exchange. It's quite correct.' I had naturally thought she was just making a local call. Apart from calling her uncles, I've hardly ever known Estelle make a long-distance call, especially on a Sunday." Beef listened patiently to this new episode. "I'll have that call traced in the morning," he said. "We can't do much more tonight. We'll see you back to your house, madam, and thank you very much for your help."

At her invitation, I ran my car into Mrs. Fordyce's drive and Beef and I returned to spend a cheerless night at Fairy Glen.

Somehow I could not rid myself of the strange feeling I had had earlier in the evening when Beef asked me to climb into the house.

"I suppose she *has* gone away, Beef?" I asked uneasily.

"Well, she's not here, is she?" he answered.

"I believe you half expected to find her corpse here, didn't you?" I said.

"When people have done one premeditated murder," Beef replied, "they seem to think nothing of doing another. I don't say I expected a body here necessarily, but I thought it was on the cards. I must say, it does seem as if Miss Pinkerton got away from here." He looked around the room as if expecting to find some answer to her disappearance.

"I'd give a lot to know what's happening to her now," he added.

20

The next morning Beef left me to clear up the breakfast—
we had raided Miss Pinkerton's larder—while he went into
the town. He had some enquiries to make, but I noticed that
he had a good look at the garden in daylight before he left.

"Looking for traces of newly disturbed earth," I said,
laughing at him, as he pounded round the minute lawn and
flowerbeds.

It was nearly ten before Beef returned, and I could tell by
his brisk walk as he strode in that he had been successful.

"Quick," he began breathlessly, "we're off back to Sussex
as fast as that car of yours can go. I'll tell you more as we go
along. You put our stuff in the car while I just have a word
with Mrs. Fordyce. I don't want her gossiping round the place
at this time. It might ruin everything."

It was a perfect day for a drive, I thought, as I got the car
ready. There had been a mist early in the morning but now
pale September sunlight was streaming down from a cloud-
less sky. I could feel a pleasant autumn nip in the air as I
carried our bags and put them in the back. Down the road

came scurrying noisily a wave of dry brown leaves, caught in a sudden gust, and I realised that autumn was fully upon us.

When Beef joined me, I lost no time in getting out of Cheltenham. As soon as we were clear of the town, Beef told me what he had discovered that morning. With the aid of the local police, which he had managed to enlist after a call had been put through to the Superintendent in charge of the Cotswold murder case, as it was called, he had traced the long-distance call that Estelle Pinkerton had made on the Sunday. It was to an hotel in Eastbourne. Fortunately Mrs. Fordyce had overheard the name of Mrs. White, to whom Miss Pinkerton had been phoning. Beef at once got through to the hotel and found there was a Mrs. White staying there.

"When at last they got this Mrs. White to the phone I had a devil of a job. To begin with she said she'd never heard of anyone called Pinkerton and she had not had any dealings with anyone at Cheltenham for many years. I was afraid she would ring off. I asked her if she'd let her house to the lady who'd phoned on Sunday afternoon. 'Oh, you mean Mrs. Welldon. Yes, I'm afraid it's gone. Mrs. Welldon, a charming old lady, called yesterday for the keys and settled everything. Only it's not a house, you know. It's only a bungalow. I said so in the advertisement.' After that it was easy. I soon got the name and address of the bungalow. It was clear that our friend Estelle Pinkerton was calling herself Mrs. Welldon. I've got the address here in my notebook. Chalk Cottage, Downland, Sussex. Do you know this place, Downland?"

"Gracious, yes," I replied with a smile. "It's only a small village. Quite near Hastings."

With the very mention of the village of Downland, I was back nearly twenty years. I could almost smell the yellow gorse and hear again the plaintive cry of the seagulls as they wheeled around those high white cliffs. How often had Vincent and I set out from Aunt Aurora's house, our lunch and bathing costumes tied to our saddles, and cycled over the hills till we came to that remote gap where then a few coastguard cottages were the only sign of human life? I could still see the wreck of a small coaster that for years rusted away against the cliffs. What dreams we had had about her in those far-off sunlit days. It was under those very cliffs, I remembered, that at the age of twelve I had smoked my first cigarette.

"We'd better stop for a bite of lunch soon," Beef said, abruptly interrupting my thoughts of the past. "We'll be in Lewes in a few minutes."

I had kept the needle of the speedometer well up as we had sped across southern England. Through Lechlade and Faringdon, past Wantage and along by the Thames to Pangbourne and Reading we had come without a pause. Guildford and Horsham were now behind us. I, too, was ready to stop for a drink and a sandwich. Neither of us, I could tell, were in any mood to linger long. Beef appeared restless and anxious, and was also feeling an excited curiosity about what would come at the end of this long quest.

At last we turned down the narrow lane that led to the village of Downland, and I was agreeably surprised to find that the place had not changed as much as I had feared. It was, of course, late in the year, but although a number of new buildings had sprung up since I was here, the village still preserved its air of lonely isolation.

"Miss Pinkerton told Mrs. White that her doctor had ordered her a month's complete rest away from everyone. It looks as if she'd get it here," Beef said, as he looked down the deserted street.

There was the usual village shop that appeared to sell everything, and Beef led the way towards it.

"We'll find out where Chalk Cottage is, anyhow," he said. "I bet it's the centre of village gossip here. We may hear something."

A middle-aged woman was alone behind the counter, and when we enquired for Chalk Cottage she came to the shop door and pointed out a small white bungalow some quarter of a mile away up the downs.

"That's Chalk Cottage," she said, seeming eager to chatter. "A lady and gentleman came there yesterday. You'd be friends of theirs, I dare say."

Beef agreed that we were on our way to visit them, and took some time over the purchase of two ounces of tobacco.

"Been empty long?" he asked.

"Ever since the end of August," she replied. "I was quite surprised when I saw the taxi go up yesterday afternoon. I mean, it's not the time of year you expect visitors, is it?"

Beef muttered some reply and then asked her if she had seen the newcomers yet.

"No, not yet," she replied. "I haven't seen them about today at all, though it's been a lovely day. They'll have to come here sometime, though, unless they want to take a bus to Hastings for every little thing."

We walked out and began to drive up the hill towards Chalk Cottage. We had only gone a hundred yards or so when the track ended and there was only a footpath with the sign "Chalk Cottage" on the gate. Leaving the car we climbed on up through the small garden that surrounded the bungalow.

There was no sign of life as we approached, and I began to fear we were going to find another empty house. Beef rang the bell and knocked loudly on the front door, but there was no answer. There was no need this time to climb in through a window, as the front door proved to be unlocked. We passed through the tiny entrance into a living-room, but here there was no sign that anyone had recently been in occupation. Beyond lay a kitchen which looked equally deserted.

"The bedrooms must be the other side of the hall," Beef said. "There are none here."

"This must be the way to them," I said, as I pushed open a door on the further side of the hall.

I walked in and then suddenly stopped. A large double bed filled most of the room and in the centre was a strange swelling. Something or somebody was in that bed. I could not move. Beef, by this time, had also entered the room. He stood looking down at the bed for a moment and then bent down and slowly pulled back the bedclothes.

There, clad only in pyjamas, lay the body of Hilton Gupp.

Beef leaned forward and put out his hand. "Cold as mutton," he said. He made a quick examination of the body and then covered the unpleasant sight up again.

"Must have been poisoned," he said. "There are no marks on the body that I can find. And a chap like Gupp doesn't just die. Not at a time like this."

I was glad when Beef left the bedroom and closed and locked the door, putting the key in his pocket. He returned to the sitting-room, sat down and began to fill his pipe.

"Beef," I said irritably, "surely there are a hundred things we ought to be doing. What about informing the police and getting a doctor?"

He lit a match and puffed slowly at his pipe. Then he began to examine a small green booklet. "Local bus timetable this," he said. "It had fallen down beside the bed.

"Is there a railway station anywhere near?" he asked.

"No," I replied. "Hastings would be the nearest. And you won't find there are many buses either."

Beef began turning over the leaves of the book.

"Ah, here we are," he said. "Downland. Good gracious, there's no bus in the morning from here until eleven-ten. She couldn't have walked because of her suitcase. Besides, there was no reason to. She couldn't have known we were coming here."

"Miss Pinkerton?" I asked.

Beef nodded.

"I see there's a bus that goes through to Seahaven. That's where the channel boats sail from. Yes, and by Jove there's a pencil mark against it. I wonder if we're going to be lucky. Do you remember how she talked about her French grandfather when she was showing you those sketches of Brittany? France, that's where she's gone, I'll bet. As far as she knows there's nothing in the world to connect Mrs. Welldon, the lady who took this bungalow, with Estelle Pinkerton of Cheltenham. All she had to do, she thought, was to stay away for a bit and come back and enjoy her money. It's a good chance she's gone abroad. Sort of thing she'd have read about. But we'll find her, wherever she's gone." He rose briskly and led the way down the hill from Chalk Cottage towards the village of Downland.

"First I'm going to phone Inspector Arnold at Hastings. He'll be able to check up on the cross-channel boats. If there's a village policeman we'd better get him to guard Chalk Cottage, but Arnold can look after the rest—doctors and so on. If she hasn't tried to slip across the channel, it may take a little time to find her."

There was a telephone booth in the village street which Beef at once entered. He was some time, but at last came out looking pleased with himself.

"I managed to get hold of Arnold himself, fortunately. He's got a description of Estelle Pinkerton and is putting it out everywhere. I told him I thought she couldn't have left this place till the eleven-ten bus. We know they didn't arrive till late yesterday afternoon and there was no bus out of here after that. We should have heard, I think, if there'd been a car around here last night. Anyway, she wouldn't want to draw attention to herself. I wouldn't be surprised if she didn't put the poison in his early-morning cup of tea. That would give her plenty of time to clear the place up and get away by that bus. Arnold looked up the boats from Seahaven when I suggested that, and he found there's one this evening at six o'clock. The one before that sailed at ten this morning, so I don't think she can have caught it. I told him that I'd meet him at Seahaven police station. We'll just see the local bobby. Arnold will do the rest."

The local police constable, whom we found in his cottage, had already had a call from Hastings, and was preparing to go up and guard Chalk Cottage until the police doctor arrived. There was nothing else for us to do in Downland and we were just preparing to drive off when the old woman came out of the village shop.

"You missed the lady at Chalk Cottage, then?" she said. "I've just heard she was seen getting on the Hastings bus this morning at eleven, but I expect she'll be back on the four o'clock. That's the last. They all come back on that when they've been to Hastings from here. If she'd got on at this stop I'd have seen her myself, but she walked along to Bylands Corner. Nearly a mile. Dragging two suitcases, too."

We were in the car by this time, and, waving goodbye, we made our escape.

When we got to Seahaven police station Beef went in to find Inspector Arnold, but it was nearly twenty minutes later before he reappeared with the Inspector.

"No reports have come in about her yet," Beef said to me, as they climbed into the car. "But we're going to watch the passengers on to the Seahaven boat."

"It seems quite a likely chance," the Inspector added, after greeting me. "That marked bus time-table and her French grandfather. All the other stations have been warned, so there's nothing else we can do for the moment."

"I've got a man watching everyone going on. There's a little spot just before they come to the customs. A disused office with glass windows. Everyone has to pass it. We often use it in cases like this."

The road came to an abrupt end at a stone wall and the Inspector jumped out and unlocked a door which led to the outer harbour. Just before the customs shed, he stopped.

"Here we are," he said, opening the door of one of the station offices. "Any luck yet?" he said to a man who was standing at the window.

"A few have gone through," the plain-clothes policeman replied, "but no one answering the description you gave me. A family, father, mother and two young girls. That couldn't have been her. An old woman about seventy, two or three business men, and a party of three clergymen."

"Well, it's early yet," the Inspector said, and we settled down to wait. As each passenger approached Beef and I looked eagerly for any sign of Estelle Pinkerton, but no one even remotely resembling her came by. I could see Beef was getting restless. He kept looking at his watch and then eagerly down the platform.

"She'll have to hurry if she's going to catch it now," the Inspector was saying, when Beef suddenly jumped up.

"Inspector, you must get me on that boat," he said excitedly, taking Arnold by the arm and dragging him out of the office. "I'm sure I'm not wrong. She's on there all right. Remember what Mrs. White said," he went on, turning to me as we hurried forward. "'A charming old lady.' I thought it was funny at the time, talking of a woman not forty. 'Course she was dressed up as an old woman. She's the old lady your chap saw go by. Naturally he wouldn't think of her. She told us she went in for amateur dramatics."

Inspector Arnold was, it seemed, well known to the officials at Seahaven and we were soon all three aboard in the purser's office.

"No," he said, in reply to Beef's eager query. "We haven't any old lady aboard this time, thank heavens. Not one. Have a look if you like, but I watched them all come aboard."

Beef thought for a moment, and then produced a photograph.

"Seen anyone like her?" he asked anxiously.

"Oh yes," the purser replied, putting down the photograph, which I recognised as one of Estelle Pinkerton that I had last seen in Fairy Glen. "She's taken a cabin. No. 34. I'll show you where it is."

Beef and the Inspector jumped up and led the way, and after knocking opened the door of cabin 34.

I never want to see again the expression I saw on Estelle Pinkerton's face as she recognised Beef. Fury. Fear. Frustration. A suffusion of blood and then a deathly pallor. At first she hardly seemed to hear when the Inspector said that he wished to question her, and asked her to accompany him off the boat. When he mentioned the name of Hilton Gupp, she swayed and I thought she would fall, but she allowed herself to be led down the gangway and into the police car that Inspector Arnold had ordered.

As we came towards my car a plain-clothes policeman came forward with a bundle in his arms.

"These have just been found in the ladies' cloak-room," he said, displaying a black bonnet and coat and a wig of silver hair.

"She had to be herself to pass the customs," Beef said. "Her passport and everything. I'd forgotten that. Besides, her whole plan depended on her going aboard as Miss Pinkerton, taking an ordinary holiday."

"It very nearly came off. If it hadn't been for you, Beef, she'd have been on her way by now," the Inspector added generously. "All I hope is that you've got all the proof you say you have. To look at her you wouldn't think she'd hurt a fly, would you? You can never tell with poisoners. I shouldn't have thought she'd had it in her to do one murder, let alone two."

"Two?" I asked.

"So Beef tells me," the Inspector replied.

Beef nodded.

21

My flat was chosen as the place in which Beef would make his long-awaited statement, and unfold the history of Estelle Pinkerton and Hilton Gupp. Two days only had gone by since Estelle Pinkerton's arrest at Seahaven, and so far she had only been charged with the murder of Hilton Gupp.

London was chosen because Inspector Arnold had to come up from Hastings, and the jovial Superintendent and the Scotland Yard detective who was in charge of the Cotswold murder case had to make the journey from Gloucestershire. Inspector Arnold was chiefly responsible for their being present. He had become quite a Beef enthusiast after we had spent the evening with him on the night of the arrest. Curiously, neither Beef nor I had met the man who had been sent down from Scotland Yard to take over the inquiry into Ridley's murder when the Chief Constable had applied for help, and, as I looked at the tall spare figure whom the Superintendent introduced to us as Chief Inspector Foster, I could see that he was not altogether pleased at the turn of events.

"I hope this is not all a mare's nest, Sergeant," he said to Beef, his thin hatchet face showing no expression except perhaps a slight distaste for everything. "If it hadn't been for Inspector Arnold's pressure I should never have come. We've got a lot of work to get through to complete the prosecution's case against Greenleaf. It's mostly routine stuff, I know, but it takes time. All that Boy Scout business of yours, Mr. Beef, trailing after Greenleaf in the dark and letting him fire a revolver that night by the Druids' Stones didn't help. We had him taped all right. It was only a matter of time. Our methods have to be slightly less spectacular than yours, but we have to be more sure. Well, let's get this over as quickly as possible. I want to be away early. I can't imagine what help we can possibly hope to get from a meeting of this sort."

He glanced round my room rather superciliously. I had taken quite a lot of trouble over their reception and I disliked the way his eyes rested disapprovingly on a side table where I had arranged a number of bottles and glasses and some very pleasant sandwiches. His disapproving glance seemed to embrace the rest of us. The rotund Superintendent, looking even more benign than usual, was sprawled comfortably in one of my big armchairs, a pint tankard in one hand and a large sandwich in the other. Beef and Arnold were equally at ease and obviously enjoying themselves standing in front of the fire and chatting happily.

"Well, Beef," said Arnold, who seemed a little embarrassed by the Chief Inspector's rudeness, for it was he, after all, who had called the meeting. "Would you like to begin now? I'm sure we're all eager to hear your theory of these murders. I know I am, even after the little that you told me the other night."

"*Theory!*" the Chief Inspector echoed. "Do you mean to say you've called me up all this way, Inspector, to listen to Beef's theories? I don't wish to be rude, but really the whole thing seems to me most extraordinary. I don't know who this gentleman is"—he indicated me—"or why he is at this meeting, apart from the fact that this seems to be his flat and we're apparently enjoying his hospitality. Beef, I'm sure, was an excellent sergeant in the Force, before he resigned, and I dare say he does a useful business as a private detective, when he's not playing darts. I'm surprised at you, really, Inspector. I'm a busy man, you know. If Beef has any fresh facts, I'm sure he knows what he ought to do. It's his duty as a citizen to report them to the police. Scotland Yard, if he prefers. But this . . . ."

He looked round the room as if unable to express what he felt.

The Inspector began to look disappointed and a little peeved at the Scotland Yard man's behaviour. Beef came at once to his rescue. He was at his best, good-humoured with just a hint of conciliation in his voice, that probably only I could tell was assumed with an inward chuckle.

"I know how you feel, sir," Beef began, "but I think it might be worth your while to wait and hear what I have to say. It won't take long. What about a nice bit of cold chicken and a drink? Then we can all settle down comfortably and I'll tell you my story."

"Well, I suppose now I'm here, I'd better wait and listen to what it is you have to say," he replied rather ungraciously, though he accepted a leg of chicken and a glass of wine. "Any new facts that you've discovered I must, of course, be informed of. Be as brief as possible, please. The Superintendent and I are eager to get back on our case."

"I'm afraid I haven't had the education of some of you," Beef began, "so I'll have to tell the story my own way.

"It all began when I was called in by the Rev. Alfred Ridley to look into his brother's death. His brother, of course, was Edwin Ridley, who had been found hanging from a beam in his house in Gloucestershire. The only thing the vicar was really worried about was whether Edwin Ridley had committed suicide, as in that case his kids would lose the very large life insurance which was due to them on their uncle's death. As you know, there was really no need for this because within twenty-four hours of his body being found the doctors all agreed that he had been strangled manually first and then strung up in an attempt to pass the murder off as suicide. I should probably have been satisfied with having done what I had been asked to do, accepted a small fee from the vicar and left the police to find the murderers. It looked a fairly ordinary sort of crime, and not particularly interesting. However, just two days after I went down to Cold Slaughter I received your letter." He looked across at me. "This was a letter written by Mr. Townsend here from Hastings to me in London, and forwarded on, saying that there was strong suspicion that his aunt had been poisoned the day before and asking me to come down and act for him and his brother as they both benefited under their aunt's Will. Two things struck me as curious after I'd read this letter, so much so that after a playful telegram to Mr. Townsend I decided to go down to Hastings.

"I noticed that both murders had taken place on the same day, the tenth of September. Nothing in itself, of course, but, taken in conjunction with the other fact which I'll tell you about later, there seemed to be some odd coincidence at work, and one thing I've learnt is to distrust coincidences. You can forget one sometimes but never two.

"However, when I got to Camber Lodge—that was Miss Fielding's house, the lady who was poisoned—I didn't for a time think much more about Ridley's murder. The whole atmosphere was so different. Ridley, by all accounts, was a mean, unpleasant, quarrelsome character, who might have been bumped off by anyone. Blackmail, theft, revenge, there could have been a dozen good reasons and no one was really sorry to see him go. Mr. Townsend's aunt, Miss Aurora Fielding, on the other hand, must have been a really good lady of the old school. You could tell that from her house, her servants and all her friends. It was difficult to think of anyone wanting to harm her, but the evidence was quite clear. Someone had poisoned her. Inspector Arnold here was quite right, of course, when he advised me to concentrate on motive. In nearly every murder the motive is either money or love. There are, of course, a hundred variations of each, but it usually boils down in the end to one or the other. In this case it clearly wasn't love and everything pointed to money. She was a wealthy old girl. Most of her money had been originally left—and this was common knowledge—in equal shares to Mr. Townsend, his brother Vincent and to a cousin, Hilton Gupp. There were other bequests I'll come to later, but the bulk went to them. At first sight these three would be the most likely suspects. Mr. Lionel Townsend, whose flat this is, I dismissed pretty well right away. I knew him too well. For one thing he hasn't the right temperament, and for another he'd have made a muck of it somewhere, I felt sure, if he'd tried. His brother Vincent was a possibility, but the most obvious suspect was their cousin Hilton Gupp. He was almost the perfect suspect. He was badly in debt and his whole future was threatened if he didn't get hold of some cash quick. His appearance was against him, too, with his dissipated good looks. Anyone could see he was a bad lot. One thing, however, seemed to clear him completely, and that was that he was nearly a hundred miles away when the murder was committed. His alibi was put to every test by the police, but they couldn't break it.

"He had recently returned with a bad record from the East Indies and had tried to borrow some money from his aunt.

He had on that visit broken into her desk and had a look at her Will to make sure he was still included. She happened to see him doing it and cut him right out the next day. He didn't know that. If she'd have told him, she'd be alive today."

"You mean that after all this you're going to tell us that Hilton Gupp murdered Aurora Fielding?" gasped Chief Inspector Foster. "We *know* that he was nowhere near Hastings."

Beef held up his huge hand.

"Hold on a minute," he said. "I'll come to everything in time. I was just going to say that I settled down to routine enquiries as prescribed, questioning the witnesses and examining what evidence there was. Just at this time I could not help wondering what was behind the behaviour of Mr. Townsend's brother Vincent and a distant relation Miss Payne, who was Miss Fielding's companion. They were obviously afraid of some discovery connected with a medicine chest, the key of which had been lost and was found on the top of Mr. Vincent Townsend's wardrobe. However, I soon got to the bottom of that. Miss Payne was an addict to sleeping tablets. The maid mentioned that Miss Fielding occasionally took a sleeping tablet, but that the last lot had disappeared unexpectedly quickly. I found an old bottle and had a word with the chemist. There was no morphia in these tablets, but he was surprised at the number which Miss Fielding's companion used to order. Mr. Vincent Townsend had discovered her weakness. They were in love with one another before the murder but didn't realise it—and he'd tried to stop Miss Payne taking them by purposely losing the key. When, just about this time, Miss Fielding was found to have been poisoned, each one feared for the other and they even began to suspect one another of the crime. That was when they hardly exchanged a word and tried to avoid each other's company. Gupp heard about the key of the medicine chest being found on Vincent Townsend's wardrobe from the cook's husband, Raikes, and when he failed one night to get a fairly large sum of money out of the Townsend brothers by threats, he went and put the wind up Miss Payne properly. He led her to believe that Vincent Townsend was about to be arrested and she, too, probably. That was when she tried to drown herself.

"I then examined the possibility that it was someone outside who had done the poisoning. The most likely opportunity for this was for someone to put the morphia in the sherry which Miss Fielding and her visitors had drunk on the morning of her death. Inspector Arnold told me that no trace of poison could be found either in the used glasses or in the decanter, but I discovered that there had been a goldfish bowl in the room—but more about that later. I then tried to question all the people who had visited Miss Fielding on the morning of her death. Three of them had fairly strong motives, one had every reason to keep Miss Fielding alive, and one could not be traced. Those who had a motive were the vicar and Miss Fielding's two great friends, the Misses Graves. Miss Fielding had left five hundred pounds to the church's restoration fund, and the vicar was crazy about restoring some old pictures on the wall. In fact later he overworked himself on this job and is still in a mental home. The Misses Graves were as poor as church mice, and very slowly coming to the time when they would be 'talked about'. There would be rumours of them 'owing tradesmen money'. For people like them this was probably the worst tragedy that could happen. Worse than death. They'd even had a summons or two which must have seemed like the end of the world. Even so I didn't really consider either them or the vicar as likely to have done a murder, but I had to keep them still in mind. Of the other two visitors, as I said before, one had every reason to keep Miss Fielding alive. Rich ladies who still employed a dressmaker like Amelia Pinhole were quickly dying out, and I bet Miss Fielding was worth quite a lot to her every year. The visitor, the lady who came collecting for missionaries, was never traced, though Townsend here found the receipt which was given that morning to Miss Fielding.

"Somehow, as I looked over my lists of suspects, I always came back to Hilton Gupp. It was you, Inspector, who first put the idea of an accomplice into my head. You remember when we were chatting after the inquest. I said something about the person who'd done it, and you put in a remark that started me on the right track. 'Person or persons,' you said. I always in my bones felt that Gupp was at the back of the murder, somehow. His story was so pat and his alibi so well-founded. He seemed almost anxious to tell us where he was when the murder was committed, didn't he? Well, I thought, he still could be involved if he had an accomplice, and there, ready-made, was one for him. I mean Raikes, of course, the cook's husband. I hadn't met him, but from all accounts he seemed to have sailed pretty close to the wind all his life. Also he was cleaning windows that morning at Camber Lodge.

"I had already guessed from that business of young Charlie, the cook's son, selling his motor-bike and the money reappearing, that Raikes had stolen the twenty quid from Miss Fielding's purse. It was only when I met him at Lewes races that I realised that he wasn't the type for murder. Too weak a character altogether. A cheap crook, a petty thief, lazy, idle, good-for-nothing, yes, but not a chap to get mixed up in murder. Even the small threat I bluffed him with sent him off in a blue funk. Afterwards I guessed a bit more why he was so frightened, but that comes in my story later. I must tell you about my win at those races sometime.

"I began then to think back about other murders, and it struck me that you don't often find a murderer with an accomplice. A murderer daren't trust another human soul with his secret. It only occurs when the two of them are involved together, when both their necks are in danger of the noose. You, Inspector Arnold, had another pair in mind, I think—Mr. Vincent Townsend and the companion, Miss Payne. I shouldn't be surprised if their getting married didn't encourage you in that theory."

Inspector Arnold nodded, and Beef went on.

"I think it was about this time that I began to realise there was a curious similarity about the crimes, apart from their being committed on the same day. Both victims were rich and all likely suspects had unimpeachable alibis. I also noted in my mind that Miss Fielding was poisoned, which was more often a woman's crime, whereas Ridley was strangled and then strung up, which could only have been done by a man. These ideas of mine were only floating about in the back of my mind then.

"I said earlier that there was another curious fact I discovered in the Cotswolds that sent me hurrying down to Hastings when I got Mr. Townsend's letter. In the room where Ridley was murdered were shelves and shelves of books. On a table was a small parcel of books still wrapped loosely in newspaper, with brown paper outside. The books didn't mean much to me and the brown paper was blank, but the newspaper was the *Sussex Gazette*, dated the sixteenth of August. But the really interesting thing that really struck me after I had received Mr. Townsend's letter was the pencil mark that newsagents so often make on the top right-hand corner for the delivery boy. It was roughly scribbled but I could still make out 'Camber Highfield'. Now Miss Fielding's notepaper, which Mr. Townsend had used for his letter, was headed 'Camber Lodge, Highfield Road, Hastings'. The date worried

me a little. It seemed a long way back till I remembered that
Gupp had paid a visit to Camber Lodge on the twentieth of
August. He had left in a hurry and might easily have used the
Sussex Gazette to pack with. Could the books have come from
him? I remembered he was staying in Oxford at the time, as
his alibi proved. I recalled then how, when I questioned him
about anything to do with his alibi for Miss Fielding's murder,
he was full of bounce, but when I touched on where he was
on the *night* of Miss Fielding's murder, he seemed nervous.
That was, of course, the night when Ridley was strangled.

"Naturally, at that time it was all vague suspicion, but my
theory was forming. It seemed far-fetched, almost fantastic.
What connection could there possibly be between Hilton
Gupp and Edwin Ridley? Gupp had been abroad for two or
three years and had no link with Gloucestershire, and Ridley
hadn't been away from the Cotswolds for several months. I
couldn't find anything in common between the two of them.
Yet there was the *Sussex Gazette* with Miss Fielding's address
on it in Ridley's house, and both these two rich elderly persons
were murdered on the same day. It certainly was a problem.
You, gentlemen, must be getting tired of listening to my voice,
and I could do with a drink."

I quickly suggested a break while we had a drink and snack.
I had looked across nervously at Chief Inspector Foster once
or twice while Beef had been talking, half expecting an inter-
ruption, but I was amused, though not surprised, to see that
he was as taken up by Beef's account as the rest of us. His
eyes never left Beef throughout this long speech.

"Beef certainly seems to have stolen a march on you,
Inspector," the Chief Inspector was saying to Arnold.

Arnold smiled. "He certainly did," he replied. "He's not
finished his story yet, though, not by a long chalk."

22

They all in their different ways seemed anxious for Beef to get on with his story, and it was not long before we were all seated again and Beef continued.

"It was, then, with all this rather jumbled in my mind that I came back to the Cotswolds. We went back to the pub I had stayed at before. Nice little place. Good grub, decent beer, and some of the chaps were pretty hot on the board. I'd like to go back there some time."

He saw me looking at him meaningly and went on with his story.

"Here again I followed the normal routine I had learnt in the Force and interviewed all the possible suspects and went into every point that came up. Although the dead man was most unpopular in the district, after I had met the neighbouring Master of the Hunt I was convinced that it wasn't just a local crime. I was sure that if there was any chance of that, you'd have known or heard something, Superintendent, and not handed the case over at once to Scotland Yard. Lovelace, the secretary, I didn't care for much, but if he did a murder it wouldn't be by strangling anyone and then tying them up to a

beam when they're dead. That was a man's job. There was all
that business about those books. I suppose he'd been pinching
'em, hadn't he?" Beef said, turning to the Superintendent.

"Oh yes, we've traced all that, but it may not come to a
prosecution. He's confessed everything and we've got some
of them back."

"I thought that was about it, but I felt it hadn't anything
to do with the murder. As you know, I was more interested
in that other little pile. They may not have been first editions,
and that Oxford bookseller sniffed at them, but they were
certainly more valuable to me. Especially the packing, as I said.

"Then of course there was Greenleaf. Well, I must say he
was a red herring to me for a long time. He could so easily
have been the type to have murdered Ridley in a fit of temper.
After I'd met him, I could see he was unbalanced about Ridley
and, I must say, he caused me a lot of thought. Fortunately,
Superintendent, you traced that car that I was lucky enough
to hear had been seen after midnight parked in a lane near
Ridley's house on the night of the murder. We were lucky,
too, that that young fellow, Bob Chapman, noticed the star-
shaped crack in the rear window. He confirmed that it was the
same car, I suppose," Beef said, addressing the Superintendent.

"He couldn't swear to it absolutely," the Superintendent
replied. "But, as he said, it wasn't likely that there were two
cars like that."

"It seemed to me that, like the rope that was used to string
Ridley up, that car was part of a premeditated murder. That
was more or less confirmed when we found that the man
who hired the car had given a false name and address. If the
car was used for the murder, and I was convinced it was,
Greenleaf was cleared. The same man who hired the car,
if you remember, did not return it until the next evening,

the evening of the eleventh of September. Greenleaf was dining with his literary agent, Mr. Thorogood, in London at that time. I may as well just finish with Greenleaf while on the subject. The Chief Inspector here talked of my behaving like a Boy Scout. I admit it. Young Bob Chapman had done us two good turns and I thought he'd like me to act up to his picture of a detective. I also wanted to know what game Greenleaf was up to. I never thought he'd be armed or I'd have tipped you the wink, Superintendent. I still think he was only putting the wind up that rascal Fagg. As it was, no harm was done and it won't do Greenleaf any harm to kick his heels in jail for a few days."

I looked across quickly at the Chief Inspector and saw him frown and lean forward as if to say something, but he evidently thought better of it and sat back again.

"Anyway," Beef said, rather defiantly, "I enjoyed myself that night. There's not much adventure about these days and the papers certainly made a good story out of it. It was about this time that I went to see Miss Estelle Pinkerton. Apart from the fact that she inherited nearly all Ridley's money, I had nothing against her up till then. One or two things, however, did come out in our talk. It seemed curious that, like Gupp, she should have an absolutely cast-iron alibi for the time of the actual murder of the person from whom she was the chief legatee. Like Gupp, too, she seemed eager to tell her story about staying with the dean of Fulham at that time. Another thing, this visit of hers was not in accordance with her usual custom. It was an extra visit to London and she was the one who had fixed to be away at that time. In other words, it was by her choice that she happened to be spending a few days with the dean of Fulham just at the time when her uncle was murdered. Again nothing much in itself. Another small thing, she purposely stayed out all day alone while she was there. Not usual, I thought. I left with the impression that she was a foolish vain creature and crazy for a man.

"One person I've missed out so far is Ridley's stepson, Major Howard. Hard up though he was for money, he certainly did not strike me as a type that would go in for premeditated murder, but there was the chance that whoever had murdered Ridley had done it almost accidentally. Ridley seemed to have been the sort of cold snake-like creature that anyone might have lost their temper with.

"I was glad, therefore, to learn, when I went to see Major Howard, that he was back in his mess for dinner at Aldershot at the time when the car, which I was sure the murderer had used, was returned to the garage.

"There was one point that attracted my attention in Major Howard's story. He said that it was a letter from Estelle Pinkerton that had first put into his mind the idea of appealing for financial help to his stepfather, Edwin Ridley. Miss Pinkerton appeared anxious that Major Howard should re-establish friendly relations with Ridley after all those years. There might be nothing in it, but it seemed strange that her letter should arrive at that particular time. Fortunately for him, though he intended to visit Ridley, he never went.

"It looked, then, very much as if Gupp was the man who hired the car in Oxford. He was there at the time, he answered more or less to the description, the car was seen outside the hotel at which he was staying, and he had no alibi for the period when Ridley was strangled. But it was all circumstantial evidence.

"Meantime another train of thought had started at the back of my mind. It must have begun after my visit to Estelle Pinkerton, but I can't remember when I really became fully aware of it. It was the word Cheltenham, I think, that first rang a bell. I couldn't at first trace any connection with the town until I suddenly remembered that Amelia Pinhole, Miss Fielding's dressmaker, had said she had once lived in Cheltenham. Straight away another thing she told us came back to me. It was that she remembered the day Miss Fielding was poisoned, because as she was going up to the gate she saw someone she thought she recognised. Estelle Pinkerton lived in Cheltenham. Could they have known one another in the old days? Was it Estelle Pinkerton that Amelia Pinhole recognised?

"I believe it was then that I began to have a glimmering of a new idea. A pact. A pact between Hilton Gupp and Estelle Pinkerton. Supposing, I thought, they each had murdered the person from whom *the other* was going to inherit money? That would do away with the one great bugbear of every murderer—palpable motive. It's agreed that any of us, the Superintendent here or the Chief Inspector, could go out of this room and commit one murder and get away with it, provided the murder was of someone unknown, and completely without motive. Well, perhaps this was how they planned to get away with it. There was only one big snag. How did a spinster in Cheltenham come to meet a ne'er-do-well like Gupp, just back from the East? Then I remembered what she said about her holidays, and how she loved to meet strangers in trains. Had they met at some foreign hotel? That seemed impossible. Then it came to me. Her holiday this summer at Estoril! I remembered seeing an advertisement about Estoril and I knew from that that it was in Portugal, somewhere near Lisbon. They'd met not at an hotel, of course, but on a boat. They must have travelled back on the same boat.

"This idea came to me about the same time as the arrest of Greenleaf. If I'm right, I thought, things'll move quickly.

Gupp will think that he's clear for the moment and that now is the time for him to act.

"I went that morning and looked back through all the passenger lists of boats from the East which had arrived about the beginning of August. At last I ran him to earth. He had come on a slow Dutch boat, the s.s. *Appeldorn*, which had put in, among other places, at Lisbon. I could hardly control myself as I looked eagerly for the name of Estelle Pinkerton among the other passengers. It was there. That meant I was right. Townsend here was fidgeting and impatient while I made the discovery, thinking that having found the name Gupp we had done enough. He little knew that this was the piece of evidence that would, so far as we knew then, put both their necks in nooses! Just to make doubly sure I took a train straight to Hastings and went to see Amelia Pinhole, the dressmaker, and asked her who she thought she'd seen that morning near Miss Fielding's house. She replied that she had at first thought it was someone she had known years before in Cheltenham, a Miss Pinkerton. It could not have been her, she added, because when she addressed Estelle, the lady, Miss Pinhole said, had said there must be some mistake and hurried away. This was only further confirmation.

"My next call was on Raikes. He was staying at Camber Lodge with his wife. I soon got his secret by pretending to know everything. I guessed he had seen something through the window that morning and told Gupp, who had somehow frightened him out of informing the police. What he'd seen did not amount to evidence, but to me it was another bit of proof of my theory. He had seen a woman whom he took to be Miss Payne—her back was towards him—doing something with a glass in the goldfish bowl. I thought for a moment and then asked him if the woman was wearing a hat. I knew neither Miss Fielding nor Miss Payne would be wearing one in the house and the Misses Graves, he had told me, hadn't arrived. When he said yes, I knew it was Estelle Pinkerton. There were no other visitors that morning. She was washing out the sherry glass that Miss Fielding had used and which would have had traces of morphia. It killed the goldfish, anyhow. I expect she did that when Miss Fielding went to fetch a book on Chinese missionary work, the one Mr. Townsend found the receipt in.

"As I travelled back to London by train I could see the whole picture. I could imagine Estelle Pinkerton getting into conversation with the good-looking tall young man who was travelling by himself. She was always crazy for a man and he probably thought she had money. They began to exchange confidences over the boat rail. Among these confidences it came out that they would both be rich when their elderly relations died. Unfortunately, they had to admit, there seemed little likelihood of either of those rich relatives dying for a very long time. By now Estelle Pinkerton had, I imagine, become infatuated with this attentive, very masculine, young man. Who made the first suggestion of hastening the death of their rich relatives, no one can say. It was probably tried out as a joke. Personally, I think the woman was behind it, but it can never be proved. So desperate for him had she become that no risk was too great. Anything rather than lose this personable young man who had so providentially appeared in answer to her prayers. Gradually the plot was hatched. Gupp probably got hold of the morphia for her in some foreign port. It was agreed that they should do the two murders on the same day. In the meantime they thought it best not to be seen together or even to meet. The date had been fixed, and we know what happened. Both murders were successful."

Beef paused and I took advantage of this to refill all their glasses.

"There were still difficulties," he continued. "I knew now all I wanted, but, though I could almost prove the Hastings murder, I only had the barest circumstantial evidence about Gupp's part in the Cotswold case. The police were sick of Gupp's name. They had tried to break his alibi and failed. Unless I could prove my case, it was no good trying Scotland Yard again. That's why I was glad when Greenleaf was arrested. I thought, and rightly, it would drive them into the open, lull them into a sense of false security. They had no reason to think that anyone even remotely suspected their reversed parts in the two murders. Gupp had gone down to Estelle Pinkerton's for the weekend probably to extract further money out of her. She, he probably pointed out, had had her benefit from the crime, she had inherited her lot. But he, by an ironic stroke of ill luck, though honourably executing his part of the bargain, had earnt nothing at all, because Miss Fielding had cut him out of her Will. Mr. Townsend had seen him splashing money about in London and I guessed where that had come from. When I heard he was away, I suspected we should find him with Estelle Pinkerton. On the Monday morning Gupp saw in the papers that Greenleaf had been arrested and, as my name appeared, he imagined that the police and I were agreed that Greenleaf was the murderer. He phoned the bank that morning, I suspect, and arranged to be away on some pretext or other. That's why the manager was a bit short with you, I expect," Beef said, looking over at me.

"The last part of this story we can only guess. Whether Estelle Pinkerton found out that Gupp didn't care tuppence for her and was only after her money, whether she realised that as long as he was alive he would bleed her of her fortune by blackmail, I don't know. Nobody except Estelle knows, and she's not likely to tell. It may be that Gupp was planning to murder her, knowing that while she lived to tell the tale he could never be free from fear. She might, he felt, break down and confess sometime. Perhaps she found out his intentions and got in first. Anyway, the cottage that she had planned as a love nest turned out to be the scene of his death. Her plan was simple enough. There was nothing to connect a charming old lady, a Mrs. Welldon from London, who rented a cottage at Downland, in which subsequently the corpse of a man called Hilton Gupp would be found, with the harmless spinster Estelle Pinkerton from Cheltenham. So she thought.

"I am going to repeat how I found out about her plans. That telephone call of hers was her only slip, but how *could* she imagine she was being followed and the number traced? Even then it was only to an hotel in Eastbourne. If it hadn't been for the curiosity of that colonel's wife, Mrs. Fordyce, we might not have found her so quickly.

"All she had to do after murdering Gupp was to disappear from the bungalow and reappear as Estelle Pinkerton on her way to her grandfather in France to spend a holiday. She would say in her letters that she felt she needed a rest after all the vulgar publicity about her uncle's death. She could then come back to Cheltenham and enjoy the fortune that had been left her. With that money she hoped to find a better man than Hilton Gupp had proved to be. Well, Inspector Arnold and I caught her just in time on the boat. We've got ample evidence against her for Gupp's murder and, if necessary, for poisoning Miss Fielding. First, her fingerprints were on the fountain-pen of Miss Fielding's which she borrowed to write that fatal receipt. They've been compared, the Inspector tells me, and there's no doubt. Second, Miss Amelia Pinhole will testify that she saw a woman she now knows to be Estelle Pinkerton coming from Miss Fielding's house on the morning of the murder. Lastly, I think you've traced the receipt itself, haven't you, Inspector? Bath, wasn't it?"

"Yes," Inspector Arnold said. "The receipt for the Church Missions Society was a fake, of course. Beef suggested it was probably printed for Miss Pinkerton down in some town near her home. Well, we found the printers, a firm in Bath. She had given the name Mrs. Welldon, the same as she used to take the cottage in Sussex. Very careless."

"It's perhaps a good thing that Gupp is dead. We might have got the garage in Oxford to identify him, but that would have been the only bit of evidence that wasn't circumstantial. What do you think, Chief Inspector?"

I was glad Beef had taken the bull by the horns.

"Very interesting story," he replied. "Thank you very much. I congratulate you on the Hastings part. How far your theories will stand any real test about our case in the Cotswolds remains to be seen. We will naturally go into the whole matter carefully. I presume you will make a written report?"

"Oh yes," Beef replied. There returned to his voice a little of the old pomposity, and he spoke as though he were endowing an orphanage. "I'm giving the whole story in writing to Inspector Arnold. That will go to Scotland Yard and you will no doubt get a copy from your headquarters."

"That'll be fine," said the Chief Inspector, but his looks did not support his words. "Come on, Superintendent. Enjoyable as the evening's been, we must get back to hard work and hard facts."

I thought I saw the fat Superintendent wink at Beef as he said goodbye. There was certainly a twinkle in his eye.

"Had to save his face," Inspector Arnold said to Beef when they had left the flat. "Greenleaf will be out in a day or two, you see."

"I thought he took it all pretty well in the end," Beef replied. "Come on, Inspector, we can have a real drink now." And they did.

23

A few weeks later Vincent, my brother, and I gave a small dinner-party at Camber Lodge. It was half-term at Vincent's public school, Penshurst, and, as he was able to get away for a few days, we decided to meet at Hastings and settle up finally the rest of Aunt Aurora's estate.

Reluctantly we agreed that Camber Lodge must be sold. We let Mary Raikes, the cook, and Ellen choose some things they treasured from among my aunt's possessions and then, after we had picked out what we both wanted, we arranged for the rest to be auctioned.

As soon as my aunt's Will had been settled, I had bought a brand new Norton motor-cycle for Charlie Raikes. He was happily dividing his time between racing on his bike and planning his new life in Canada. Their passages, his mother's and his, had been booked, and they were due to sail in a fortnight. Tom Raikes, the husband, had gone off again, with, I suspected, some portion of the money my aunt had left Mary his wife. Nothing more could be done for him.

Vincent and I were both a little worried about Ellen when we decided to close down Camber Lodge. Her whole life had been spent there with my aunt, and, though we agreed to give her a substantial cheque, we knew that money would be no real consolation. She had decided, however, where her duty lay. "I must go and look after those poor Misses Graves," she told us. "They're all right for money now, thanks to Miss Fielding. That's one thing. But they've aged terribly since your aunt's death. They were such friends, you know, all those years. I'm sure Miss Fielding would want me to do it. I shall find the difference in that house, I know. They won't be considerate, like your aunt, to work for. One of them can hardly move by herself now, and the other's a bit queer in her head ever since they had the bailiffs in. But I must do it. I shouldn't be easy in my conscience if I didn't carry on Miss Fielding's good work, now she's not here to do it herself."

Christian charity I felt could go no further. Of the vicar, too, we heard better news. The restoration of the murals in his church had been completed. He had been taken from the private mental home to see the work. And this had brought about a wonderful improvement. It was hoped that he would be allowed to leave the home very soon. All this Vincent and I had found out on our arrival in Hastings, and we were now sitting comfortably in front of a fire, drinking some of my aunt's excellent sherry, waiting for our guests. Beef, of course, was to be there. He and the Reverend Alfred Ridley were due any time from the station. Inspector Arnold was coming, and Beef had insisted on our asking Amelia Pinhole. "A good feed and some drinks will do the old girl a pile of good," he had said. "It'll mean a lot to her, and, after all, she did help us clear it up. I can just hear her telling her friends about the party afterwards."

Alfred Ridley, the vicar, had really behaved very well in settling up his murdered brother's estate. He had gone carefully into the whole publishing racket which his brother had carried on as Thomas Thayer, Publisher, and made restitution where he could. He had changed the name of the firm to the Church of England Theological Publishing Company. I had a feeling, remembering the man, that it would prosper. Greenleaf, too, he had helped; and, as Michael Thorogood had prophesied, Greenleaf already promised to make a name for himself. He had, as Inspector Arnold foretold, been released almost at once after the meeting in my flat.

When all our guests had arrived and sherry had been served, we went in to dinner. Mary, given carte blanche, excelled herself.

It was genius on her part. The whole dinner was period, an early Edwardian dinner. It was exactly like the illustrations to an early copy of Mrs. Beeton. Soup, fish, loin of veal, pheasants, a medley of sweets and cheese, cooked in her inimitable way and served in almost forgotten profusion. Wines, that would have even won George Saintsbury's approval, were served with every course, sherry, hock, claret, champagne and a really excellent brandy that Mary must have found in some far corner of my aunt's cellar. How Aunt Aurora would have enjoyed it all, I could not help thinking. Her dining-room with its solid comfortable furniture and glass chandeliers was the setting. For this atmosphere Amelia Pinhole seemed just right. Her large bust and old-fashioned coiffure blended with the scene and the dim light of the candles softened her heavily rouged features. She and Beef were the life of the party. We all drank a lot of very good wine, and the last scene I remember of the party, after Ridley's clergyman brother had gone to bed, was Beef thumping away accompaniments on the piano and Amelia Pinhole singing. When she was too hoarse to continue, with an exaggerated old-world leave-taking she left us, and with her went Inspector Arnold who had offered to drive her home.

"I'm going home in the arms of the law," were her final words as the front door closed behind them.

Vincent and Edith claimed they were tired and also departed to bed. Edith had slightly improved with marriage, but I still could not understand my brother's choice and, from the few words I had had with her, nor could the matron or the boys in his House.

Beef and I were at last left alone.

"Just a nightcap," he said, pouring out two large liqueur brandies. There was no sign that he had drunk the best part of a bottle of champagne in addition to a number of glasses of sherry, hock and claret.

"I suppose now you've got all this money you won't want to bother with writing up my cases any more?" he said, and for the first time I thought, though it may have been the drink, I detected a note of regret in Beef's voice.

"Oh, there's not as much money as all that," I said. "The death duties were heavier than we thought, and most of my aunt's shares are well down. No, I shall carry on."

"Well, in that case," he said, "we'll get back to London tomorrow. You can then lock yourself up in that flat of yours and write up this case. Should make a good story, if you tell it right. I'm getting tired of people not having heard of me and having to play second fiddle to all these other clever detectives."

"All right, Beef," I replied. "I'll do my best."

As I turned to go upstairs and looked round the house I could not help thinking of Estelle Pinkerton in some lonely cell, but then I caught sight of a portrait of my Aunt Aurora and the momentary feeling of compassion passed.